Virginia ANDREWS

HOUSE OF SECRETS

**SIMON &
SCHUSTER**

London · New York · Sydney · Toronto · New Delhi

A CBS COMPANY

First published in the USA by Gallery Books, 2018
An Imprint of Simon & Schuster, Inc.
First published in Great Britain by Simon & Schuster UK Ltd, 2018
A CBS COMPANY

1 3 5 7 9 10 8 6 4 2

Simon & Schuster UK Ltd
1st Floor
222 Gray's Inn Road
London WC1X 8HB

Simon & Schuster Australia, Sydney
Simon & Schuster India, New Delhi

www.simonandschuster.co.uk
www.simonandschuster.com.au
www.simonandschuster.co.in

A CIP catalogue record for this book
is available from the British Library

Hardback ISBN: 978-1-4711-7404-9
eBook ISBN: 978-1-4711-7406-3

Printed and bound by CPI Group (UK) Ltd, Croydon, CR0 4YY

HOUSE OF SECRETS

Virginia Andrews Books

The Dollanganger Family
Flowers in the Attic
Petals on the Wind
If There Be Thorns
Seeds of Yesterday
Garden of Shadows
Christopher's Diary:
    Secrets of
    Foxworth
Christopher's Diary:
    Echoes of
    Dollanganger
Secret Brother

The Audrina Series
My Sweet Audrina
Whitefern

The Casteel Family
Heaven
Dark Angel
Fallen Hearts
Gates of Paradise
Web of Dreams

The Cutler Family
Dawn
Secrets of the Morning
Twilight's Child
Midnight Whispers
Darkest Hour

The Landry Family
Ruby
Pearl in the Mist
All That Glitters
Hidden Jewel
Tarnished Gold

The Logan Family
Melody
Heart Song
Unfinished Symphony
Music in the Night
Olivia

The Orphans Series
Butterfly
Crystal
Brooke
Raven
Runaways

The Wildflowers Series
Misty
Star
Jade
Cat
Into the Garden

The Hudson Family
Rain
Lightning Strikes
Eye of the Storm
The End of the Rainbow

The Shooting Stars
Cinnamon
Ice
Rose
Honey
Falling Stars

The De Beers Family
"Dark Seed"
Willow
Wicked Forest
Twisted Roots
Into the Woods
Hidden Leaves

The Broken Wings Series
Broken Wings
Midnight Flight

The Gemini Series
Celeste
Black Cat
Child of Darkness

The Shadows Series
April Shadows
Girl in the Shadows

The Early Spring Series
Broken Flower
Scattered Leaves

The Secrets Series
Secrets in the Attic
Secrets in the Shadows

The Delia Series
Delia's Crossing
Delia's Heart
Delia's Gift

The Heavenstone Series
The Heavenstone
    Secrets
Secret Whispers

The March Family
Family Storms
Cloudburst

The Kindred Series
Daughter of Darkness
Daughter of Light

The Forbidden Series
The Forbidden Sister
"The Forbidden Heart"
Roxy's Story

The Mirror Sisters
The Mirror Sisters
Broken Glass
Shattered Memories

The Girls of Spindrift
Bittersweet Dreams
"Corliss"
"Donna"

Stand-alone Novels
Gods of Green
    Mountain
Into the Darkness
Capturing Angels
The Unwelcomed
    Child
Sage's Eyes

HOUSE OF SECRETS

Prologue

I HAD ALWAYS suspected that there were dark and forbidding secrets in Wyndemere House, a nineteenth-century Gothic Revival mansion that had been in the Davenport family for nearly eighty years. The secrets lingered in every corner like old spiderwebs catching dust in an attic long after the spider had died, and they echoed in every footstep as if they followed everyone about the house. As a child growing up there, I feared learning what they were. At times, when I thought a shadow had glided across the walls in my room like sliding ice or when I thought I heard the sound of what I imagined to be sobbing leaking through the ceiling from one of what I knew to be empty bedrooms above, I shuddered, embraced myself, and tried to avoid dreams.

Because the house was old and the stories

about the Jamesons, the people who had lived in it even before the Davenports, were legendary tales about witchcraft and lost children, it never occurred to me as I grew up, living with my mother in what were the help's quarters, that the one secret that would most affect my life was kept locked up in my mother's heart. No matter where we lived, that secret would have festered until, like the black flower in *The Scarlet Letter*, it blossomed and left me naked and defenseless in a world where eyes could condemn and voices could sting like angry hornets.

The dark-gray stone-faced house with its louvered black vinyl shutters, towering brick chimneys, and gargoyles replicating those on Notre Dame in Paris couldn't help but be forbidding, despite the great care that was taken to surround it with a variety of flowers, manicured hedges, beautiful fountains, and rolling green lawns perfumed with the aroma of early spring whenever the grass was cut. During the coldest wintry nights, the elaborate outside lights desperately tried to warm the mansion and help it look welcoming. Deer would come out of the surrounding forest and pose like models for statuary, as if they understood that the house loomed with as great an importance as anything else nature had chosen for their world.

Situated on more than fifteen acres abutting Lake Wyndemere, a five-mile-long lake on the border between New York and Massachusetts, the house was over fifteen thousand square feet and had seventeen bedrooms, six baths, and eight fireplaces. It had an elegant beige foyer with a Louis XVI console; a very large living room with neoclassical sofas, chairs, and tables; a dining room that could seat twenty; and a library, which Dr. Davenport used as an office, too. It was semicircular, with a wood-paneled ceiling, a fireplace, and walls of bookcases. All the rooms had intricately designed parquet floors. The main entrance had an open staircase, molded cornices, and a red-marble fireplace. Many rooms were warmed with Persian rugs and stuffed with antiques. There were elaborate chandeliers that drizzled light everywhere in the evening and on dreary winter days.

Throughout the spring and summer, there was always a variety of flowers in vases in every downstairs room and every bedroom in use upstairs. The flowers were changed weekly so that there was an ongoing mixed aroma that sweetened the air and subdued any stale odors that might come from vintage pictures, furnishings, and antiques, many created long before the house was built. Whenever windows could be thrown wide open, they were.

Most of the bedrooms were closed off and used rarely except for the occasional guest. When I was little and often followed my mother upstairs, Mrs. Marlene, the cook, whose parents had emigrated from Cork, Ireland, teased me by warning me never to open any of those closed doors, or "a ghost could fly out."

If I looked too frightened, she would laugh and recite a limerick: *A ghost in the town of Macroom one night found a ghoul in his room. They argued all night as to who had the right to frighten the wits out of whom.*

Then she would laugh and hug me. I might smile, but I still never opened a closed door.

Now, as for almost the past ten years, my mother and I occupied two bedrooms at the rear of the mansion on the first floor, and we had our own small kitchen and den, all of it originally created for live-in household servants. Dr. Davenport and, my mother said, his first wife did not want any other strangers besides us living in their home. His second wife definitely did not. If anyone else was to live here, he or she would have to have one of our bedrooms. No workers, except my mother when the Davenport children were infants and she was their nanny, would be permitted to inhabit an upstairs bedroom. Instead, a team of maids and Mrs. Marlene, who had been working at Wyndemere for over twenty years, came and went six days a week.

On Sundays, my mother would take over most of the meal service, but Dr. Davenport and his wife would usually go to dinner at a restaurant

Sunday night and my mother would have only the children under her watch. There was no cleaning on Sundays, nor was there anyone working on the grounds.

Years before I was born, Dr. Davenport, a cardiovascular surgeon, married Samantha Avery, the daughter of a prominent dental-equipment manufacturer. His parents approved the marriage and were supposedly even instrumental in bringing their son and Samantha together. Dr. Davenport's father and Samantha's were close friends and partners in some business ventures. My mother told me that what she called "posh families" often engineered marriages between their daughters and sons. It provided them with a sense of security to know that the expanding family would be like new branches on a well-established, firmly planted tree. "Birds of a feather stick together," she said.

"But that doesn't sound very romantic," I said.

I was fourteen when my mother described all this with more detail than she ever had previously. It had become more important for me to hear about love and marriage, so I asked as many questions as I could about everyone, especially the Davenports. Overnight, it seemed, I was capable of falling in love at the wink of an eye and with a soft smile singling me out from my tuft of girlfriends. My girlfriends and I emerged from the same cocoon of puberty held together with strings of desperate phone calls about potential boyfriends, pajama-party confessionals, and flowering hormones. We were at the age when one mutual giggle could sweep us—a special cluster of smiles, swaggering hips, budding breasts, and growing self-confidence—down a school hallway. Other girls in our freshman high school class envied us, and older boys began to stop to take notice.

"Romance, Fern," my mother said in her inimitable dry way that some claimed was natural to British people, "is the least of it when it comes to marriage."

"Not for me," I replied. "Nothing will be more important. How can anyone permit her parents to decide with whom she should spend the rest of her life? Ugh."

I was more like a rubber band these days, snapping back. Defiance had become instinctive and necessary in order to assure myself, my friends, and any boy who would show interest in me that I had matured and had a mind of my own. I wanted everyone to believe that I could say things, tell things about myself, without having to run home to my mother to first get confirmation. I was headstrong and determined that people should see me for who I really was and not lump me in with some stereotype assigned to girls without fathers. With the air of independence I was projecting, I might as well have already been eighteen and out on my own in the world.

All my girlfriends, some coming right out and admitting it, were jealous of my poise and assurance.

"You're not afraid of anyone or anything," Evelyn Porter told me when I cut Barry Austin, a senior, down to size after he had made a disgusting remark about my rear end. I told him his nose was longer than his penis so he could walk safely into a glass door when he had an erection. He turned a new shade of bloodred, looked at the surprised delight on my girlfriends' faces, and fled.

"If you act like sheep, they'll act like wolves," I quoted from my mother's repertoire.

"I wish I had your nerve," Evelyn said.

All the girls around us nodded, wishing they were more like me, but then later they would surely comfort themselves with the knowledge that, unlike them, I had no father, and my mother was someone's nanny before she had become a house manager. Although that sounded important on the surface, I knew that most thought of her as just a glorified housemaid. The more painful reality was that we never had a home of our own or a family in the United States.

My mother had never been married.

I was a mistake, the result of some unexpected and overwhelming rush of passion that pressured her to close her eyes and cast caution to the wind. She was so adamant about not discussing it with me, no matter when or how I brought it up, that I began to feel like a virginal conception. Whenever girlfriends who thought they had become intimate enough with me asked about my father, I answered the way I always had: "I don't know, and my mother has sworn to herself never to say."

"Doesn't it bother you?" most of my girlfriends wanted to know.

"Why should it?" I countered defensively. "It's too late to matter," I'd say, even though in my heart of hearts, I knew it still did and always would. It kept a haze around me, staining me with subtle condemnation. People were supposedly more liberal-minded about such things nowadays, but I was more often than not the target of hypocritical eyes or words like *not that it matters to me*.

Oh, it mattered.

In fact, after I had first landed on the beaches of adolescence and I realized that boys were hovering around me more than they ever had, I became keenly aware that some of them had the impression and shared the belief that a girl born out of wedlock had inherited promiscuity and was an easy score. They believed that, like my mother, I would definitely go all the way, likely on the first date, something my very existence acknowledged for them. I had to be stronger and defiant. They could whisper about my mother and me behind my back, but few had the nerve to say anything nasty on the topic to my face.

Besides, my mother did not sleep around. She had no dirty reputation. People who had gotten to know her well respected her. None saw her as a loose woman. In fact, I couldn't find much evidence of any boyfriend in her life, no old pictures or old love letters tied with a pink ribbon and stuffed in a carton of memories. That part was frustrating. I needed clues. How did all this happen? How did I come to be here with her?

My mother had left her home in Guildford, England, when her music teacher, Mr. Wollard, convinced her she could be a singing star in America. She was the lead in all the school musicals. She told me she had even sung in a pub occasionally on weekends. My grandparents were against her stopping her education and rushing off to get her name in lights. My grandfather was a banker and, according to my mother, very conservative. She called him a typical Royalist. When she finally decided to follow her dream and quit school to go to America, my grandfather became very angry. But she was stubbornly ambitious and wouldn't back down.

"Your grandfather Arthur showed me the door like he would some ragtag beggar," my mother told me. "It broke my mother's heart. He forbade my even writing a letter. I left with whatever I could pack in a beaten old suitcase that had belonged to your grandmother. If it wasn't for my older sister, Julia, I wouldn't have even known when my father passed away four years ago. Now, when I think about it, I don't know what was in my head besides those soapy ambitions. I really never got past being a waitress. So much for Mr. Wollard's prediction that I'd be the next Madonna."

"But why Wyndemere? It's not close to New York City. What brought you here?" I had to know.

She told me that when she was really down and out because the girl with whom she was sharing rent on the small apartment in New York had left and she had gotten nowhere with her singing, a friend of a friend introduced her to Dr. and Mrs. Davenport, who were in New York at the time. They were looking for a nanny, and both liked her and were impressed with her enough to hire her. My mother said she took the job to care for the Davenports' baby son, Ryder, who was due in two months. She thought it would tide her over for a year or two and she would save enough money to return to New York and continue pursuing her dream.

But then, on a particularly icy winter afternoon a little past the first year, Samantha Davenport lost control of her vehicle while coming down a particularly steep hill and ran off the road and down an embankment, the car doing a somersault and landing on its roof. She wasn't wearing her seat belt and broke her neck. She was dead for hours before the vehicle was located.

I never knew her, of course, but from the pictures I had seen of her, I thought she had been a very attractive light-brown-haired woman who never seemed to have lost her little-girl eyes and smile. When I mentioned that to my mother once, she said, "That's exactly who she was, a little girl, so protected and spoiled she didn't have to grow up. You grow up when you need to face challenges, especially challenges when you're alone. I had to grow up fast," she added, but not bitterly. Of course, I wanted to know all about that, every nitty-gritty detail of her journey that brought her to who she now was.

However, getting my mother to talk about her past was like pulling pieces of packing Styrofoam off your clothes. Her standard reply to a question about her history, and therefore mine, when I pursued more detail was, "I'll tell you some other time."

"Some other time" seemed to move further and further into the distant future, and after a while, I stopped asking questions. I was too busy now writing my own history. Helping me do that was Ryder Davenport, who was two years older than me. When he was six and I was four, we began to play together. It wasn't until Dr. Davenport remarried that the boundaries for me in the mansion were more strictly enforced. In fact, Bea Davenport, his second wife, wanted my mother and me out of the house entirely, but by then, my mother was managing the staff and assisting in the kitchen and was available to be a nanny again, this time to Dr. Davenport's and Bea's daughter, born a year after their marriage.

I never understood why she agreed to it, but Bea Davenport permitted their daughter to be named after Dr. Davenport's first wife, Samantha. Ryder almost immediately began to call her Sam, and the name, despite Bea's objections, stuck. In fact, when Samantha entered school, she enjoyed her friends calling her Sam, even though her teachers refused to do so. Of course, I called her Sam, too, which was another thing that didn't endear me to Bea Davenport.

Bea wasn't as pretty as Samantha Avery, but she, too, came from a posh family. Her father was head administrator at the hospital where Dr. Davenport operated on his patients and through various charity events became acquainted with Bea Howell. My mother told me he was a man who simply had no patience for what she called "the courting game." Although she didn't say it in so many words, I knew she believed Dr. Davenport married Bea Howell because it was convenient. A man like him needed a woman at his side who could qualify as an important doctor's wife, and it wasn't terribly long afterward that he became the head of cardiology at the hospital.

Bea had gone to Vassar but had no interest in developing any sort of career besides becoming a doctor's wife. Dr. Davenport wasn't the first to date her, but he had the most impressive status and was already quite wealthy, two qualifications she required before she would give a man a second look.

"She's the type who holds her head up and back so high that you can examine her sinuses," my mother once muttered. I had no idea what she meant then, but she warned me not only to keep out of the new Mrs. Davenport's way but to avoid her shadow as well.

I know Ryder never liked her. It was something that helped make the two of us closer allies in the big house. As soon as Sam was old enough to understand, she wanted to be our ally, too. She looked more like her mother than she did her father. She had her mother's coffee-bean brown eyes, her slightly long, thin nose and thin lips. Bea's dark-brown hair was closer to black, and so was Sam's. But regardless of how her mother treated Ryder and me, Sam craved our friendship and followed us about like a puppy.

For some reason, she didn't inherit the doctor's or Bea's height and was always tiny, fragile. Ryder nicknamed her Sam the Bird. Her mother hated the way she would trek behind us everywhere, especially me, and often came to our quarters to drag her back into "the house," as she called it, threatening to lock her in her room if she left the house again. It was as if my mother and I lived in a truly separate building, with dandruff as well as dust floating in the air. Bea was not above putting Sam immediately into a hot bath as soon as she discovered she had been here.

So there we were, the three of us, growing up in one of the area's most famous houses on beautiful property but with me always feeling worse than a poor relative, especially with my mother continually warning me not to push too hard to do too much in the great house. She was keenly aware of Bea Davenport's disapproval of our being "underfoot," as my mother would say. That meant I would have to tiptoe and never raise my voice. I was to be "easily ignored."

"She should be as surprised to see you as she would be if you had just moved in insidiously," my mother told me. I was only ten at the time and had to rush off to my computer to look up the word. My mother, although she really had not gone further than a public-school education, had the vocabulary of a college graduate and loved to read, which probably helped make me an A-plus student.

I tried to follow my mother's wishes for how

I should behave in Wyndemere, but despite what Bea wanted or my mother's thoughts about how discreetly we had to live in this great house, destiny, woven in secrets, had other plans for us all, and especially for me. What I learned before I was very old was that every day you could be reborn through the education you had and the work you did, or you could simply disappear with the memory of you absorbed in some soon-to-be-forgotten cloud drifting off to the horizon.

Can you ever remember a cloud?

What I finally realized was that life was simply the challenge to be meaningful to someone else besides yourself.

Because of the way we lived and how I was brought up, and especially because of the great secret I would someday know, no one would be more surprised than I would that I was ever meaningful to anyone besides my mother.

There were times I felt I wasn't even meaningful to myself and never would be.

1

FOR MOST OF my youth, Saturdays and Sundays were not the jewels of the week that they were for my classmates and friends. Unlike other girls my age, I couldn't invite anyone to sleep over or have a birthday party with my classmates as guests. Bea Davenport had laid that rule on my mother. She didn't want strange children coming to the house and gawking at Wyndemere or disturbing the grounds. I couldn't have breakfast, lunch, or especially dinner with Ryder or, for that matter, Samantha when she was no longer an infant. Bea Davenport wouldn't permit me to be in either of their rooms by the time Ryder was eight and Samantha was five, and she continually discouraged both of them from coming to mine even when they were older.

For Samantha, that was like reaching into the candy jar when no one was looking. The moment her mother left the house, she would drop what she was doing and sneak through the hallways to stand in my bedroom doorway, hoping I would invite her in to play or just to talk. When Ryder was older, he was more in his stepmother's face about it, marching right past her to come to see me and often, again out of spite, inviting one of my friends to go rowing with us on the lake. Bea was furious about that and got Dr. Davenport to discourage it by telling Ryder there were insurance concerns. He was to use the rowboat only when either he or Bea was present, which was rare.

I did recall the two times Dr. Davenport took my mother and me, Ryder, and Samantha out in his motorboat, but we were all very young and he wasn't as busy as he was now. In fact, his motorboat was so neglected; it was in need of repair. It bobbed at the dock like some forgotten relative trying to get his attention.

Bea Davenport did other things to keep us in our place. To this day, my mother and I were forbidden to enter the house from the front. Even when there was two feet of snow, we would have to go around to the rear entrance to get to our rooms. It was the same entrance where most deliveries were made, with my mother there to accept them. If Bea could, she would have stamped our foreheads with the word *servants*.

With a voice that was strident and nasal, Bea would snap the rules at us frequently, especially adding newly conceived prohibitions like staying out of the gazebo and off the tennis court. If I did go through the house for any reason, I wasn't to touch anything. I recalled how she had one of the maids clean and polish the banister after I had gone upstairs with my mother, especially when my mother was caring for Sam. My mother always had my hands washed before we approached the Davenport children, but that didn't matter. It was as if I had some disease inherent in my skin. I remember feeling very dirty whenever I was in Bea's presence. She looked at me closely, searching for some blotch, some smudge, anything to confirm her suspicions that I was not only imperfect but infectious.

My mother was never to touch her jewelry and, of course, to be sure no maid ever did. Because my mother was the house manager, a title Bea would never pronounce, any mistake was her fault, down to having what Bea considered the wrong brand of margarine. It did no good, either, to protest that Mrs. Marlene had been serving it for years. There was a new sun shining on this house now. Furniture and paintings were shifted about, and window shades were opened and closed differently to move shadows from their traditional nests. Bea was always redecorating something. Only Dr. Davenport's office was off-limits to her.

If there was even the smallest impression that my mother and I were a little more than household servants, that impression was crushed the way you might stamp down on an insect. I think that was the reason she made the front entrance so sacrosanct. We couldn't come through if we took off our shoes. We couldn't come through even if we could remove our inferior souls.

Most of the time, the pathway to the rear was cleared of snow. Mr. Stark, who managed the grounds, the long driveway, and all the outside fixtures, was very fond of my mother and me and was at the house especially early on weekdays in the winter to be sure we had an easy time going in and out. He was twenty years older than my mother, but I was sure, being a widower, he dreamed of her being more to him than simply a fellow employee. He'd leap at an invitation to have dinner with us and never forgot my mother's birthday or mine. Despite his balding head of gray hair and the deep wrinkles worn into his face, he was stout and fit. My mother called him a walking tree trunk, even to his face.

"George, you have bark for skin," she would say, half-kiddingly, especially when he wore a coat too thin for the colder weather. But there wasn't anything she could say that wouldn't bring a smile to his face.

In fact, there were times when I wondered if George Stark might be my father. He had been working at Wyndemere long before my mother arrived here, and once, when my mother was in the mood to tell me about her early days and my birth, she admitted she had needed help caring for me as well as caring for Ryder when I was born about two years after him.

"Mr. Stark's daughter Cathy helped me out for your first year. She stayed in what is your room. Dr. Davenport approved, but of course, that was before his second marriage. By the time his new wife moved in, I was able to handle both you and Ryder, so Cathy went home."

"I wondered why you always had me call her Aunt Cathy," I said.

"Just a kindness. She has a younger brother, Stuart, but they don't see each other much. Sometimes you have to adopt a family," my mother said. "It's too bad some nice young man in Hillsborough hasn't discovered how wonderful a wife Cathy Stark would make. The hospital here is lucky to have her nursing in the ER. Whatever she does, she does with great dedication and responsibility."

Aunt Cathy was always so glad to see me

and never forgot to bring me a present on my birthday and Christmas, just as her father never forgot. Suspicion ran deep, but I didn't see much resemblance between myself and Cathy or with Mr. Stark. Maybe that was because I romanticized too much about my real father, dreaming of a handsome and exciting young man who had swooped in one day and swept my mother off her feet. It was why I searched so hard for some clues, a letter, something. It was easy to imagine what it would say. Sometimes I invented the idea that he was already married at the time or that he was from a family so rich and powerful that the idea of his marrying my mother was practically science fiction.

In fact, I used to compose the love letters I imagined he would sneak into the house.

Dear Emma,

I was thinking so hard about you today and remembering how comforting and wonderful your smile for me could be that I forgot an important appointment. My wife was upset and demanded to know what I was thinking. I am so tempted to tell her. I am thinking about the most beautiful woman in the world. I am thinking about her kiss and how she

*embraced me. I am thinking of the minutes
and hours that were precious jewels in
my bank of memories, and I am thinking
about the child we created out of our love.*

I made up different names to use as his signa-
ture, most taken from great romances I had read
for extra credit in literature class, like Antony from
Antony and Cleopatra or Tristan from *Tristan and
Isolde*. I even signed one *Romeo*. As soon as I finished my letter and had read it at least ten times, I
would tear it into shreds, afraid my mother would
find it and be upset. It was always like ripping up
a beautiful dream. Yet it was something I thought I
might never stop doing, even when I was older and
entering high school.

Hillsborough was the township we lived in, and
Ryder, Sam, and I attended Hillsborough Central
School, which had the elementary school adjacent
to the junior-senior high school. I went to school
on a school bus, but Ryder and Sam were driven
to school by Dr. and Bea Davenport's limo driver,
Parker Thomson, a forty-five-year-old African-
American man with premature chalk-white hair
that made it look like a piece of a cloud had settled
on his head. He had been one of Dr. Davenport's
patients and was devoted to him. He was always
very nice to me, waving and smiling whenever he
saw me, but less so when Bea was present.

Ryder wanted me to ride with him and Sam, but Bea Davenport forbade it, and to my surprise and disappointment, Dr. Davenport rarely challenged anything she had decided regarding the house or the help. I thought he might make an exception when it came to me, but he didn't and was quick to dismiss Ryder's appeal to override his stepmother's rules. When I complained to my mother, she said perhaps he didn't want the distractions that came from domestic arguments.

"A cardiac specialist and surgeon like Dr. Davenport certainly doesn't want to leave the house for the hospital with any unnecessary worry on his shoulders. He could miss something important, and someone might die."

I couldn't deny he was a very busy and dedicated doctor who, according to my mother, "took his responsibilities as seriously as a bishop who had to report to the Almighty. Few men have life and death in their hands as many times a week as Dr. Davenport has," she said. But that still seemed like a weak excuse for his disinterest in what went on at Wyndemere.

From what I knew of him and from the way I heard people in the community talk about him, it did seem as if he walked on water. If there was anyone I really tiptoed around, it was Dr. Davenport, but he really never chastised me for anything more than not listening to my mother or obeying her strictly. From time to time, whenever he did see me, he asked how I was doing in school, but his questions were quick and to the point. Invariably, he would simply say, "Keep up the good work," quickly stroke my head like he might pet a kitten, and that would be that. I didn't think he really cared all that much whether I did well in school or not. He was simply being polite. For some people, good etiquette was sewn into their skin. It was as automatic as breathing. Still, it meant something to me to catch his attention, even if only for a few seconds a week, usually outside the house and away from Bea Davenport's disapproving eyes.

Dr. Davenport stood just a little over five foot ten, but he always seemed taller to me. I was always afraid to look him in the eyes. When I was little and my mother told me he operated on people's hearts, I thought he could see and know everything about someone, even his or her thoughts. His eyes were sterling-silver gray and piercingly intense whenever he spoke to anyone, especially me. He was very handsome in a distinguished sort of way, always closely shaven, his lips firm and straight. He went to an old-fashioned barber who cut his pecan-brown hair so precisely that there was never a strand too long or too short. Everything about his appearance was perfect. He wore a shirt and a tie like a uniform. My mother said he was one of those rare doctors "who actually practice what they preach."

His day began with an early-morning run along the banks of the lake, even on very cold days, and he watched his diet. When he did have a day off, he would go rowing on the lake for hours. As a consequence, he had a lean body and a ruddy complexion. What attracted my attention especially when I was little was how long his fingers were. If he shook hands with someone, his hand seemed to wrap completely around the other's. Everything he did, he did purposefully, slowly, as if placing something on a table was as critical a motion as the first incision to begin a heart operation.

He was as careful about his words as well. Whenever I heard him talking to Ryder or Sam, I smiled at how precise he was about what he wanted them to do or remember. He always repeated the important things, and when I asked my mother about that, she said, "Dr. Davenport believes few people listen the first time, and he's used to dictating medical information, how many pills to take, how often, and what to avoid while taking it."

"Maybe he thinks everyone's his patient, even his children," I said. "Even me!"

She gave me a strange look and then nodded. I caught her smiling to herself and wondered what I had said to bring some humor to mind. Maybe it was because she had thought something similar about Dr. Davenport but would never say it. She would never do or say anything even slightly disrespectful when it came to him. I don't think it was because she thought he was so much better than everyone, including herself, as much as it was because she had been here when he had suffered the loss of his parents and his first wife and then had cared for his children.

I used to be jealous of how well and lovingly she took care of Sam especially. I was three when Sam was born, and for those early years, at least, because my mother had me to care for, too, when Aunt Cathy wasn't available, Bea Davenport permitted me to be beside my mother when she looked after Sam. But I was forbidden to touch her. Sometimes when Bea wasn't in the house, however, my mother let me hold Sam's bottle while she drank. A real live baby, as opposed to a doll, was fascinating to watch. My mother assured me that Sam recognized me and smiled at me. I think she was trying to contain my jealousy.

Anyway, that was also how Ryder and I were able to spend more time together when we were little, when I accompanied my mother to do something for him or care for Sam, especially when Bea Davenport was out of the house. She was always attending this or that charity function and getting her picture on the society page of the local newspaper. Ryder got used to me being around him and loved to teach me how to work some of his toys. We would watch television together often during those years, too. Until Bea Davenport built "the Berlin Wall" between us in the house, Ryder used to say, "We're all like brother and sisters."

He wasn't saying that now, and it wasn't only because Bea Davenport insisted there be boundaries between us. No, there was another reason, or at least I hoped so. Deep in my heart, I felt it when he looked at me thinking I wasn't aware of it, but, like other boys at school, he suddenly realized I was capable of stirring him up, and maybe I could even be found in one of his sexual fantasies. I knew I had some about him. Well, maybe more than some.

One day recently, when he came to my room after school because I had asked him to help me with my math homework, which was really just an excuse to be close to him, he appeared sooner than I had expected. I had just started to change my clothes and was in my bra and panties when he stepped through my open doorway. My mother was in the kitchen helping Mrs. Marlene.

"Oh," he said, his face bursting with what I thought was delightful surprise, a rich crimson shade.

I shrugged and reached for my sweatshirt slowly. "It's the same as my two-piece bathing suit," I said. Of course, it wasn't. My panties were almost transparent, but I wanted to impress him with how sophisticated I was and how mature my body had become.

He nodded and went to my desk to look at my math text while I put on my jeans. He concentrated on explaining my math problem to me, but both of us sensed something had changed between us. Suddenly, he was affected by how close to him I stood and if we touched our arms or grazed our shoulders. It seemed like he couldn't wait to leave that afternoon, but I was confident it was because of how he was reacting to me rather than any displeasure with me.

"I've got a ton of homework myself," he blurted when I assured him I understood the math problem. I had to shout "Thanks!" after him. He was practically running down the hall to get away from himself as much as from me. Anyone else might have been offended, clamoring with annoyance. *What, do I have bad breath or something?* But not me. I knew Ryder too well. Something unexpected had stirred inside him, something that had already stirred in me as well.

It was true, I thought, that girls grew up faster than boys.

My girlfriends would often tease me about Ryder. They had all sorts of romantic scenarios in mind because we lived in the great house. Most of what they imagined were really wishes for themselves, understandable wishes. Ryder was even more handsome than his father, and he had the same firm, athletic build. I was sure he had inherited his father's intelligence, being a straight-A student.

I don't know when exactly I had begun to notice the smallest things about him, delicious things. I liked the way he would sweep his dark-brown bangs away from his eyes when he grew serious about something. Ever since he was fourteen, Ryder had wanted his hair longer than his father wanted him to have it. I think that was more a result of his stepmother Bea's negative comments about how he dressed and looked. I knew he often did things just to displease her, which usually resulted in Dr. Davenport having a heart-to-heart talk with him in his office. Ryder told me that it was almost like being called to the principal's office in school. I was fascinated with his descriptions of these sessions.

"He looks like he's about to take my pulse first, and he asks me questions like a doctor trying to diagnose what's wrong with you. 'Why did you do this? How do you feel when you do things like this?' By the time he's finished, I do feel sick," Ryder said. "I always expect him to say 'take two aspirins and behave' or something."

I felt sneaky knowing all this. After all, it wasn't my business. It was as if I had listened at the door. I never told my mother what he had told me, however. I didn't want her to think ill of him, not that she could, and to me it always seemed Ryder had more affection for my mother than he certainly did for his father's second wife. After all, my mother had practically brought him up herself. I knew Bea resented that, and it was probably why she was so adamant about keeping us in our servants' mode. We weren't permitted to forget that we were the hired help, not for an instant, even on our birthdays. Ryder would get us presents and usually say, "This is from my father and me," making a point of not including Bea.

Ryder had his mother's eyes, which were a soft blue or what my girlfriends called "dream eyes." His smile always started with those eyes and then rippled out over his high cheekbones and his nose with its high, prominent bridge, down to his firm, straight, "kissable" lips. He had a slightly cleft chin and was self-conscious about it, probably more so when he entered his teenage years. Nervously, he would put his right forefinger over it whenever he was in deep thought. No one else but me seemed to notice that. His mother had also had that cleft chin. I could see it in the beautiful headshots of her in frames on Dr. Davenport's office walls the few times I had been in there. But her cleft was even slighter than his.

Once, years later, when I was more comfortable talking to him, I put my finger on his cleft chin and told him what I had noticed him doing. He shrugged and revealed he had studied up on it.

"In Persian literature, you know, the chin dimple is considered a facet of beauty." He leaned toward me and, in a whisper that titillated me as much as a kiss might, added, "It's a well into which the poor lover has fallen and become trapped."

I was self-conscious about the way I blushed, so I snapped back at him with, "Yes, but yours isn't deep enough to trap a fly."

Ryder could be arrogant sometimes and too full of himself. He was honest enough to admit that to me and tell me, "You're the only one who reminds me I put my pants on one leg at a time."

I wasn't sure I was happy about that. It wasn't how I wanted him to think of me. It sounded too much like being a good friend, even a sister, and I was dreaming of more. But those feelings were yet to come. They were still embryonic, inside an egg far from being hatched. And boy, were those thoughts forbidden in the world of Wyndemere

House. Nothing could damage the Davenport image of being special.

Inside its walls, we were truly a world unto ourselves. Sometimes I believed the Davenports thought their personal history was as important as the country's, especially as it involved Dr. Davenport's father and mother. Awards, plaques given to them from high government officials, huge portraits of ancestors who looked like noblemen or princesses, even queens and kings, hung over fireplaces and in the entryway. When I was five my mother told me most posh families felt that way about themselves. "The blue bloods," she said, "think they were chosen to have special privileges."

"Why do you call them blue bloods?" I asked. I had seen Ryder cut himself and knew his blood was as red as mine.

"Aristocrats in the Middle Ages thought their blood was blue, and the term stuck," she said.

"This isn't the Middle Ages," I said. Even back then, at the age of eight, I didn't want to criticize Ryder and Sam, and I especially didn't want to think badly of Dr. Davenport.

My mother shrugged. "You could never convince Simon and Elizabeth Davenport of that."

I really didn't know Dr. Davenport's parents. His mother gave birth to him when she was nearly forty and his father was fifty. By the time my mother came to work for Dr. Davenport and his first wife, Samantha, his father was seventy-eight and a severe diabetic. There was a full-time nurse caring for him back then. According to my mother, Dr. Davenport's mother was one of those women determined to defeat age.

"She practically put her plastic surgeon's children through college singlehandedly and would spend hours in the morning working on her makeup before she would leave the house, usually to meet women overly made up like herself for lunch at some expensive restaurant. Her skin had been pulled and stretched so much it was practically transparent. You could see the veins in her face, which were always blue, convincing her she was truly a blue blood."

Mrs. Marlene told me Elizabeth Davenport interviewed undertakers to find one who would be skilled enough to make her look alive in her casket. She said, "The woman actually went to funerals if there was an open casket to inspect the work they had done. I wanted to tell her what my grandmother had told me: Never resist growing old. Many are denied that privilege."

These little stories about Dr. Davenport's parents trickled down to me as I grew older. I knew they had slept in separate bedrooms almost the day after returning from their honeymoon. I was told that they always dressed formally for dinner, something Dr. Davenport still did, and they were always wealthy. Simon Davenport had assumed control of his father's export-import business and had doubled its value. He had wanted Dr. Davenport to assume it, too, but Harrison Davenport was a brilliant student determined to become a cardiac surgeon. In the end, the business was sold, for what my mother called "an outlandish amount of money, enough to choke a horse."

Simon Davenport died before I was born, and Elizabeth had a stroke and lived in her room with around-the-clock care until I was six. I saw only glimpses of her when I was still permitted to go upstairs to either Ryder's or Sam's room when my mother cared for them. My memory of her was of a tiny woman practically swallowed up in a bed with huge pillows and a headboard with embossed angels. I thought they were there to carry her to heaven, but when I told my mother that, she shook her head and said, "Too heavy a load."

Too heavy a load? She looked like she was put together with chicken feathers.

I never realized she had died until weeks later. To me, the house wasn't any quieter or darker, and I saw no one, not even Dr. Davenport, crying. Later, my mother told me she and Mrs. Marlene had gone to the funeral.

"Did she look alive?" I asked.

She smiled. "I thought she was going to sit up

and complain about the uncomfortable coffin half-way through the service."

I knew my mother was just being funny, but for a long time afterward, I had dreams about this wisp of a woman with her styled and lacquered rust-brown dyed hair wandering through Wynde-mere House at night looking for some jewelry she was always accusing maids of stealing. When I told my mother about my dreams and visions, she did not laugh.

"Most ghosts," she said, "are visible only to children. But you have nothing to be afraid of, Fern. Elizabeth Davenport thought children were a nuisance and wished people were born grown-up. I don't think she was much of a mother for Dr. Davenport. From the way he talks sometimes, it was like she had completely forgotten she had given birth. Maybe she didn't," she added in an almost inaudible mumble.

There was another dark secret, I thought. It was no use to keep asking about it, either. My mother refused to follow and encourage gossip about the Davenports, especially when other members of the staff asked her questions.

"Never you mind," she'd tell them. "Manage yourself. You've got enough there to occupy your mind for a lifetime."

Even as they grew older, neither Ryder nor Sam seemed to care all that much about their grandparents and their family history. Sometimes, I thought because of my mother, I knew more than they did about their grandparents. Because I had so little when it came to family, I enjoyed the fact that they didn't talk about their own very much. Their world, like mine, was quite enough, even though we practically lived on separate planets. With Bea Davenport's heavy unwritten but clearly stated rules governing my behavior, it really was like visiting another house whenever I did cross over, either to help my mother with her chores or during a rare time when she and I were invited to participate in something. It was why I wasn't very helpful when the girls in my class asked me questions about Wyndemere.

"I really don't live there," I said. "I live in the afterthought, a part of the building created when the original owners realized they needed a place for their live-in help. Two maids slept where I sleep, and another maid and the cook back then slept where my mother sleeps."

It didn't sound good and certainly not like anything any of my friends would envy, but I saw no reason to lie about it. Someday I'd be leaving Wyndemere, and so would my mother. We'd be more like normal people then, I thought, although deep in my heart, I had a fear. I feared my mother would fade and die if she ever left Wyndemere.

I had no idea why.

It was another secret and one maybe not too far from the secret that squirmed restlessly just beyond my reach but was growing closer and closer with every passing year, and this year seemed to be going faster than the previous. Maybe that was because I was doing more with my friends. One thing I was going to do that I had never done was attend the prom. It would be my first formal date.

At Hillsborough, the senior class ran the school prom. Others attended, of course. Ryder was a senior this year and president of his class. Although he was always popular and invited to many parties and had many friends, he hadn't dated one girl as steadily as he did this year, Alison Reuben.

Alison Reuben was definitely the prettiest girl in Ryder's class. She had light strawberry-blond hair that floated around her cameo face dominated by her kelly-green eyes, and there was no other girl with fuller, more perfect lips. The patches of freckles at the crests of her cheeks and the richness of her complexion made any makeup extraneous. She didn't even have to put on lipstick, because her lips were so bright, a sort of reddish orange. I wanted so much to hate her, because she was one of those girls who knew they were beautiful and let everyone else know it, too.

Ryder was blind to any faults in her character, and I was certainly not going to be the one to point any out. Whenever I was near them, she was pleasant enough to me but always acted toward me the way someone much older and more sophisticated would. Although she never came right out and said it, I sensed she saw me as only the little girl whose mother worked for Ryder's parents.

So I was very surprised when one night after dinner, when I was doing some homework and lying on my bed in my pajamas, I heard a soft knock on my not-quite-closed door and looked up to see Ryder peering in.

"Hey," he said. "Can I talk to you?"

I slammed my history book closed so fast and hard that I almost caught a finger in it. "Come in," I said, sitting up. He stepped in. "Close the door."

He thought a moment, as if he had to step over hot coals, and then did so.

"What's happening?"

I brought my knees up and embraced my legs. He came closer and, after a slight hesitation, sat on my bed. My pajama top was open more than it should be, but I didn't rush to button it. I saw how his eyes were drawn to the growing fullness of my breasts.

"What do you think of Paul Gabriel?" he asked.

"Paul Gabriel? He's a senior."

"Right."

I shrugged. "I don't think of him at all," I

replied, tucking the sides of my mouth in. That triggered a dimple in my right cheek, the same dimple my mother had. I supposed one of the things that made it easier to ignore wondering who my father might be was the strong resemblance I bore to my mother. We had the same violet eyes and raven hair, with curls that were always a little frizzy and untamed. Our foreheads were a little too wide, but we made up for it with perfect, diminutive features, high cheekbones, and full lips.

"Yeah, well, he's noticed you," Ryder said.

"Really?" I searched my memory for any snapshot visions of Paul Gabriel. He was tall, over six feet, with an awkward gait. I vaguely knew he was one of the best pitchers on the school's baseball team, but I couldn't recall ever speaking to him.

"He's a nice enough guy, actually shy."

I nodded. "So?"

"So he came to me to ask if I thought you would go to the prom with him."

"Paul Gabriel? I don't think he's said two words to me."

"I told you he was shy. I think you'd have a good time. I bet not too many girls in your class are being asked," he added.

"I don't know."

"If you agree, he'll drive. He's got his own car."

I started to shake my head.

"And we'd double-date," he said. "There's an after-party at Shane Cisco's house."

"Really? Is Alison all right with that?"

"She will be. I haven't told her yet. Paul called me again about it tonight. So what do you say? C'mon. It'll be fun. Paul's okay. I wouldn't set you up with anyone who wasn't," he added.

"I'll ask my mother," I said. "But I know I don't have the right sort of dress."

"I've got an idea," he said, leaning forward, his hand on my knee. "I know where my mother's dresses are stored in the attic. We'll find one that works, and you can get it fitted. Okay?"

"I guess," I said, shocked and delighted at how determined he was to get me to go, determined enough to want me to wear one of his mother's dresses.

"Great." He stood up and started out.

"Hey," I called when he opened the door. "You didn't arrange all this just to get a ride to the prom, did you? Because I know you wouldn't want Parker driving you like some snobby rich kid, and your father hasn't bought you your car yet."

He smiled. "What a terrible thing to think," he said, widening his smile, and he left.

Did I know him, or did I know him? Whatever, what did I care about his reason? We'd be double-dating! It would be my first formal date, too.

I lay back and looked up at the ceiling.

It all sounded wonderful, but how was Alison going to react to this? I could count on the fingers of one hand how many conversations she'd had with me so far this year, and those were usually "Oh, hello." I wasn't exactly the choice she would make for a girl to share her big night. She had many close friends in her own class.

And then I wondered, what would it be like going to the prom with a boy I hadn't even spoken that much to all year? And anyway, could I give Paul Gabriel the attention my date should have if I was with Ryder? Every time he kissed Alison, I would imagine he was kissing me.

Could I hide that from Paul Gabriel? What if he realized it and blurted out something like "Hey, she's jealous"?

Alison might tell him to take care of his own business, meaning me. What would I do then? I had yet to kiss a boy the way I dreamed of kissing Ryder. And the prom . . . what if it led to something further? Would my resistance fit Alison's view of me perfectly?

She's just a little girl. Why did Ryder arrange this?

I might spoil their night with my innocence.

My worries fit. After all, this was virgin me afraid of justifying the dirty thoughts boys whispered behind my back because I was a mistake.

Was I a mistake?

And was it true that girls who were mistakes had a tendency to be more promiscuous after all? I was always worried about my sexual thoughts and the fantasies I couldn't seem to stop lately.

What did this really mean?

Maybe I didn't have long to find out.

And maybe that frightened me more than anything.

2

PAUL GABRIEL WASN'T just physically awkward, walking as if one of his legs was shorter than the other; he was socially awkward as well. Shy wasn't the right word for it. Ryder had searched for a euphemism for crude, unsophisticated, and as far from romantic and graceful as the planet Mars was from Earth. I knew shy boys who had a sweetness about them. Shy fit them as well as a perfectly sized shoe. They were cute. Paul wasn't ugly, but he certainly wasn't cute. I couldn't imagine that Ryder was that close to him, either, or at least any closer than he was with other boys in the senior class. Truthfully, I hadn't seen them together that much.

Ryder was correct in saying that few, if any, other girls from my class would be asked to the prom, but what he didn't understand was that I would go not just to be one who was invited but because I would be with him and Alison. I was confident that Paul Gabriel took it the way he thought any girl might, that I was excited enough to go on a date with him because he was one of the school's sports heroes.

The following day, Ryder invited me to sit with him and Alison in the cafeteria. I was surprised. Ryder and Alison were always surrounded by friends who were either seniors or juniors. A seat at their table was cherished as if it was a seat with royalty. This particular day, no one was walking toward a table with them. I saw Ryder nudge Alison when I entered the cafeteria. My eyes always went to Ryder when I was in the same room with him in school, whether that was the gym, the auditorium, or the cafeteria. She rolled her eyes.

I was keenly aware of how much closer his relationship with Alison had become, practically counting how many times he pressed his shoulder against hers or snuck in a peck on her cheek like someone stealing a grape off a vine. I realized their affection for each other was maturing into love. They were behaving more and more as if there was no one else in the room. I think there were times when my eyes were soaked in jealous tears that I couldn't stop. I was watching a star grow dimmer and dimmer in the night sky, a star certainly out of my reach.

Maybe my jealousy colored how I viewed Alison. Did she sense that, and was that why she deliberately treated me as if I was still in grade school? I never wanted to dislike someone Ryder liked. I was terrified of his being disappointed in me if I even hinted at something unpleasant about her.

Instead, if anything, I tried to emulate Alison, even to walk like she walked or keep that Madonna smile on my face, too. I was hoping that someday Ryder would say, "You're just like Alison." He would give me a longer second look and maybe think, *I have someone very precious right under my eyes.*

Timidly, I approached them. Now that they were drawing me into their circle, even if only for a short time, the possibility that Alison would take one good look at my face and know how jealous I was worried me. She wouldn't want anything to do with me then. No girl would want someone too close who was competing with her for her boyfriend's attention.

"Hey," Ryder said. "Grab your lunch and join us."

"Really?"

"No. Pretend," he said. He smiled. "Of course. C'mon. Just join us, Fern."

I watched him discourage other boys from sitting at their table. Whatever he had said to them didn't upset them. Naturally, I rushed to get my

food and nearly tripped carrying my tray over to
their table.

"Hi," I said stupidly, as if I was just meeting
them. I was that nervous. I knew all my girlfriends
were watching and wondering.

Just as I sat, Paul Gabriel approached and sat
beside me. Alison still didn't look terribly happy
about my joining them, but Ryder was smiling
in anticipation. So that was why he invited me, I
realized. The prom invitation was to come here
and now. I held my breath, wondering if, when it
came right down to it, I would back out and maybe
make Alison happy.

"Hey," Paul said. I turned to him. *Hey?* Great
way to start a conversation, I thought. On the
other hand, my mother had told me that *hey* in
Swedish meant *hello*. Not that Paul Gabriel was
Swedish.

The awkwardness in his movements, however,
seemed to have invaded his face. When he smiled,
it influenced only the right side of his mouth, his
lips parting enough just at the corner. I had never
noticed the color of his eyes, having hardly given
him a second glance, but now I noted how they
were a dull, faded blue. He had a thin nose and
slim cheeks that flowed down to his angular jaw.
He wore his long light-brown hair unruly, looking
like someone who brushed it quickly in the morning with his fingers.

Ryder said Paul had the perfect baseball pitcher's body, tall with good shoulders and long arms and hands. He had already broken the school's record for strikeouts when he was only a sophomore, and there was real talk that a major-league team was scouting him. Right now, he wore a Hillsborough T-shirt and jeans. He had an expensive-looking watch that I would learn was given to him on his sixteenth birthday, more as a celebration of his athletic achievements than for his special year.

"Hey," I replied, and looked at Ryder, who gave me a slight nod of encouragement. Should I want this more than I was demonstrating?

I turned back to Paul and smiled. For a moment, I thought he had used his entire vocabulary. I saw him glance at Ryder, maybe for help. Now that I gave him more thought, I realized Paul had no special girlfriends, no one special cheering for him at games. When it wasn't baseball season, he was practically lost in the woodwork, as my mother would say. Maybe going to the prom with him was so far from an achievement in the eyes of my girlfriends that no one would be jealous. Of course, I wasn't doing it to draw their envy. I liked to think I was doing it for Ryder.

"So what's up with you, Paul?" Ryder asked. He tilted his head toward me.

"Huh? Oh," he said. He turned back to me. "So, Fern, anyone ask you to the prom yet?"

"Not yet," I said.

Ryder's smile widened. "You'd better move quickly, then," he told Paul.

"Yeah, so I was thinking that maybe you'd go with me," Paul said.

Like Ryder, there was a part of me that enjoyed teasing sometimes. "Go where?" I asked, and put on a face of confusion that even I had trouble not laughing at.

"The prom," he said, as if there was absolutely nowhere else in the world to go.

"Oh, the prom. No," I said. "No one's asked me to that."

"Well, do you think you would go with me?"

"Yeah, I think so," I said. "When you ask, I'll know for sure if I would."

Alison couldn't hold back a laugh this time.

Ryder threw a piece of carrot at Paul. "Ask her, already. I've got to finish lunch."

"Would you go with me to the prom?" Paul asked, like a line he had been practicing all night.

"I will go with you," I said, as if I had memorized the next line.

Maybe imagining we were in a play together wasn't such a fantastic idea. I felt like I was taking on a role just so I could be on the same stage as Ryder and Alison after all. Most of the time, we were all performing for each other around here anyway, I thought, and it did make this easier.

Paul smiled. "That's great. We'll double-date with Ryder and Alison. Okay?"

"Ryder?" I said, looking at him. "You're going to the prom?"

"Smart-ass," Ryder said.

Paul laughed. He did look very pleased, like he had just saved the ball game. Maybe it would be a fun time after all. Ryder would help me find the dress up in the attic. Perhaps my mother would let me have my hair done at a beauty salon. It would be exciting to try a new style, one that would reduce the frizziness. My mother had some earrings and necklaces that might work. She never told me how she had gotten them and never wore them herself, but when I was little, I'd put them on and pretend I was going to a charity ball like Bea Davenport, who was always so bedecked in jewelry that I thought she would sink if she fell into a pool. I started to realize that the glamour of the prom, staying out late, and going to an after-party had the potential to make this the most exciting night of my life up to now.

Ryder winked at me. Then he and Paul began talking baseball. Ryder was the starting third baseman.

"Boys can be so boring," Alison said. "And some are too spoiled," she added, throwing a look back at Ryder.

"What do you mean?" I asked.

"I think it would be cool to go to the prom in a chauffeur-driven limousine, but just because he comes and goes to school in it, Ryder thinks it's no big deal. Instead, he hatched this plot to double-date with Paul just to have him drive us."

"Oh," I said.

"I mean, he could have had Paul take you anyway if that was important to Paul, and we wouldn't have to ride in his old car."

I didn't know what to say. Did she think I had put Ryder up to it? "You saw I didn't try to arrange this, right?"

"Whatever," she said. "I hope you have something good to wear. I'm getting a new dress just for the prom."

"Oh. What's it like?"

"I'll let you know," she said. "Ryder told me about getting you one of his mother's gowns. I don't know why he's so excited about that. It could be very wrong, too old-fashioned."

"Is he very excited about it?"

She paused and pursed her lips. "I've never seen him so excited about a woman's dress. He never gets that excited about what I wear."

"But it is his real mother's dress, after all," I said. "I'm excited about it, too."

All my girlfriends looked surprised at how intense my conversation with Alison was getting. Most looked a little jealous. I wasn't thinking of her as much as I was thinking about the actual prom date. I felt as though I had made a leap for myself, a giant leap for womankind. This would be the first time I would be out with Ryder at night, and for me, even though I wasn't his actual date, that was like reaching the moon.

"Yes, well, maybe I'll have to help. If you look stupid and we're together, I'll look stupid," she said, and walked off to class.

At the end of the day, I couldn't wait to get home to tell my mother. She was having a cup of coffee with Mr. Stark in our small kitchen. The moment I entered, I paused, checking my excitement. I believed that some of us were born with sharper instincts than others or at least developed those instincts sooner. One thing I had grown up being alert to in Wyndemere was when someone was talking about me. Even when I was only seven or eight, I could sense when I had been the topic of discussion. I knew Mrs. Marlene was always concerned about me, as concerned as a mother or a grandmother might be, and when I walked into the kitchen and everyone would grow silent and busy, I knew my name had been on everyone's lips.

It seemed to me that this attention was directed at me because I didn't have a father. For most of my time living in Wyndemere, because of the demands that were made on my mother, I was left alone to fend for myself far more than most girls my age.

I was the object of some concern, even some pity. At a much younger age than any of my classmates, I had to start preparations for our dinner or help to look after our small section of the great house, vacuuming and washing down the kitchen floor and counters as well as the windows. None of the maids was permitted to do any cleaning for us, but my mother was keen on us keeping the old and worn furnishings immaculate. She wanted to take another possible criticism out of Bea Davenport's bag of complaints for sure. While my mother was off supervising their care of the grand mansion, the washing and drying of clothes and the preparation and serving of meals, I was left with much more responsibility than any other girl my age.

I didn't mind it. I was never lazy or neglectful. I think some of my determination to do well came from my reaction to Bea Davenport's obvious condescension, the way she looked down on us and especially me, making me feel as if I might contaminate Sam. I never felt the doctor was looking at us that way, but he wasn't home as much as Bea was, of course, and when he was home, he rarely came to our section of the house or had much to do with the servants. I knew that he usually retreated to his office-library. Ryder told me it was very rare for his father to relax with him and his stepmother in the living room to read or watch television. The truth was, both he and his father went to their respective private places, which was why Sam wandered down to my room so often, especially when Bea was out at one of her social events.

I was sure that Mrs. Marlene and my mother, and even Mr. Stark, were worried that I wouldn't grow up normally in this environment. Not being permitted to have friends over and being caged in the way I was, I would surely develop all sorts of complexes. I was already heavily weighted down with the stigma of being what Bea Davenport had no trouble calling "an illegitimate child."

It made me wonder what a legitimate child really was. There were religious people who believed I had been born without a soul. Some of Bea Davenport's posh friends looked at me as if I were no better than some wild animal born in the forest. I knew they were expecting me to be uncouth and ill mannered and have the poorest hygiene. When I was five years old and my mother had bought me a new dress for my birthday, I overheard a woman named Clair Edison, who saw me playing out front in my new clothes, say, "You can put lipstick on a pig, but it's still a pig."

When I told my mother what I had heard Clair Edison say, her eyes turned into knives for a moment. She looked like she was going to charge out to confront both Mrs. Edison and Bea Davenport, who were sitting on the veranda having afternoon tea. She even went to the door, opened it, and took a step out before pausing. I was too young to understand why, but whatever had changed her mind saddened me. From that day on, I tried to avoid doing anything in Bea Davenport's presence. I embraced my mother's warning to stay out of her shadow.

Right now, when I stepped into our kitchen and saw my mother's and Mr. Stark's faces, I felt my heart skip a beat. I closed the door behind me softly.

"What's wrong?" I asked. I borrowed one of Mr. Stark's favorite expressions. "You both look like you've been nursing the same beer for the past three hours."

Mr. Stark smiled, but it was just a flash. He turned to my mother, the look of concern returning.

"Mrs. Davenport was here about an hour ago," my mother began. "Why didn't you tell me you were going to go on a double date with Ryder to the prom?"

"I wasn't sure until today. Why?"

"Dr. Davenport informed her this morning, and she's upset."

"Ryder must have told his father a friend of his was going to ask me, and he must have told her," I said, putting my books on the counter. "Why would that matter to her, anyway?"

"Dr. Davenport told her Ryder asked permission to let you use one of his first wife's dresses. I don't think that went over very well with her."

"More like a lead balloon," Mr. Stark said.

"She accused me of putting you up to asking, since I would know there were dresses in the attic."

"So?" I leaned back against the counter and folded my arms across my breasts. Defiance stiffened my whole body. "I still don't get it. What put a hot poker up her—"

"Fern!"

"Why is she upset?" I asked.

"She says I should have first asked her permission. She's the mistress of Wyndemere. I told her all of this was news to me, but she doesn't believe me, of course. She thinks I deliberately went around her. She's someone who stands on ceremony. She'll never eat salad with anything but a salad fork. She'd rather starve."

"It was Ryder's idea," I said. "Why doesn't she ask him?"

"I imagine she will," my mother said. "But she probably won't believe him. She won't want to believe him."

"So what does this mean? I shouldn't go to the prom?"

"When were you going to tell me about it?"

"Right now. I was only asked at lunch. Bugger!" I added, mimicking one of her favorite British exclamations.

Mr. Stark started to smile but stopped when he glanced at my mother.

"I didn't say you can't go. I'll just get you your own dress, Fern. Mr. Stark will be glad to drive you and the boy who asked you."

"My pleasure," Mr. Stark said. "I've never been to a prom."

"The boy's name is Paul Gabriel. He's a senior, and he has his own car and can drive at night. Ryder wanted us to go together so he wouldn't have to be driven by Parker."

"That's his battle to fight, Fern," my mother said. "You just stay clear of that woman until Dr. Davenport decides what's what."

"Ryder wanted me to wear one of his real mother's dresses," I said, the tears starting to burn my eyes. "That's important to him, and that's what I'd like to do, too. I don't think there are many alterations to do."

My mother shook her head. "Don't push, Fern. A branch that bends in the wind lasts longer."

"I'm not a branch. I'm a human being with blood as red as hers," I said sharply, then scooped up my books and went to my room, shutting the door behind me before falling onto my bed and embracing my pillow. Hours ago, I felt I was flying like an eagle. Now I felt I was crawling like a worm, a worm under Bea Davenport's foot. I was hot with rage. My mother should find a job somewhere else. *We should get out of this house*, I thought. Why didn't she ever try? *She's not appreciated and I'm certainly not.*

I turned on my back, folded my arms under my breasts, and sulked. What gave some people the right to believe they walked with angels? Was it simply a matter of money? This was America. We were all supposed to be equal, even me, an "illegitimate child." Maybe that was only something taught to grade-school children so they would recite the Pledge of Allegiance enthusiastically.

My mother knocked on my door and then peeked in. "Don't get so upset over this," she said. "You'll have many more dates, dates without Bea Davenport putting her nose where it doesn't belong."

She sat at the foot of my bed and put her hand on my leg. One thing my mother had taught me without formally doing so was that when you wanted to reach someone, really reach them, it helped to take their hand while you spoke or gently touch their arm. The physical contact reinforced your sincerity. I always wanted to do that whenever I spoke with Ryder, but I was afraid he would shake me off, and that would nearly bring me to tears. Something always kept us from getting too close, even when we were little. Would that always be true?

And why were we both like that, anyway? Did

we realize that if we opened up just a little to each other, a flood of emotion and affection would follow and be so strong it would overwhelm us both? I couldn't even begin to imagine Bea Davenport's reaction to that. Might as well try to imagine a hydrogen-bomb explosion.

"As long as we're under this roof, she'll sneer down at us," I said. "And Dr. Davenport doesn't do enough to stop her. I don't care how busy he is."

I realized there were many more words and feelings of rage bottled up inside me. I was always afraid to be too bold about my complaints or, as my mother might say, cheeky. The very thought of drawing Dr. Davenport into my tantrums was terrifying, not that he was any sort of ogre. He was more like some sort of king who shouldn't be bothered with the day-to-day problems of his lesser subjects.

"The best way to handle snobs is to pretend they don't exist," my mother said. "Nothing infuriates them more than being ignored. If I tried to convince her about the dress, she'd enjoy lording it over us, Fern. Believe me, it will bother her more to see you buy your own beautiful gown."

I looked away. How could I explain my feelings about it without revealing how much it meant to me to be wearing Ryder's mother's dress? If I looked beautiful in it, he would look at me so differently. The dress had a special meaning for him.

The very idea that he would think of this, would want me to wear it, had filled me with such excitement. And here was Bea Davenport ruining it.

"Tell me about your date," my mother said.

I'd better not say Ryder had arranged it, I thought. It wasn't easy, but I dressed Paul Gabriel in what we had learned was hyperbole. "He's the star of our baseball team, a senior, Paul Gabriel, and will probably become a major-league player and have his face on boxes of cereal someday. He's polite, a little shy, but very popular at school because of his achievements on the baseball field. We might look funny dancing together, because he's six foot four. In heels, I might reach five foot five, so maybe we'll look all right, maybe even cute together. His father owns Gabriel Insurance."

"He sounds like the bee's knees," my mother said. She slapped my knee lovingly and stood up. "We'll go dress hunting this weekend. Oh, when is the prom?"

"Weekend after next," I said. "It's at the school. The senior class has to design it. Ryder's president of the class, you know."

"Yes. He's definitely the bee's knees. Well, I'm sure it will be a special night for you. Forget about the rest of this."

"There's an after-party, too." I thought it best to reveal this while she was trying to cheer me up.

"Oh? Why is that?"

"The prom always ends early, and rather than drive around looking for something else to do, there's this party."

"Where?"

"At someone's house, Shane Cisco. He's one of Ryder's best friends in school."

She thought a moment. "Well, if Dr. Davenport approves of Ryder going, I suppose I can approve of your going. What time is all this over?"

"It could go all night," I said. "It's a tradition."

She stood there staring at me in a funny way and then shook her head.

"What?" I asked.

"My father loved that word. He used it to stifle any and every new thought my sister and I had or explain away anything he wanted us to do without really justifying it. His answer was always because it was traditional. Just be wary of anyone who wants you to do something because it's traditional. But," she said, changing her dour expression and tone instantly, "I'm sure it will be a wonderful night for you. I wish I'd had a prom."

"Didn't you have any nights like that back in England?"

She looked thoughtful again. Was she about to reveal that part of her past that she had kept so long under lock and key? She shook her head. "Sometimes remembering the past makes the present unbearable. That's not unusual, Fern. Your childhood, these years, are meant to be golden. Then you become an adult, and suddenly you can no longer be oblivious and carefree. Don't rush to get there. I'll start on dinner," she said, and left me feeling so twisted up inside that I wished I had no feelings for anything, anything at all.

Later that night, after my mother had gone to bed and I had just slipped under my covers and was about to turn off my night-table lamp, I heard my bedroom door being opened. I sat up as quickly as I would if I believed one of Mrs. Marlene's famous ghosts had arrived.

It was Ryder.

His face looked flushed with excitement. He was in his robe and pajamas.

"What's happening?" I whispered. With all the commotion Bea Davenport had stirred up, I knew my mother would not be happy about his sneaking down and over to our side and giving her another reason to complain.

"My father just had a big fight with my stepmother. First time I've heard him like that. And it was all about the dress for you to wear to the prom."

"Really? You know she came over here to complain to my mother?"

"No," he said. "Why?"

"She thought my mother had come up with the idea and told your father. From what she said, my mother thought he was the one who might have complained to your stepmother and sent her here to bawl out my mother."

"He only told her about it. He didn't complain. Tonight she started to rant and rave about it, and they had the fight. Believe me, he thought it was okay for you to wear my mother's dress."

"Oh. So what do I do? My mother wants to take me shopping for a dress this weekend, and she thinks you won't be able to double-date with Paul and me now."

"Forget that. I discussed it with my father, and he's approved. Tomorrow you're coming home from school in the limousine with Sam and me and Alison."

"Alison?"

"Yes. As soon as we're home, the three of us are going up to the attic to choose the best gown. And if my stepmother doesn't like it, she can . . . go to another charity luncheon," he said, and smiled.

"Alison wants to do that?" I asked. I tried to hide my disappointment. I was dreaming of Ryder and me alone in the attic, rifling through clothes and in a unique way being more intimate than we had ever been. I was sure he would share his feelings about never knowing his real mother. He would tell me things that he had never told anyone, maybe even his father.

"Sure. She wants to be in on the decision, and besides, what do I know about women's clothes? We'll talk more about it at lunch tomorrow," he said.

"I hate to have been the reason for a fight between your parents."

"She's not my mother, so I don't think of her as a parent. Forget about it. I'm glad my father finally spoke up."

"I suppose," I said.

He stepped a little closer and looked at me so softly that my heart began to race. Then he touched my hand and smiled. I wanted him to kiss me, and I think he wanted to do that, too, but he pulled his hand back.

"See you in the morning," he said, and left as quietly as he had come.

I lay back on my pillow and thought about what he had told me. It was all making me nervous now. Dr. Davenport had never interceded to take my side or, as far as I knew, my mother's side in any dispute that involved Bea Davenport. Was this his way of revealing how much he really missed his first wife? Maybe my mother was wrong about all that; maybe he was pointed in Samantha's direction, but he had honestly fallen in love with her. I decided I would ask my mother more about it. She was certainly going to be surprised at the outcome about the dress.

On the other hand, she'd remind me that a poked snake never forgets. You could win a battle but lose the war, and in this house, there seemed to be continuous hostilities going on, with constant skirmishes about how things were cleaned, how dinners were served, and how the servants behaved in general. Whenever it was to her advantage to do so, Bea Davenport would remind my mother she was supposedly the house manager or something. Therefore, any problem, no matter how small, had to be her fault. It was as if from day one, Bea Davenport was out to build a case to justify dismissing my mother and evicting us from Wyndemere. Perhaps my mother's compromise, at least regarding the dress, was the best way to go for now.

How had something that had loomed so wonderful become the cause of so much turmoil? I knew Bea Davenport well enough to believe she would not accept defeat when it came to ruling what she surely believed was her kingdom, Wyndemere. I had seen my mother verbally abused by her, and I had seen how my mother did not fight back. Perhaps she knew that was exactly what Bea Davenport hoped for, a defiant, disobedient house manager who would not work well with her. She always looked more frustrated by my mother's retreat, at least whenever I had witnessed one. This had the makings of being different. It wasn't over, not by a long shot, and it made me very nervous.

Maybe it would even ruin our special night.

At breakfast the following morning, I told my mother about Ryder's visit and what he had said. As I anticipated, she did not look happy about it.

"What do I do?" I asked.

She sat with her cup of coffee silently for a few moments.

"Ryder never accepted Bea Davenport," she began. "Even as an infant, he seemed repulsed by her. In those days, when I was caring for Ryder and you, I expected she would assume some of a mother's role, do things like shop for him, look after his eating and hygiene, and perhaps even play with him, show him some attention. She didn't have Samantha until nearly a year after she and Dr. Davenport had married, and when she did give birth, she repulsed Ryder even more."

"You were more like a mother to him once his real mother died. I'm sure Dr. Davenport realizes that, too."

"Yes." She looked up at me, her eyes narrowing. "I have great fondness for Ryder. He's a wonderful young man, but you have to be wary of one thing, Fern."

"What?" I asked, feeling like my heart had paused in anticipation and fear.

"Be wary of him using you to strike at his step-mother," she said.

"I don't understand."

"I'm sure he would like nothing more than his father driving her out of their lives. This dress could be a way of building a wedge between them. And I'm sure he'll be on the lookout for other ways."

"He's not that conniving, Mother," I said, a little outraged at the suggestion.

She shrugged at my indignation. "It's not neces-sarily a weakness to be good at conniving in this world, Fern. Perhaps I know Ryder better than anyone."

"He's not a mean person," I insisted.

"I didn't say he was. What he wants to do doesn't come from meanness. It comes from want-ing more love."

"His father loves him, doesn't he? Even though he's not the most emotional man. I guess he's like that because of what he does, right? I mean, a doc-tor who has patients who might die and do die can't be emotional. Am I right?"

She rose and went to the sink. "You don't want to miss the bus," she said.

"Well, what do I do about the dress? Ryder wants to have me and Alison Reuben choose one today."

She turned and looked at me, obviously deciding.

"If it's what Dr. Davenport wants or approves, then damn the torpedoes, full speed ahead," she said.

I started to laugh and then stopped, wondering just what those torpedoes would be like.

3

RYDER DIDN'T INVITE me to go to school in the limousine with him and Sam. I waited for the bus at my usual spot in front of Wyndemere and watched as he and Sam were driven off. The windows were tinted, so I didn't know if either was looking my way. For years, it was like this, even if it was raining. My mother gave me an umbrella, and I stood under an old maple, but in the late fall and winter, with the leaves stripped away, that provided little shelter. Usually, I didn't have to wait much longer after they had left in the Davenports' limousine. Ryder had told me his stepmother had mentioned that the one and only time his father suggested I go to school with them.

"She has only to wait another five minutes," she

had said. "We must draw the line between what we give our servants and what we give ourselves."

My mother would surely call her a Royalist, I thought, and imagined she did, if not to herself, then to Mrs. Marlene.

Today I was more disappointed than ever about not going in the limousine to school, however. But then I thought Ryder might not want to telegraph his plans to his stepmother, which, I'd have to admit, was somewhat shrewd on his part. He didn't want to give Bea another opportunity to stand in our way by complaining to Dr. Davenport about how Ryder and I were defying her orders every chance we had. My mother probably did know Ryder best of all. Still, despite his cleverness, I couldn't help but be nervous about what we were planning to do after school.

Once again, the four of us sat at the same table during lunch. I could feel we were the center of attention. All my friends were looking our way and chattering like excited sparrows.

"How big is the attic at Wyndemere?" Alison asked me. "Wyndemere is such a huge mansion."

Ryder waited for me to answer, but I shook my head. "I don't remember ever being up there. I don't even know exactly how you go up there, where the stairs are."

"It's about a third as big as the house, like a loft," Ryder explained. "Some of the things up there go back to before my grandparents owned the place, furniture, armoires full of old bedding and stuff. There's nothing terribly valuable, as far as I know, except, of course, my mother's things. But they're valuable only to my father and me," he emphasized.

"Maybe there's some buried treasure," Paul suggested. "Or a dead body, a skeleton." He grimaced as if he was telling a story on Halloween.

"Thanks. I'm taking these girls up there. You're not helpful."

Paul shrugged and laughed.

"There's a stairway on the east end of the upstairs, just beyond the last guest bedroom," Ryder said, more to me than to Alison. "I haven't been up there that much, either. Almost all the times I went up when I was younger were with your mother."

"My mother? Why was she up there?"

"I don't know. She was looking for something or other. There were some old toys she thought I'd like, I guess. I don't even know whose they were. My father didn't seem to know when I showed them to him, so they weren't his. I did go up there with my father a year ago. He didn't tell me why he was going up. He just invited me to go with him, and when my father invites me to do something with him, I drop everything I'm doing to go."

"Yeah, when my father invites me to go with

him someplace, it's to help with something, do some work," Paul said. "I hide."

Alison laughed, but I wanted Ryder to stay on the subject and tell more.

"Why did Dr. Davenport go up there?" I asked.

"He went through my mother's things looking for something. That's how I learned about the dresses."

"What was he looking for?" I asked.

"I don't know. Some jewelry, maybe, or some picture. I wasn't paying all that much attention."

"It's nice your father still thinks about her," Alison said.

I looked at her. I wished I had said it because of the smile Ryder gave her and how he reached for her hand. He behaved as though he thought there was magic in their touch. It brought a glow to his face.

"He's pretty busy, but when he has a chance to relax and do nothing, I believe that's all he thinks about," Ryder told her. "I'm kind of like that with you."

Alison's smile deepened. She glanced at me with a look in her eyes that told me, *See? He's clay in my hands to mold.*

Ryder paused, a little embarrassed at how he and Alison were behaving as if Paul and I weren't there, too.

"Okay," he said, turning back to us. "So we're set. Paul, did you get your tuxedo?"

"Huh? Oh, yeah. I gotta buy one of those."

"You rent it, Paul, with tuxedo shoes. Next time you use a tux will probably be your wedding," Ryder told him.

Alison laughed. "He'll probably get married on a baseball mound," she said.

All the blood in his body seemed to rush into Paul's face. I actually felt a little sorry for him.

"You own a tuxedo, don't you, Ryder? You don't rent one, right?" I asked.

"Yeah, but that's because of the charity events my father and Bea make me and Sam attend. Paul's luckier."

"Well, maybe you should go with him to pick one out and all that comes with it," I suggested, sounding like I was defending and looking out for Paul, I'm sure. Ryder's smile widened at how quickly I got concerned.

"You should," Alison said. "He's liable to get something with pins and stripes."

"Huh?" Paul said.

"Well, I guess I will," Ryder replied. He saluted us both, and Alison and I started to laugh. "We've got our marching orders, Paul. This Saturday, we get you fitted. Don't make any other plans."

"Yes, sir," Paul said, saluting, too.

"We're going to have the best time of anyone at the prom," Ryder promised. "Dressed like penguins or not, Paul. Of course, the women will be dazzling."

"They are now," Paul replied, and Ryder looked surprised at his sharp, clever response, but very happy.

For me, it was as if I had stepped on a cloud.

However, despite Ryder's assurance that his father not only approved of my using one of his first wife's gowns but seemed pleased by the idea as well, I was still quite anxious and edgy at the end of the school day. What if he had changed his mind while we were in school, or once we chose a dress and he saw which one it was, he told us to put it back? I'd be devastated, and it might be the cause of a bad argument between Ryder and his father. How would I feel then? What a damper that would put on the prom.

Nothing was as simple as it seemed, especially within the confines of Wyndemere. There were no normal expectations. Mrs. Marlene's ghosts were always in the shadows, and I was always walking on thin ice.

All my girlfriends, most of whom had been cross-examining me about every detail related to the prom, were surprised when I veered off the path to the school buses and headed for the front of the building, where Parker usually parked to wait for Ryder and Sam. I had said nothing about it, realizing this might be the one and only time I would go home in the limousine. It was painful to explain to them how my mother and I were treated at Wyndemere, painful and difficult, because I didn't want to blame the doctor for anything, and I certainly didn't want gossip to get back to Bea Davenport.

Alison, Ryder, and Sam were already waiting at the limousine.

"C'mon," Ryder urged, holding the door open for me. It felt like some kind of urgent escape.

I slipped in to sit between Alison and Sam. Ryder sat across from us.

"All aboard?" Parker asked.

"And ready for takeoff," Ryder replied. He took one look at my face and shook his head. "Stop worrying so much, Fern. Follow Bea's instructions, and never grimace with concern, or you'll get wrinkles."

He looked at Alison.

"She even avoids smiling, because she read an article about how it, too, can hasten wrinkles. She cross-examined my father about it at dinner one night."

"What did he think?" I asked before Alison could.

"He thought it was ridiculous, but whenever he contradicts something she's read or believes, she tells him he's too much of a specialist to know. Like a cardiac surgeon wouldn't have the basic medical education," he added.

I glanced at Sam. I often wondered how she

reacted to Ryder's criticisms of Bea. After all, she was Sam's mother. However, Sam, like the two of us, had gotten more attention from my mother than her own when she was an infant. I knew she idolized Ryder and looked up to me as well whenever she could, even now. I thought the fact that she would disobey her mother to spend as much time with either Ryder or me proved where her real loyalties lay.

"I want to go up to the attic, too," Sam said. "Can I?"

Ryder looked at me for help.

"You'd have to get your mother's permission first, Sam," I said.

"Dad didn't say I could bring you," Ryder quickly added, "so Fern's right. Ask your mother."

"What if she's not home?" Sam asked, the unhappy thought rearranging her entire face, her eyes narrowing and looking like they were on the verge of flooding with tears, her lips twisting, and the tip of her nose dipping. When something upset her, she was almost a mirror image of her mother.

"If she says yes whenever she is home, I'll take you up to explore," Ryder promised.

"I want to go with all of you today. I want to see the dresses, too."

"Oh, Ryder, why can't she?" Alison asked. "If it's that disgusting up there, how can we expect to find anything suitable for a prom now?"

He thought a moment and shrugged. He looked

like he would challenge anything and anyone to please Alison. "I guess when you're already in the doghouse, breaking another rule won't matter. Okay, Sam, but try not to get dirty and dusty, and don't tell your mother you were up there unless she asks, okay?"

"Okay," Sam said, bouncing a little on the seat and smiling at Alison. I wished I had fought harder for her.

When we pulled up to the front of the house, I took a deep breath. I remembered the last time I had entered Wyndemere this way. It was when I was a little more than five and Dr. Davenport had come home just after I had cut myself on a jagged branch. My mother didn't know I was playing out front. I held my hand up, fascinated with the stream of blood rushing down my palm. I heard him step out of his car and saw him look my way.

"Get over here," he ordered. I rushed to him. He seized my wrist and held my hand up. "How did you do this?"

I shrugged and looked back at the branch I had been using for a magic wand. He didn't wait for my explanation. He took out a handkerchief, wrapped it around my hand, and then led me quickly up the steps to the front door. I was afraid my mother would be very angry. I wasn't even thinking about Bea Davenport, but she seemed to pop out of a wall, her eyes wide.

"Why are you bringing her in this way?" she demanded.

"She cut herself," he said, and hurried me to the powder room, where he carefully washed my hand, examined the wound, and then reached under the cabinet for a first-aid kit. Even though my cut stung, I was very quiet and more fascinated with how efficiently he worked sterilizing the area and then fixing the Band-Aid. When he was finished, before he did anything else, he washed my blood off the inside of the sink.

"My blood's red," I said.

He paused, a slight soft smile on his lips. "And so?"

"I'm not a blue blood."

It was the first time he had ever laughed at anything I said. It wasn't a loud laugh; it was simply a widening of his smile and a slight sound that he seemed to want to swallow. "I wouldn't worry about it," he told me. "Go back and tell your mother what happened, and next time, you be more careful about what you pick up, understand?"

I nodded.

He thought a moment. "Let's be sure you've had your tetanus shot, too," he added, more to himself than to me.

When he opened the bathroom door, I shot out and ran through the house to our section, more excited about what had happened than I was about Christmas. My mother seemed even more intrigued by it all than I was. She was especially interested in how Bea Davenport had reacted, but I really hadn't paid much attention to her. I was mesmerized by everything Dr. Davenport said and did.

My mother chastised me for playing in front of the house, more than she did about my getting cut on a broken branch. "You have to stay where you belong," she told me.

I didn't fully understand what she meant. To me, when I was little, I belonged everywhere something amused or fascinated me.

I mentioned what Dr. Davenport had said about tetanus, which I pronounced as "tet-us."

She smiled and said, "He forgot he had set up your appointment with Dr. Bliskin himself. But he's a very busy man," she added, which was something she always said practically every time any mention of Dr. Davenport was made.

I relived all this in my mind, from the moment we all stepped out of the limousine to the moment we walked through the grand front entrance of Wyndemere. I couldn't imagine the doors of heaven being any grander or more impressive.

One of the maids, crossing the hallway to the living room, glanced our way but kept going. I knew that Alison had been here on a few occasions, once or twice for dinner. I didn't want to

cross-examine her or Ryder about how well that
went, but I knew how snobby Bea was, of course,
and Alison's family was not wealthy. Her parents
would surely not be attending the costly charity
affairs Bea helped organize and attended with Dr.
Davenport. Alison's father was a UPS deliveryman,
and her mother could take only part-time work
because Alison had a ten-year-old brother and a
seven-year-old sister. They lived in a modest Queen
Anne house in a far poorer neighborhood of Hillsborough, although you couldn't tell how modest
from the way Alison behaved in school.

I saw that regardless of how many times
Alison had been here, she was obviously still over-
whelmed with the size of Wyndemere and the elaborate decorations, chandeliers, paintings, and rugs.
Mrs. Marlene would say, "She looks google-eyed."

"It's like walking into a museum every time I
come here," Alison said.

"Well, we do have a mummy," Ryder quipped
in a whisper. I was still holding my breath. "Let's
just go right up," he said. I held Sam's hand, and
we all headed for the stairway.

We had just started up when we heard Bea
Davenport shout, "Samantha! Where do you think
you're going?"

It was impossible to have known if she was
home or not. She had her own late-model Mercedes sedan and used it whenever she was unable

to have the limousine, but the garage was on the east end of the mansion, and the doors were shut. She had stepped out of the living room and stood there glaring up at us, with her hands on her hips, her posture as erect and stiff as a sentry's at a military compound. I sensed she had been lying in wait, anticipating that we might permit Sam to go up with us and even that I might be brought home in the limousine.

Sam looked terrified. My heart was thumping, too. She tightened her grip on my hand.

"She's going up to her room, I imagine," Ryder said nonchalantly. His casual tone took the air out of Bea Davenport's swollen face.

"You make sure that you do only that, Samantha. Change your clothes, and come right down here. I want to talk to you," she said. "And no one else is to go into your room."

Sam looked like she would cry. I smiled at her, but she lowered her head.

"And, Ryder Davenport, I don't recall giving permission to have Parker drive anyone else in the limo but you and Samantha," Bea said.

Ryder stared down at her.

No one spoke; no one breathed. Would she use this as a way to stop us?

"C'mon," Ryder told us after another silent moment. We continued up the stairs, but I knew from the way she treated my mother that Bea Davenport's temper tantrum would burst into more of a rage when she was ignored.

As soon as we were out of Bea's eyesight and hearing, Ryder turned to Sam and said, "I'll take you up to the attic when she's not home. I promise."

It was something, but going up with us was everything. She peeled off to her bedroom, her head down, dressed in disappointment.

"Why is she like that?" Alison asked. When I didn't answer, she turned to Ryder. "Why is she so angry about your being with Fern? Did you do something that upset her?" she asked me.

"Yes, I was born," I said dryly.

Apparently, he hadn't warned her about any of it.

"No. What Fern means to say is my stepmother was born on the wrong side of the bed," Ryder told her. "Forget her. This way," he directed, and we walked down the long, somewhat dark corridor to the stairway that led up to the attic.

It was a short stairway with banisters that looked like they were the originals, never reinforced. They were a bit shaky. Unlike the marble stairway, these steps were wood without the benefit of even a thin carpet. Every one of them moaned beneath our feet. There was even less light guiding our way. I had no doubt that Bea Davenport would have little interest in upgrading anything about the attic or in approaching it. Everything in it predated her, and she didn't want those memories to live in any form.

The dark oak door was wide, however, probably with the anticipation that the attic would be used to store furniture and other sizable things, like the old-fashioned luggage trunks and large cartons of forgettable items people couldn't bring themselves to throw away. It was the headquarters for hoarders. The door's hinges squeaked like a sick cat.

Ryder entered first and found the switch that triggered a line of dangling naked light bulbs the length of the attic, at least two of which needed to be replaced. Alison and I paused behind him. It was vast, with no apparent organization of what had been brought up and stored in it. Cartons were scattered among articles of furniture, some covered in dust-laden vinyl. There were standing lamps that looked helplessly inefficient and stacks of bed frames and bedsprings. Since there wasn't a single window, the air reeked of age itself. Small clouds of dust particles danced around the limited circles of illumination under the light bulbs.

"Ugh," Alison said. "I can't imagine finding anything suitable up here."

"Let's try. My mother's things are off to the right here," Ryder said. Actually, he whispered. It gave me the feeling that he felt something holy and special about his mother's possessions. It was as if we had entered a cathedral.

Do people live on in the things they once possessed? I wondered. Clothes especially were like part of your body. Maybe that was why when someone died, the people who loved him or her were anxious to give their clothes away. They were too vibrant a reminder, teasing with the flood of images that they could engender. Perhaps their perfume or cologne was still strong. A whiff of that would release memories and visuals, even the sound of a voice, and some memorable words.

What about a strand of hair still clinging to the material with the desperation of someone who refused to be forgotten? Our English teacher, Mr. Madeo, in a lesson about poetry, showed us something called a haiku, a three-line, seventeen-syllable poem that captured an image, a feeling. Right now, one of the ones he had read came right to mind: *The piercing chill I feel: my dead wife's comb, in our bedroom, under my heel.*

Ryder seemed hesitant. He still hadn't stepped forward.

"If you don't want to do this," I said, "it's all right. My mother wants to buy me a gown."

"That's probably a better idea, now that I see what this is like," Alison said.

"What? No. Of course not. These clothes cry out to be used," Ryder insisted. "Everything was quite expensive." He looked at me. "It's all right; it's fine. It's what my father wants, too. It bothers him that all this is never used."

"Well, let's look and get it over with," Alison said.

Why did she insist on coming? I wondered. What did she think it was like up here, Bergdorf Goodman?

Ryder moved quickly now and paused at a three-door armoire with a full beveled dressing mirror and what I thought were ornately carved side doors.

"This is beautiful," I said, running my hand over the surface. "Why was it moved up here?"

Ryder blew air through his lips. "Are you kidding? Anything that had the slightest to do with my mother was excommunicated when Bea became the mistress of Wyndemere."

He opened the center door and stepped back.

"Ladies, welcome to Ryder Davenport's department store."

Alison moved to it first and began to sift through the dresses and gowns. I had never gone to a formal party, much less a prom, so I thought I should let her make the decision. She was grimacing and rejecting everything—and quickly, too.

"Out of style. Too gaudy. Too simple. Ugly," she recited.

I plucked a dress out from under her and held it

up. "I like this," I said. "Couldn't it work?" It was an A-line, sleeveless, sheer-neck chiffon. I knew it wasn't really out of style.

She scooped it out of my hands and held it up. "It's so long," she said.

I had not told anyone that I had gone on the Internet and studied prom gowns. "It's supposed to be," I said. Ryder's eyebrows lifted. "It's a brush-train dress."

"You'll be swimming in it," Alison said. "How tall was your mother?" she asked Ryder.

"Five-ten," he said.

Alison looked at me. "She's at least five inches shorter, and you know how tall Paul is."

"I can pick some of that up with shoes."

"Exactly. You'll need shoes to match. You might as well—"

"Wait," Ryder said. "My father told me my mother had a small foot. You might be the same size. We'll check the armoire that contains her shoes. There's probably a pair made for this dress."

"That would really be lucky," Alison muttered, but she sounded disappointed.

"Serendipity," Ryder said, more to himself.

I held the dress up in front of me. "Don't you think the bodice will fit perfectly?"

She nodded, grimacing.

"I might only have to shorten it. I bet I won't have to take in the waist very much," I said.

"You can go to Bea's tailor," Ryder joked.

"You really do want to give her a heart attack," I said. "Should we check the shoes?" I was getting very excited now, and Alison was losing her resistance.

He led us to a matching chestnut rotating shoe-rack cabinet. It had three levels, each with three rows of shoes. He pulled open all three, and Alison plucked out the pair that matched the dress.

"Try them on," she said reluctantly. "They look perfect."

I gazed around and sat on a black trunk. The two of them hovered over me as I took off my Skechers and then slipped into the right shoe first. It had a two-inch heel. I looked up at Alison. It felt good. I tried on the other, and then I stood.

"Well?" Ryder asked.

"Serendipity," I said.

He smiled. "My father's going to love this."

"Really?"

"You bet. I love it. All I have are pictures of my mother. I'm sure I have one where she's wearing this dress. It's in an album my father lets me look at, an album he keeps in his office."

Neither Alison nor I spoke. Ryder looked away to hide the sadness he felt. It had simply never occurred to me that a child could feel a connection between himself and his dead mother whom he couldn't really remember or know except through videos and pictures. When he watched a video and heard her voice, it would almost be like watching a famous movie star, maybe, maybe for me; but for Ryder, there was definitely something more, something he knew he had missed and wanted dearly.

He turned back to us, gathering himself together quickly. "What else, Alison?" he asked.

"You should have the dress dry-cleaned for sure and checked for stains."

"Yeah, sure. What else does she need?"

She looked at me as if to say, *A new body and, for sure, a new face.* "I'm getting my hair done next Saturday. If you want to do something special for the prom, you have to schedule an appointment somewhere right away," she told me.

"Okay. I'll ask my mother."

"I think she could use a nice pair of earrings," Alison added. "I don't think she needs a necklace."

Ryder thought a moment. "I think my father put all my mother's jewelry in a bank safety-deposit box. I can ask him." He smiled. "Maybe Bea will offer you some."

"With poison on them. No, thanks. My mother has some jewelry, too," I said. "I'd worry about losing one of your mother's earrings. I'm sure your mother's jewelry is way more expensive."

"Okay," Ryder said. "Girls, I leave the rest up to you," he declared.

I folded the dress to carry and changed back to my Skechers. We started out of the attic.

Ryder slipped back for a moment to whisper, "You're going to look beautiful, Fern, as beautiful as my mother looked."

"I doubt that," I said quickly.

"No matter. Paul's a lucky guy," he said.

His lips grazed my ear.

The thrill that passed through me woke me in places I never expected.

But I had no idea why it also frightened me.

Bea Davenport seemed to have been waiting at the bottom of the stairway the whole time. Sam was nowhere in sight.

"Hello, Mrs. Davenport," Alison said as we descended. "I'm sorry I didn't get a chance to say hello before."

"Let me see that dress," she demanded, ignoring her.

I unfolded it and held it up.

"You'll look absolutely foolish in something like that," she declared, and then she smiled with ice, as though such a possibility was very pleasing.

I saw Alison nod.

"I'm sure my mother never did," Ryder countered.

"She's not your mother," Bea said.

"No," Ryder replied. "No one is."

Bea's eyes flared, and then she spun around and went into the living room.

"Ouch," Alison said. "If you weren't persona non grata before, Fern, you certainly are now."

"C'mon," Ryder told her. "I'll have Parker take you home and go along. You okay, Fern?"

I nodded, but I was still quite frightened. It wasn't the first time I'd seen or heard Ryder defy his stepmother, but this time, it seemed like a deep slice severing anything that even slightly joined them together as a family. Would I somehow be blamed for that, blamed by Dr. Davenport?

"I'll call you later," Alison said, sounding like the reluctant draftee who realized she had to co-operate. "If your mother doesn't have earrings that work, I might, and maybe I can get you into my hairdresser, too."

"You two are treating Paul too well," Ryder joked—or maybe not. I hoped not.

Alison grimaced. "I still think we'd all look better in your family limousine."

"We'll be fine. You'll have another ride in it now. See you later, Fern," he said, then took her hand, and they walked out to the limousine.

I glanced at the living-room entrance and then hurried through the house to our living quarters. My mother was in the kitchen working on a meat loaf for us. I burst in, undecided about what I should tell her first.

"Here's the dress Ryder and Alison helped me pick out," I said, holding it up.

"Alison?"

"Ryder's girlfriend."

"Oh, yes." She took the dress and held it out in front of her. "It's beautiful. I'll have Mr. Stark take us to Mrs. Levine after you return from school tomorrow. She'll do what has to be done. And those are the shoes? They fit you?"

"Perfectly. Ryder calls it serendipity."

"Does he?" She handed the dress back to me.

"Do you have a pair of earrings that might work with it?" I asked.

"I think I do," she said. "They're not real diamonds, but they're pretty. A young man gave them to me when I was working in New York."

"You never told me you had a boyfriend in New York," I said.

"It was weighted too heavily on one side."

"What's that mean?"

"He thought he was my boyfriend more than I did, but I couldn't break his heart and not accept a birthday gift, could I?" she asked, smiling.

"Can I have my hair done for the prom?" I asked.

"Oh, I don't know where to go for that," she said. "Mrs. Marlene, as you know, cuts my hair."

"Alison's calling her hairdresser to see if she can get me in."

"Sounds like you have a good friend," she said. "If not, we'll figure something out. That dress will need to be cleaned, you know, but Mrs. Levine will take care of that, too."

"Thanks, Mummy."

She turned back to her meat loaf preparations.

"Bea Davenport was quite unhappy about all this, and she and Ryder had some words," I said. I thought she had better know so she could be prepared for the nastiness that was probably on the horizon.

"Oh. That's too bad."

"Maybe Dr. Davenport needs to operate on her heart," I said.

She started to smile, even laugh, but stopped herself. "Now, don't you go and fan the flames, Fern Corey," my mother warned.

"I won't, but I don't think anyone really has to fan them. They've got their own winds."

I went to hang up the dress.

After dinner, just as I had begun my homework, Alison called to tell me she had persuaded her hairdresser to work on my hair right after he worked on hers. She made it sound like she'd had to move heaven and earth.

I thanked her as profusely as I could.

"I'll bring some ideas for the cut and style that he gave me last week. You can look at them tomorrow at school. He's very good, as you can tell from how he does my hair."

"Thanks."

"Is everything all right there?" she asked. I knew what she meant.

"Bea Davenport won't be any sweeter to me or my mother, if that's what you mean. I'm sure Ryder will be having a talk with Dr. Davenport, though."

"Ryder really dislikes her," Alison said. "He told me some other things about her on the way to my house, things you might not know."

She was making it clear that she had Ryder's deep trust and knew more about what went on in the Davenport family than I ever could.

"Probably not."

Whatever she believed, I still felt that I had shared something with Ryder in the attic that was very special, something neither Alison nor any other girlfriend he might have could share. It was as if we were on a different radio frequency, one not within their reach. I did feel from her tone and the looks she had given me that Alison sensed a bond between Ryder and me, a bond she didn't understand and didn't care to understand.

"I often wonder why Dr. Davenport married her," I said, "but then there's Sam. She's a great kid. I love Sam."

"Maybe that's how your mother rationalizes you," she said.

"What?"

"No matter how you came about, she's pleased with you, isn't she?" she asked.

"Yes, of course."

"So? Well, let's not depress ourselves or talk about this stuff, especially in front of Ryder, and make him unhappy. What about the earrings?"

"My mother has a pair for me."

"Good," Alison said. "Thank your lucky stars. You're going to have a lot of fun, Fern, even with Paul Gabriel. I remember my first prom. I wasn't crazy about going with Jason Marks, but I practically ignored him and enjoyed myself."

"You won't be ignoring Ryder," I said.

"Of course not. And he won't be ignoring me," she added.

"No," I said. *Of course not,* I thought, which was why she would have much more fun than I would.

"Anything else I can do for you?" she asked. Whom was she out to impress now?

"No. I'm fine. Thanks, Alison."

"See you tomorrow," she said.

After I hung up, I lay back on my bed and looked up at the ceiling, thinking.

Why did she have to say that about my mother? Was that a common thought among people who knew me, knew us?

Everyone, especially people my age, struggled with the question *Who am I?* There were so many other questions dependent on the answer. *Where do I belong? Whom should I be with? What should I try to make of myself?*

We fluttered about, twisting and turning, starting down one path and then another, terrified we
would make a decision that would ruin the rest of
our lives. Maybe we didn't say so aloud, but I was
certain that fear was in everyone's heart.

Here I was, sixteen, and there were still so
many questions, things about my mother I did not
know. I was around enough adults to know that
most of them enjoyed cherry-picking their pasts to
recall and share events that had pleased them, moments they cherished.

My mother seemed afraid to do that. Every
time she began, she stopped and retreated to talk
about something minor, something that would enable her to forget.

But forget what?

Years from now, would I be like that, too, perhaps with my own daughter?

How would I describe the first prom, the first
real date I had gone on? I liked the boy I would
dance with enough, but my eyes would be on another, someone in love with someone else, someone
he wouldn't mind remembering. His date would be
the same. She would have no trouble talking about
her prom.

I would try not to be, but I knew I would be
jealous.

Look happy and as beautiful as you can, I told
myself, *and don't for a moment appear dissatisfied*

and ungrateful. Think of it as a coming-out party. You're emerging from one of the forgotten places in this great house, and you're going to stir memories that were sleeping too long in the corners. They were memories surely filled with music and laughter.

Bea Davenport might hover like a large, angry cloud over everything in Wyndemere, but a ray of sunshine would drill through and light a path toward resolving the ever-present question, *Who am I?*

Should I continue on this path?

I must not stop searching for the answer. The only thing slowing me down was my fear of it.

4

IT WAS A week of preparations and so much excitement at school that it was almost impossible to concentrate on schoolwork. I was on the phone almost every night with one of my girlfriends whose envy practically dripped through the receiver. I tried to remain modest about all the attention I was getting, but it wasn't easy to control my own enthusiasm. Our lunch table remained confined to Ryder, Paul, Alison, and me the whole week, but our friends hovered around us. Some, like the girls on Ryder's prom committee, interrupted every day to ask a question that had an obvious answer. Every girl in the school who had not yet been asked searched the remaining uncommitted boys in the senior class, practically begging for an invitation. A few actually initiated the invitations themselves.

All week, I moved through the hallways like a queen bee surrounded by drones buzzing with questions about my clothes, my hair. Many made comments about other girls who were going, to provide me with information about their preparations, as if I was in some grand competition. It was all quite new for me. In science class, Mr. Malamud's description of how a caterpillar morphs into a butterfly had an unexpected meaning. It was suddenly a way to view myself and what was happening to me. When he said the caterpillar first digests itself, but certain groups of cells survive to turn it into the beautiful butterfly, I thought maybe I was doing that.

To fully grasp the responsibility of becoming a young lady, the princess all of us young ladies thought we were becoming, I had to put away childish things, digest them. Suddenly, being loud and giggling over silly comments and clownish, immature actions had to stop. I became more aware of how I dressed every day and what I said to anyone. I wanted to be more demure, move more gracefully, and care about my posture. I studied Alison continuously, trying to capture that same soft smile, that look in her eyes that, without being arrogant, clearly said, *What you're complaining about or wanting to do is childish.*

By midweek, I thought I had aged a decade more than my juvenile, self-indulgent classmates. Some of the more jealous ones were already whispering behind my back, conspiring to have me clearly labeled snobby. How ironic, I thought. It wasn't long ago that my being what Bea Davenport practically shouted in the halls of Wyndemere, an illegitimate child, had me traveling on a level quite a bit below most of my classmates. Maybe I was a real Cinderella after all.

This infatuation with a newer, more mature self-image reached a climax on Thursday, when I nearly failed a math test. Mr. Wasserman, my teacher, scowled at my paper when he handed it to me.

"You know this material, Fern," he said. "These are careless errors."

"I'm sorry."

I was sure he knew the reason for my inattentiveness. Students weren't the only ones who gossiped about their activities in our relatively small school.

He shook his head. "Compartmentalize," he prescribed. "When you're in my classroom, you're nowhere else."

"Okay," I said. He was one teacher I didn't want to disappoint.

Pamela Sommes overheard him and had a broad smile on her envious round face. If she were the last girl on earth, the last boy would force himself to turn asexual. It wasn't only my thought, either, but that didn't lessen my embarrassment and regret. The truth was that I was nearly in tears by the time the bell rang. I didn't know how many times during classes I had doodled images of myself in my new dress and failed to listen.

After school on Monday, Mr. Stark had driven my mother and me to Mrs. Levine's home. She was an elderly lady who operated a tailor shop out of her house, actually not too far from where Alison's family lived. Ten years ago, my mother had a box of clothes for me that needed some tailoring, and she had brought me to Mrs. Levine's shop. Apparently, from what I could remember, the clothes were of some high quality and worth adjusting and fitting for me. When I recalled that, I wondered if they could have been something else discovered in the attic. Perhaps my mother had been told where to look for them. I couldn't imagine her simply going up there to forage about with clothes for me in mind.

On the way to Mrs. Levine's this time, I asked her about it and quickly saw from the way Mr. Stark looked at her that the answer was something neither cared to explain. That only sharpened my curiosity.

"Why are you thinking about that now?" my mother asked, sounding suspicious.

"I don't know. It just came to me. Whose

clothes were they? Why is it such a secret, anyway? Whose hand-me-downs were they?"

"They were all like new, Fern," my mother said. "I wouldn't call them hand-me-downs."

"Yes, I remember that. I never really thought of them as used clothes, but whose were they? Why is it such a secret?" I cried again, exasperated.

"You might as well tell her," Mr. Stark said. "She's old enough now and knows how to keep things to herself."

I looked at my mother with anticipation.

"Dr. Davenport had a younger sister," my mother said softly. "She died when she was about six. He was about nine at the time."

"What? I never heard any mention of her. I never saw a picture of her. I don't understand. How did she die?"

"She had a malfunctioning heart valve. She died in her sleep one night. Elizabeth Davenport's way of handling her sorrow was to deny that her daughter had ever existed. She closed up her room, which is still closed today, and got rid of anything and everything that belonged to the child. Except some of the clothes that for some reason were stored in the attic. I think Simon Davenport insisted on holding on to something."

"What was her name?"

"Holly," my mother said. "I believe it was Simon Davenport's grandmother's name."

I sat back, shocked. How could someone's, a little girl's, existence be completely erased? What a horrible thing. I sat up quickly.

"Where was she buried? There was a grave for her, right? Does the doctor visit it? Has he brought Ryder there?"

"Oh, Fern, why bring all this up now?" my mother moaned. "It was a horrible tragedy for the Davenports. Everyone has his or her own way of dealing with such things. My own father was like that. If something annoyed or displeased him, he simply denied it existed."

"Like you?"

"Exactly."

"But where is Holly buried?"

"She wasn't buried, Fern. She was cremated. I think her remains are in some vault. Can we stop talking about this?" my mother pleaded.

Mr. Stark nodded. "You should listen to your mother," he said.

"But Dr. Davenport gave you those clothes for me?"

"Yes," she said.

I thought about it some more. "I bet that was why he wanted to be a cardiac surgeon. I bet every time he helps someone, he brings his sister back to life."

My mother turned sharply and looked at me, surprised at my quick analysis.

"Right?" I asked.

"Maybe," she said.

"Does Ryder know this? He's never mentioned it."

"I don't think so, Fern. Don't you be the one to mention it to him, either," she warned.

"What about Bea Davenport?"

"I don't know who knows what now, Fern. If I had to venture a guess, I'd say she doesn't know and wouldn't care about it anyway."

"Does Mrs. Marlene know?"

"Oh, Fern, please."

A heavy silence fell over the three of us for a few moments.

"How strange all this is," I thought aloud when I realized something else. "I'm going to wear Dr. Davenport's first wife's dress to the prom, and when I was little, I wore his sister's clothes. And it all came from the attic. Secrets. More secrets," I muttered.

My mother bit down on her lower lip and turned away.

Later, I tried to concentrate on what we were doing at Mrs. Levine's, but it was difficult to forget what my mother had told me. It was actually more of the reason I was so distracted at school, but I couldn't mention it, of course. I began to rake through all my childhood memories, especially the ones that involved Ryder, but I could think of nothing, not a reference, and not anything in the house that suggested Dr. Davenport once had a younger sister.

Mrs. Levine raved about Ryder's mother's dress and how beautiful I was going to look in it when she was finished with the adjustments. Every time she referred to how she remembered me as a little girl, I thought about Holly Davenport. It gave me an eerie feeling to think that perhaps all those times when I was little and felt a shadowy presence moving about me in the house, I was sensing Holly's spirit.

That following day at lunch, Ryder had noticed something different about me. Despite Bea Davenport's efforts to build a chasm between Ryder, Sam, and myself, Ryder and I were often sensitive to each other's feelings. Just like I could look at him and read that he was upset about something, he could look at and read me.

"Are you feeling all right?" he asked me when the bell rang ending the lunch hour and we had started out.

"I'm fine," I said.

He thought for a moment and must have concluded that I was simply very nervous about attending the prom. He knew, of course, that this was my first formal date, too. Like everyone else, I had met boys at the mall or at sporting events, but none of those budding little romances ever flowered. I had no expectation of developing a romance with Paul, either.

Ryder had another suspicion about my subdued manner. "Bea is not going to cause us any more trouble," he promised as we walked in the hallway. Alison caught up. "My father and she had another argument. He didn't think she should have prevented Sam from going into the attic with us."

"My mother says she scowls at her more, but she hasn't said anything or increased her complaining. She hasn't reduced it, either," I added, and he laughed.

"Paul will come to Wyndemere first on Saturday and pick you and me up, and then we'll go to Alison's house to get her," Ryder said. He thought a moment and added, "I want you to come into the main house when you're ready. We're not having Paul go around to the servants' entrance to pick you up. I'll tell you exactly when Paul's arriving."

"Are you sure?"

"This is not a delivery," he replied, his eyes sharp and determined.

"Okay," I said.

"Well, I don't think Bea Davenport can make a fuss over that," my mother said that afternoon when I told her what Ryder wanted me to do. "But I've often been wrong about how picayune that woman can be. She'd make a good drill sergeant for someone's army."

The next day, Ryder laughed when I told him what my mother had said.

"I keep her out of my room," he bragged. "And lock my personal things in a trunk in the closet just so she can't get her snoopy nose into it."

"Everything is set at the beauty salon for Saturday," Alison piped up. I could see that she didn't want to hear anything more about Bea Davenport. I was sure Ryder and she had exhausted the subject between the day in the attic and now.

I had to get myself more into all this, I thought. I had to do what Mr. Wasserman told me to do in class, compartmentalize and shove all the static out of my mind. I was going with my mother after school to do a final fitting of the dress at Mrs. Levine's on Thursday. Both Alison and Ryder knew.

"Can't wait to see you in it," Alison said dryly. I sensed she didn't really think it would look good on me.

"Me, neither," Ryder added as we separated for our classes. The look on his face gave me a chill. Ordinarily, I would have been happy to hear him say such a thing, but for some reason, I felt I was facing an unexpected challenge. It was as if he really expected I would look as beautiful in the dress as his mother had, that I was somehow worthy of the dress.

But what if I didn't look anywhere nearly as attractive in it? What if I looked silly in it or something? Maybe he should have offered the dress to Alison instead of me. Why didn't he if it was so special to him? Surely, he thought Alison was very beautiful. She was. Everyone said so. Was it that he wouldn't want her to wear a hand-me-down? Did he see my mother and me the way Bea wanted him to see us, as the poor servants living in the rear of Wyndemere? Was he hoping that I, like some mythical Cinderella, would, when I put on the dress, magically rise out of the ordinary, if only for one night?

And as soon as prom night was over and I took off the dress, would I return to that second-class person Bea Davenport insisted my mother and I were? I was afraid of that moment when the prom and all that followed had become a memory. I'd hang up the dress, put away the shoes, and return to childish fantasies and, more important, perhaps, my place in Wyndemere, even my place in my school.

Ryder didn't even mention my riding to or from school in the limousine again. I thought that prohibition remained to placate Bea Davenport and give her some small victory. After all, from what Ryder was telling me, Dr. Davenport was criticizing her not for how she had treated me but for how she had treated Sam. His usual aloofness, especially when it came to me, would continue except for one small but surprising moment.

Ryder came to see me during dinner Friday. My

mother and I were in the kitchen. He knocked and entered.

"Sorry to bother you, Miss Corey," he told my mother.

As always, when she saw Ryder, especially without his father or Bea present, her face lit up. She was as excited as she would be to see and speak to her own child. No matter what he did when he was younger, and even now, she was always one of the first to defend him, especially in front of the other servants. Of course, it was difficult to defend him when he was insolent to his stepmother in front of a maid or Mrs. Marlene, but rather than criticize him, my mother would remain silent. Her look was enough. Everyone understood. The only face that truly smiled at Bea Davenport in Wyndemere was the face Bea saw in the mirror.

"It's all right, Ryder. We're just having a quick nibble. Fern is too nervous to eat, and she makes me too nervous to eat as well," she added.

Ryder looked at me and smiled. "I'll be sure she's fed well at the prom and after," he promised. "I just wanted to stop in to tell Fern that my father has asked for her to stop by his office just before Paul arrives. He'd like to see her in the dress, so she should plan accordingly."

My mother froze with the bowl of salad in her hands. "Oh?" she said. She looked at me. "That's very nice, right, Fern?"

For a moment, I couldn't speak. It was one thing for Ryder to see me in the dress and say something cute or funny or even very nice, but Dr. Davenport would be looking at me and thinking of his first wife. If he thought I did his wife's memory a disservice, he might just nod and turn away. It would be devastating, right before I was going to leave for the prom. How would the rest of the night feel? My depression would drag everyone down, especially ruining Alison's night, and she would never let me forget it.

"Yes. Very nice," I managed to say.

I should have had more confidence, I know. Both my mother and I loved the way Mrs. Levine had adjusted and fitted the dress to me. She had insisted on taking a picture of me for her shop wall. For her, it was a work of art. My mother was staring at me in a way I had not seen her stare.

"What?" I asked her, afraid she thought wearing Samantha Davenport's dress was a mistake after all.

She shook her head. My heart began to sink. How would I get a nice dress now and the shoes to match?

But then she smiled. "I'm thinking of how sad and unfortunate it was for my father never to have set eyes on you. You resemble his mother in so many ways. She was a very beautiful woman."

"And so are you, Emma," Mrs. Levine said.

"I'm not surprised at how Fern's turned out. The apple doesn't fall far from the tree."

"Unless the tree's at the top of a hill. That's what my father would say when explaining me to his friends."

"Well, he'd be wrong," Mrs. Levine insisted.

To have such a wonderful reaction from Mrs. Levine and my mother was great, but it wasn't the same thing as having Dr. Davenport consider me.

"I'll stop in my father's office with you," Ryder said now. He knew I was nervous and even a little frightened about it. "He likes to check how I look, too. I don't think he'll carry on about my hair. He's given up on that. Okay?"

He looked at my mother.

"She'll have a great time. I promise," he told her. "And I'll look after her."

"That's good," my mother said. "Thank you, Ryder."

"See you soon," Ryder told me, and left.

I turned to my mother. "Now I wish we had bought me my own dress," I said.

"Oh, don't be foolish, girl. That dress cost ten times what we would have spent, and you look beautiful in it. Dr. Davenport will be proud of how you wear it. It will do his wife's memory justice. I remember her well, and you look just as good in it, if not better. And that's that," she said.

Maybe she was right. Maybe I was being unnecessarily nervous and looking for excuses for myself. After all, I was going to be double-dating with Alison. Her beauty would overshadow me— anyone—anyway. Why wasn't I more worried about that?

"Mr. Stark will be by to take you to the beauty parlor tomorrow," my mother said. "I won't be going along, you know. I have work to do here."

"Did you really like the style I chose?"

I had shown her the half dozen pictures Alison had given me.

"Certainly did." She paused to think. "I haven't been to a real beauty salon since I worked in New York."

"Whose fault is that?" I asked. For as long as I could remember, Mrs. Marlene cut her hair and she cut Mrs. Marlene's. She had always cut mine. She told me her father wouldn't even permit her mother to spend money on a beauty salon. Her mother, her sister, and she had to learn how to cut and trim their own and took turns doing it for each other.

She pulled her shoulders up. "Ain't you the smarty-pants now?" she said, half-kidding. She glanced at her reflection in the one kitchen window we had, which was over the sink, and fluffed her hair. "I might just make my own appointment. George saw a few nasty little gray strands sneaking in."

"He told you that? Cheeky," I said.

She laughed. "George Stark and I have long since stifled any pretense between us."

"Did you know his wife well?" I asked, my old suspicions reviving.

"Not well, no," she said. "She contracted a vicious cancer, and from the time she was diagnosed to the day she passed, it was barely four months. Very difficult time for Mr. Stark," she added. "You weren't born yet, but I had Ryder to care for, so there was just so much I could do to help. His way of dealing with it was to work harder here," she added. "And Cathy was a big help to him, too. But let's not talk about sad things now. You have a wonderful event ahead of you."

She smiled.

"You know, the word *prom* can be different in England. There, the Proms are daily orchestral classical music concerts. I went to one in the Royal Albert Hall when I was a few years younger than you. I loved all music. That was very exciting for me, but not like the excitement you're having at your first prom."

"You must have had some formal dates before you left England," I said. I was determined to get her to tell me more intimate things about her life.

She nodded and sat at the table. "There was a young man who haunted my front door. He was wary of my father, who looked at every possible beau I might have as if he was a potential rapist. But this young man was undaunted."

"What was his name?"

"Nigel. Nigel Douglas. Nigel Ashley Douglas, to be exact. His father owned a pharmacy, and he worked there until he went to college. He went to Oxford for pharmacology. I'm sure he took over his father's pharmacy."

"You don't know?"

"No. When I left, as I told you, only my sister stayed in touch with me, and secretly, of course. She could whisper news about me to my mother whenever my father wasn't around."

"Did she ever come to America to visit?"

"No. My sister was doomed to be a spinster. She was a slave to my parents. I shouldn't say 'slave'; I should say 'dedicated.' I was more selfish."

"And now?"

"And now she takes care of my mother, who really needs to be in a home."

"Don't you ever want to go see her?"

"She suffers from serious dementia. She wouldn't know I was there, Fern. It's better that if she remembers anything, she remembers me before I left. Oh," she said, snapping out of her reverie quickly. "There you go again, getting me to talk about the saddest things. Live for today, not yesterday, Fern. That's what I do now. You're what matters and what will matter, and that's that."

After dinner, I put on my prom dress again and stood before the full-length mirror my mother had given me long ago. I imagined Ryder standing beside me in his tuxedo, looking smart and handsome. I had seen him wearing it and knew how distinguished he could look, even with his rebellious hairstyle.

When I closed my eyes, I imagined dancing with him, not Paul. How hard that was going to be, and how foolish I might look in Paul's arms, I thought.

My mother knocked and peeked in. "Well, this is truly a dress rehearsal," she said. I must have looked embarrassed. "That's all right, Fern. I'd be doing the same thing. Anyway, I just wanted to let you know that I was going to O'Heany's tavern for a little while with Mr. Stark."

"You are?"

"Well, I should. Today's his birthday," she revealed. "He wouldn't let me or Mrs. Marlene make him a cake. He's really a shy man."

"Wish him happy birthday for me. I would have tried to get him something if I had remembered." If I hadn't been concentrating so much on myself this whole week, I would have, I thought.

"Oh, I got him something from us, his favorite aftershave lotion. Actually, I got him to make it his favorite, English Leather."

"Did your father wear that?"

"No," she said. She paused, started to close the door, and stopped. "It was something Nigel wore," she said, and closed the door.

I stood there for a moment staring at the closed door. What if she lied to me? What if Nigel Ashley Douglas did follow her to America, followed her here?

What if he was my real father?

I took off my prom dress slowly and then looked at myself in the mirror. Was it terribly wrong, narcissistic, to gaze at yourself, delighted at how your figure was forming, perhaps more than simply nicely? My breasts were round and firm and felt fuller just these past few weeks. I was developing what my mother called "an hourglass figure."

Preparing for bed now, I undid my bra and turned to look at my side profile when I pulled my shoulders back. I imagined Ryder opening my door the way he once had and bursting in on me again, only this time, he would see me half-naked. He wouldn't speak; he wouldn't even swallow. He'd barely breathe. And instead of rushing to cover myself, I would turn slowly to face him fully.

The images sent wave after wave of erotic feelings up my legs to the insides of my thighs. When I gazed at myself in the mirror, I saw how flushed I'd become. Was this the way my mother was a little over sixteen years ago? Whoever had come upon her when she was undressed would have had every iota of self-control diminished.

They had embraced each other under waves of passion as strong as an undertow at sea. Resistance was futile, really unwanted. There were no thoughts about tomorrow, only thoughts about the moment. My lips were salty with the images, my father's strong body pressed gently against her softness. What words did he whisper, what did she whisper? Were there any promises? Did either offer a *wait* or a *no*?

Most of, if not almost all, my friends did not obsess about the sexual moments that resulted in their conception. From the way they spoke, I sensed a resistance against thinking of their parents in that way. For me, because of how forbidden it must have been and still was, there had to be an undeniable and persistent fascination.

Would I ever feel sexual and not think of it? At night, when I closed my eyes and had my sexual fantasies, I often envisioned my mother much younger and as defiant as she had been when she left England against her father's wishes. Never once, perhaps because the possibilities weren't yet there, did I sense her concern that I might have a moment of sexual surrender and weakness like she had.

But surely it would begin to have a seat at the table now. Her questions about my dates and places I wanted to go would be sharper, closer. She would wonder if she indeed saw too much of herself in me. Yes, there was that apple that didn't fall far from the tree. Was I wiser, stronger, and more alert to the dangers because of what she had done and who I was?

I was confident now that she would talk more about herself. I had reached a place where she was unafraid of damaging childhood innocence. We were growing closer. A part of me welcomed it, but a part of me regretted losing the comfort of make-believe.

I lay back on my bed, naked now, and kept my hands at my sides. There was such a strong urge coming from every erotic place, calling for my touch. *Conquer it first in yourself*, I thought, *and it might be easier to conquer it when it comes with someone you like, someone you want very much to touch you and make you cry with delight and wonderful fear simultaneously.*

I closed my eyes and thought of other things. Minutes passed. I heard the sounds in the house and my own heart thumping. I crawled beneath my cover and turned off my light. I was poised, waiting for the sun to give birth to tomorrow. The ghost of Dr. Davenport's first wife and the ghost of his sister, Holly, were making their way through the walls of Wyndemere to wait with him in his office, wait for me to come walking through that door.

I must not disappoint them.

That was how I began my prayers. I fell asleep listening to the whispers promising me that I would not disappoint anyone, especially not Ryder.

Were they the whispers of the ghosts of Wyndemere, or were they my own?

5

MR. STARK WAS more excited about my going to a beauty salon than I was. From the way he spoke, I wondered if his daughter, whom I always called Aunt Cathy, had ever gone to one, especially before or when she was my age. Did she have any real dates or boyfriends? She never had mentioned any romances to me, high school or otherwise, and I never thought it was my place to ask. I feared she might somehow consider the question a criticism of her lack of relationships. Or maybe she would think I suspected her of being gay.

As far as I knew, Mr. Stark never complained about his daughter's anemic social life. He was proud of her accomplishments in nursing and talked about the good work she did for charities run by their church. She seemed to be one of those women destined to be spinsters from the day they were born. And it wasn't because she was particularly unattractive. She was certainly as pretty as many of Bea's friends. The only hint Mr. Stark ever dropped was to say, "Cathy's very particular about who she spends her time with, maybe too particular."

Thinking about Cathy Stark from time to time often caused me to wonder about my mother. It wasn't only because she was my mother that I thought of her as an attractive woman. She still had a very nice figure, probably because she worked so hard that she burned away calories before they could even contemplate adding to her weight. I couldn't recall a time during my sixteen years when she looked any heavier. Except for the few times she was sick with a cold or the flu, she always had a vibrant, healthy complexion. She certainly didn't look her age. I had friends who told me she could easily be mistaken for my older sister.

Because she had the courage to attempt to be an entertainer, and in a different country at that, she was certainly not shy. She was forceful when she had to be in the house with the staff, and wherever we went, she would not avoid conversations with strangers, even men she didn't know. But when it came to these men and their obvious interest in her, she had a way of putting a quick *Don't bother* into her demeanor. Maybe it was the sharp chill she would bring into her eyes or the way her smile flew off her face.

Why wasn't she interested in them? Didn't she dream of some man coming along and whisking her and me off to a wonderful new life where she wouldn't be a servant to anyone anymore? Did my father make her a promise that she still believed would come true? Recently, I wondered about her sexual needs. Had all that somehow died when I was born? Was her self-confidence when it came to romance shattered with the realization that she had given in to hot passion too easily, and was she afraid it would happen again if she began a relationship? How could I ask my mother such questions without causing her to feel even worse about her past?

I couldn't, but I could listen for clues, not only in what she told me but in what she said to others, especially Mr. Stark. There were mysteries swirling around him as well. For starters, he rarely talked about his son. When I asked my mother about it, she said it was one of those cases of oil and water and left it at that. Of course, I wouldn't dare directly ask him anything so personal, although I believed he would never resent anything I did or said. It wasn't hard for me to see how much he enjoyed my company. He was very excited for me today. It drove him to think about his own high school romances.

"On my first real date, I was so nervous that I forgot to put enough gas in my car."

"What happened?" I asked.

"I ran out on the way to my date's home, and that wasn't an excuse her father would accept if we were late for her curfew, so I had to call my father to come and bail us out."

"Was he angry?"

"Oh, no. My dad was quite a great guy. He thought it was funny, but he felt sorry for us and stayed with my car while I used his to take my date home to make her curfew. Then I went for a can of gas and returned. Every time I went on a date or out with friends, he'd always smile and say, 'Hey, George, you got enough gas?' "

"I wish I had met him."

"Oh, you did, when you were about three," he said. "Of course, I don't expect you to remember, but he gave you one of those very big lollipops, one almost as big as your face."

It was on the tip of my tongue to ask more questions about the days when my mother had first come to Wyndemere, but I was afraid of stepping into forbidden territory, afraid to hear things that might deeply disturb me, especially today.

"I'll be waiting for your phone call," he told me when he dropped me off at the salon. "Just going to spend some time with one of my old friends, Tony Gibson. He hears out of his left ear, and I hear out of my right, so we get along. You have my cell number, right?"

"My mom had me put it in my wallet some time ago," I said. I paused when I opened the car door to get out. "She told me that if I was ever in trouble and she wasn't around, you'd be the one I should call."

"Absolutely," he said. "Night or day."

"I'd hate to bother you."

I waited to see if he would say anything more, but he only nodded. "Have a good hairdo," he said.

"Thanks."

I couldn't imagine a conversation between me and my father being much different. I was sure he would have that same special look in his eyes as he contemplated his little girl being turned into a young woman. I had seen that look on the faces of some of my friends' fathers. They were excited for them but also a little regretful. Every father wants his daughter to be his little girl forever. How lucky they were to have someone who loved them so much that they couldn't help but have those feelings.

Now I was really nervous about all this. I always had my hair washed and cut at home, but to have someone who not only made his living doing it but also had a reputation for doing it well was intimidating. Had I chosen the right style? Was I too young for it? Would he embarrass me?

Alison was just being finished up when I entered the salon. Her stylist and now mine, Richard Boxer, paused to gaze at me. He looked at me so long I thought he was deciding whether he should even try to do anything with my hair. All my fears were being realized, I thought, but he surprised me.

"I just love it," he said, "when I'm given great raw material to work with."

I blushed because of the way other women in the salon were looking at me, too, but Alison looked skeptical. I thought he had done a wonderful job with her hair. I didn't think it was possible for her to look more beautiful, but she did. She decided to stay while he worked on mine and talk about the prom, the after-party, and all the gossip leading up to it. Whenever she paused, Richard asked me questions about Wyndemere.

"How many bedrooms are in that place?"

"Seventeen," I said, "but not all are used."

"The first time I saw it, I was about seven, I think. My parents were driving by, and I looked at it and thought surely a king or a prince lived in it. Now I see it is a princess," he added, looking at me in the mirror as he began to cut and style.

"I don't really live in it," I said.

"Oh?"

I described the help's quarters. I looked at Alison as I spoke. I didn't know what she had told him to get me the appointment on such short notice. Maybe she'd made me sound much more important than I was. He was quiet a moment after I finished.

Then he stepped back, looked at me in the mirror, and said, "By the time I'm done with you here, you will look like the princess I imagined whether you sleep in one of those fancy bedrooms or not. I'll make sure of that."

It was as if I had challenged him. I was more nervous than ever. It did seem like everything I was doing to prepare for this date was another test. Did I deserve the dress? Would a new hairstyle change everyone's perception of me? Would I look foolish on the dance floor with Paul? Would I make a fool of myself at the after-party? Could I really be anything like Alison? Could I have her poise and self-confidence? Most of all, perhaps, would Ryder laugh at me, shake his head, and regret bringing me along? I was too young and innocent after all. A hairdo did not a prom date make, I told myself, but I soon changed my mind.

Richard Boxer was truly an artist. He used his scissors and brush with a graceful expertise. I felt myself being remade right before my eyes. When he was finished, others in the salon paused to look our way and offer compliments.

"You look nice," Alison said. "Thanks, Richard," she told him, as if he had been doing her a great favor and not me.

"Thank you, Alison," I said.

She smiled. "You do look good. Ryder's right," she said. "Paul Gabriel is one very lucky guy."

"Ryder said that?" I asked.

She nodded.

I spun around and looked at myself again in the mirror. Maybe I didn't have the strength to be modest, I thought. I wasn't falling in love with my own image like Narcissus in Greek mythology, but I was suddenly confident enough to believe that Ryder really would look at me with new eyes.

Everyone would.

"I'll call you later to see if you have any questions," Alison said, and rushed off.

Two of the women leaving at the same time paused to tell me they wished they were my age again and going to a prom.

When he returned to take me home, Mr. Stark lavished compliment upon compliment on me, adding to my swelled head. "You've really grown into a beautiful young lady," he said the moment he set eyes on me. "It's a joy to be around to see it happening. Don't forget, I knew you when you were still in diapers. You have your mother's beautiful eyes. That new hairdo brings it out."

"I guess my birth came as a shock," I suggested, hoping he would lower his defenses and reveal more to me about myself and my mother.

"Not a shock. You didn't exactly appear over-night. Last I heard, it still takes about nine months."

"Well, I imagine I was a shock to someone," I said.

He didn't say anything.

"Probably my real father most of all," I suggested.

He glanced at me. We had never spoken about any of that. It was as if he accepted that I was simply always there.

"Did you know him?" I pursued.

I didn't know why it was suddenly more important than ever to talk about my father. Maybe I really regretted not having him to celebrate the steps I was taking into womanhood. All over Hillsborough tonight, most of, if not all, the girls going to the prom would have both their parents standing in doorways watching them leave in their gowns, their escorts in tuxedos, their childhoods retreating like snails into shells. Whose hand would my mother be holding when I left? Who would celebrate and comfort her? Who would share her pride?

Yes, something had come over me in that beauty salon. I didn't only feel beautiful; I felt older, mature. Although asking Mr. Stark this question had come into my mind before this, especially when he was doing something with me or I was watching him fix something to do with the house and he said something about what I was like when I was an infant, I never had the nerve to ask it until now.

After a long pause, he said, "That's something for you to discuss with your mother, Fern, not me."

I sat back. He'd surely tell my mother. That was good, I thought. Maybe she'd decide it was time for her to tell me more.

In the meantime, when we arrived at Wyndemere, she was very excited about my hairdo. In fact, she was so embarrassed about her reaction she turned to Mr. Stark, who was smiling and chuckling, and regained her composure quickly.

"You know what they say, George," she said. "You relive your youth through your children."

"Yes, well, I wouldn't doubt you were as beautiful at her age, Emma," he replied. "You're still quite beautiful."

"Oh, go on with you," she said, waving at him as she would at a fly.

From the way he had reacted to my question in the car and the way they were looking at each other now, I was convinced there was something more between them than simple friendship, if not in the past, then in the present.

"You go rest now, Fern," my mother ordered. "You have quite an evening ahead of you."

It seemed to me she wanted me out of the moment she was sharing with Mr. Stark. In fact, I had never seen my mother look as embarrassed. The tailoring of my beautiful dress, the styled hair, the prospects of the prom and the after-party, preparing to be viewed by Dr. Davenport, Ryder's compliments according to Alison, and now what I sensed in my mother—all of it was emotionally overwhelming. She was right. I needed some quiet time.

I went to my room, but I was afraid I would do something to mess up my hair, so I didn't lie down. I sat with two large fluffy pillows behind my lower back and tried to meditate, but it seemed an impossible task. My body felt electrified. I was sizzling with images and things that had been said to me and about me. A little while later, my mother knocked and then came in with a cup of herbal tea.

"This will calm you a bit," she said. It was always a joke between her and Mr. Stark that the English thought a cup of tea could solve every-thing.

I took the cup and looked at her. Even as a little girl, I always sensed when my mother was debating with herself whether to say or do something, and she was doing that right now.

"Mr. Stark said you asked him some personal questions. He'd never tell you, but he was a little embarrassed."

"Why?"

"They're not questions for him to answer."

"Then who will answer them?" I countered quickly, maybe a bit too harshly.

She continued to stare at me for a few moments and then nodded. "This is a big night for you, Fern. It's almost like a coming-out party, something they used to do for debutantes. You're making an entrance onto your social stage at an age when I believe you're most vulnerable emotionally. I'll know when it's right for you to get the answers to questions that hover above us both. Trust me," she said. "Please."

"Okay, Mummy. Of course, I trust you."

She smiled. "You sounded like me at your age just now. We Brits always call our mothers Mummy, even when we're old enough to be grand-mothers ourselves."

She stepped forward to hug me and kiss me on the forehead.

"Don't worry. I didn't mess up a strand," she joked. "Call me if you want help with anything."

"I will, Mummy. Thank you."

She walked out, her head a little lowered, her shoulders up, feeling much older herself, I was sure. It brought tears to my eyes. I never wanted my mother to age a day, but my pushing myself into a woman's state of mind was going to cause just that. It was inevitable, sad and wonderful simultaneously. Someday all this would happen again, only I would be the mother.

I looked at the clock. It was time for my shower and then my careful and timid application of whatever makeup I thought I needed. I would probably call my mother back to help me decide. When she was in show business or tried to be, makeup was surely a major thing for her. We did have some pictures of her when she worked in New York and trying to get a foothold on a singing career. She was stunning.

Just before I got ready to shower, my phone rang. It was Alison. She surprised me with her confession.

"Now that I've seen how good you look, I'm nervous," she said. "I hope my hair is right, and this dress . . . my mother helped me choose it, but . . ."

"You can't be anything but beautiful, Alison," I said.

Me, giving her courage? Were we always to be this way, self-conscious and, when it came right down to it, insecure, no matter how pretty we were and how often we were told?

"You did go last year," I reminded her. "At least you know what to expect."

"Yes, but that was different."

"Why?"

"I didn't go with Ryder Davenport, president of the class. There'll be a spotlight on us all night."

I knew she didn't mean to, but she did sound like she was complaining about it, whereas I'd scrub every floor in Wyndemere on my hands and knees if I could be his date.

"There's always a spotlight on you two, Alison," I said. I hoped I didn't sound as jealous about it as I felt.

"You're right, of course. Just pre-prom jitters. Anyway, I'm looking forward to seeing you in your gown."

"My mother thinks it fits perfectly."

"Does she? Your mother was a professional singer once, right? Ryder told me that."

"She tried to be. She worked in New York when she came from England."

"Ryder says you have a beautiful voice, too."

"He does? I don't remember singing that much in front of him."

"You're in the chorus."

"But I'm not the one Mr. Jacobs calls on to do the solo parts."

"Ryder thinks you will be once Carly Daniels graduates."

"He said that, too?"

"Why are you so surprised? You don't live in the main part of the house, but you live in Wyndemere, and you two were practically brought up together until you were old enough to be on your own, right?"

"Yes," I said. I wanted to say more, but I was afraid of revealing too much.

"Anyway, see you soon, Princess of Wynde-mere," she added, but it didn't sound like a compliment.

"Don't tell anyone that, or it will get back to Ryder's stepmother and I'll be assassinated," I said.

"Why don't you and your mother leave that place? She could probably get a similar job some-where else, maybe in one of the bigger cities?" She sounded like she wished we would leave, espe-cially me.

"Someday, maybe," I said.

She grunted and said good-bye.

I turned to look at myself. My face was flushed. Her words, despite the insecure way I sounded to her, had excited me more than even I realized. *Time to get ready*, I thought. *This will be quite a night.*

My mother did help me with my makeup. She helped me choose the right shade of lipstick. She knew how to emphasize my eyes, which every-one thought was the feature I should highlight. She said it had always been the same for her. I watched how she used a dark eyeliner pencil carefully, from the inner corner of each eye to the outside edge. As she worked, she talked about what she was doing.

"I was very lucky," she said. "I had a makeup artist who liked to practice on my eyes before I went for an audition or sang in some club when I did get a job. She was just starting out in the in-dustry, too."

"What happened to her?"

"She went to Los Angeles, and the last I heard, which was years and years ago, she got jobs on television shows. You're so lucky you have long eyelashes. I knew some girls trying to be models who'd kill for your eyelashes," she said. "You don't need to curl them. They already make your eyes look bigger."

She stood back and looked at me in the mirror.

"I wouldn't do much more," she said. "Subtlety is always more effective."

She paused and simply stared. It was one of those times when my mother looked at me and surely was thrown back to her memories of herself at my age or a little older. How frustrating it must have been for her to be failing at her dream, especially in light of how her father had treated it and her. In the end, she was surely haunted by the question of whether her defiance was worth it. She had lost so much and was somewhere she had never intended to be, with no husband to help her care for their daughter.

And yet she never ever made me feel unwanted. She would rather die than call me a mistake. I was sure her resistance to talking about how she became pregnant was tied to her worry that I would feel inferior. No one wanted to be known as an accident, and once the details of it were spelled out, the sense of being just that would be more vivid and impossible to ignore. And yet I would be a liar to deny that I wanted to know it all, every second. Of course, question one was, who was my father? Then, where did my mother meet him? How long had she been seeing him? Was it that unlucky first time parents worry their daughters will have? Did she love this man? Was she being rebellious and defiant? Was she drunk or even on some drug? Did she keep her pregnancy a secret from her lover? Did he even know that I existed?

Who, standing in my shoes, wouldn't have these questions invading every thoughtful moment of her life?

I looked away, took a breath, and rose.

"Time to put on my gown," I said.

She nodded. I went to the closet. When I slipped it on, she did the zipper in the back, and then we both looked at me. Her smile said it all. I put on my shoes. She gave me the earrings and watched me put them on.

"Mr. Stark would like to see you before you go see Dr. Davenport," she said. "He's waiting in the kitchen."

As soon as I walked in, he stood up. "Wow!" he said. "Is this the little girl who used to follow me around, wearing my tool belt, when she was about seven?"

"Same girl," my mother said.

"You look beautiful, Fern," he said.

"Thank you."

"Let me get a quick picture for your mom." He took out his smartphone and took a few, which he showed us. "I'll get them printed out," he said. "Maybe frame one, huh?" he asked my mother.

"That'd be nice, George. Thank you."

We heard a knock and saw Ryder standing there in his tuxedo. He was carrying the corsage he would give Alison.

"You look mighty handsome, Ryder," Mr. Stark said.

"Thank you, Mr. Stark," Ryder said, but his eyes were locked on me. It took him so long to comment that I was sure he was dissatisfied. But then he smiled and said, "It looks like my mother's dress was made especially for you, Fern. You look great."

"Thank you."

"Ready?" he asked. "Don't worry. I think my father's more nervous about it than you."

"That only makes me more nervous," I said.

I looked at my mother. She nodded, her eyes narrowing with that look that told me to be proud, and then she hugged me. "You two have a great time," she said, "but . . ."

"But be careful," Ryder finished for her. "Don't you know that's my middle name, Miss Corey? Ryder Careful Davenport."

"Never you mind what's your name. Keep your wits about you."

"We will," he promised. He reached for my hand.

For a little while, at least, I could pretend I was really his date.

Then Mr. Stark did something that would keep this moment forever for me. "Hold on," he called as we started out the door to the hallway that led into the main house. He took out his smartphone again. "A quick picture of the two of you, all grown up," he said.

Ryder looked at me, smiled, and then put his arm around my shoulders as we turned toward Mr. Stark.

"Got it," he said.

We continued out. I thought Ryder would let go of my hand after we had left the help's quarters, but he held on as we walked toward his father's office door. Before we got there, Mrs. Marlene stepped out of the kitchen and looked our way.

"My, my," she said. "What a pair of young beauties we have here. You two have a whale of a time." One of the maids peered at us over her shoulder. "Go on," Mrs. Marlene told her. "Don't gape at them like they're in a zoo." She smiled again at us and disappeared.

We paused at the door. Ryder knocked. We heard Dr. Davenport say, "Come in." Ryder glanced at me and opened the door. Dr. Davenport was behind his desk, leaning forward, his reading glasses lower on the bridge of his nose so he could look over them as we entered. I had never realized he wore reading glasses, but it had been some time since I had stepped into his office. He sat back. He was still wearing a tie and a white shirt, but he had his jacket off.

"Well," he said. "Come in, come in."

Ryder let go of my hand, and we drew closer to his large, dark oak desk. I glanced at the framed picture of Samantha Davenport that hung on the wall to our left. She was dressed in her wedding gown. My first thought was to wonder if Dr. Davenport had a picture of her in the dress I was wearing. Would he be making an immediate comparison?

On the desk, he had only a book and a yellow legal-size pad. He pressed his long fingers together in a cathedral shape and looked at me with such intensity I couldn't help but hold my breath.

"Who tailored the dress for you?" he asked.

"Mrs. Levine. She's done things before for me and for my mother."

He nodded. He still neither indicated in his face nor said anything to indicate whether he thought it looked nice on me. He wasn't looking at Ryder at all, however. Then he turned slightly to him.

"The first time your mother wore this dress

was when we attended a gala in honor of the governor. She looked so beautiful that she could stop clocks."

I glanced at Ryder and saw how fascinated he was with what his father was saying. I could only imagine that references to his mother were few and far between.

Dr. Davenport turned back to me. "What did your mother say when she saw you in the dress?" he asked.

"She said it looked very nice on me. Mrs. Levine took a picture of me in it to frame and put on her wall," I added. I thought he should know that, especially if he wasn't going to compliment me very much.

"That's not surprising," he said. "My wife would have been very proud of how you're wearing it."

"She sure would," Ryder said. He said it like he wanted his words nailed to the wall.

Dr. Davenport didn't look like he was smiling, exactly, but there was something in his face that told me he was very pleased about what Ryder had said and how he had said it.

"Thank you for coming to show me how the dress was fitted for you, Fern. I like what you've had done with your hair, too," he said. "Very becoming. I wish someone else worried more about what his hair looked like."

Ryder smiled.

"Who is your date tonight, Fern?"

"Paul Gabriel," Ryder answered for me. "He's our star pitcher."

Dr. Davenport nodded. "I believe I've seen him pitch. Impressive. Let's see how impressive he is tonight," he added. If he hadn't smiled, I wouldn't have realized he was kidding. There was always so much firmness and authority in his voice, even when he said a simple "Good morning."

"I'll make sure he's impressive," Ryder said.

"I believe you'll have your own date to impress," his father said quickly. "I expect you to enjoy yourselves, but take care. Life is a very fragile thing," he added, glancing, I thought, at Samantha's portrait.

"We will, Dad," Ryder said.

Dr. Davenport nodded. "Thank you for stopping by, Fern," he said. He didn't dismiss us, but we knew the visit had ended when he raised his glasses on his nose and looked at his notepad.

Ryder nodded at me, and we walked out.

"If you weren't wearing that dress, I'd never have known where my mother wore it," he said as soon as he closed the door behind us. "He doesn't like talking about her too much, and not because Bea would be jealous. Even when we're alone, he avoids any reference to her."

"It's like you're a virginal conception, huh?" I asked.

"Yes," he said, nodding and smiling. "Sometimes it is."

"That's the way I feel. How ironic. My mother avoids any possible reference to who my father might be. She might change that soon."

"Aren't we a pair?" Ryder said.

We heard the bells ringing from the front entrance.

"Paul's here," he said. "If he does something you don't like, just say, 'Ball one.'"

"Ball one?"

"Yes. Four balls, and he takes a walk," he added, smiling. "Keep everything in baseball lingo, and you'll do fine."

As we approached the door, Bea Davenport began to descend the stairway with Sam right behind her.

"Just a moment," she called to us. "You could think of your little sister, who was waiting to see you all dressed," she added as she continued coming down.

"Sorry," Ryder said to Sam. "What do you think of us?"

"Cool," Sam said, which made us both smile.

"That's not a word to express a compliment," Bea told her. She turned to me. "Your dress isn't exactly what I would call fashionable today, but your mother's tailor did a good job on it."

"That's not a way to express a compliment," Ryder parroted.

Before she could reply, he opened the door for Paul.

"Hey!" Paul cried, looking at us. "Let's play ball!"

He held up my corsage like he was going to throw it at home plate.

Ryder glanced back at Bea, who had stepped closer with Sam, I was sure to see what sort of boy would want to take me to the prom.

"You have to pin that on her, Paul," Ryder said in a little over a whisper.

"Oh, yeah." He took out the pin and held it and the corsage up, obviously not sure where it would go.

"Let me help you," Ryder offered, and pinned the corsage carefully to my dress.

"Thank you," I said, looking at Ryder.

"Look all right to you?" Ryder asked Paul.

"Sure," he said, nodding.

Ryder and I laughed.

Paul leaned forward, looking behind us at Bea. "That your mother?" he whispered.

"Hardly," I said. "My mother's a human being."

I didn't know if Bea had heard me, and I didn't care.

Ryder, smiling, closed the door behind us. "Let's go have a great time," he said.

"Will do," Paul said. He started ahead of us for his car.

Ryder looked at me and shrugged. But he took my hand to do what Paul should have done, and I couldn't have been happier about it.

6

I HAD BEEN in Alison's neighborhood many times, but when she had begun to date Ryder steadily, I paid attention to the addresses and noted her family's home. Mr. Stark's house wasn't far from it, either, and I had taken rides with Aunt Cathy and him often, so I knew what Alison's neighborhood was like. Most of the homes were modest two-story Queen Annes like hers, and most were kept nicely, with patches of lawn and some landscaping. Very few were new structures, but there were many that had been somewhat upgraded with improved landscaping and better siding.

Once, when my mother was with us and we were passing through this area on our way to a mall to shop, she wondered aloud what it would be like to live in a house that wasn't a mansion. Maybe these houses situated closely to each other on quiet streets brought back memories of her own home back in Guildford, England. On more than one occasion, she told me that although her father had been a banker, they certainly didn't live in a posh mansion.

"It's noisier than it is at Wyndemere, that's for sure," Mr. Stark had told her. "Ryder Davenport could play drums in his room and no one would notice. There was a joke about Wyndemere. Old man Davenport could invite guests for a few days or so and never know if they had left or not."

My mother didn't say anything more when he had told her that. She stared out the car window with a slight smile across her lips when we saw children on a front lawn running in a circle around a woman who looked like their mother. It had gotten me thinking. What, I wondered, did my mother really miss? How close were she and her sister and parents when she was young? How brokenhearted was her mother when my mother left? Did she think her father would regret casting her out of their family and contact her? Were he and she, as Mrs. Marlene would say, cut from the same cloth, both too proud to compromise or apologize? For years, all these questions surely haunted her. It was no wonder that she resisted reminiscing with me. It was like salting a wound.

All these feelings and questions returned to my memory as we continued to Alison's house.

Ryder mistook my introspection for nervousness. "Hey," he said, reaching forward to touch me on the shoulder. "Relax. You're going to have a lot of fun."

Paul looked at me as if doubting that was the strangest thing possible.

"I'm not nervous," I said. Of course, that was a lie.

"You're in good hands tonight," Paul assured me with a gleeful smile. "Right, Ryder?"

"Just keep them on the steering wheel," Ryder said.

"Until we stop," Paul replied, and laughed at his own joke, if it was a joke.

When Paul pulled into the Reubens' driveway, Ryder opened the door almost before he had come to a stop. He stepped out quickly and hurried to the front door. In my heart of hearts, I wished he was rushing to my door with that much enthusiasm and excitement. He disappeared inside for a few moments, and when he reemerged with Alison, her parents were with them.

Alison's father was a tall, stout man with broad shoulders and hair closer to Alison's color than her mother's, which was a darker brown, but it was obvious that Alison had inherited most of her pretty features from her mother, who really did look like she could be her older sister. Ryder gestured for us to get out and approach them.

"What's up?" Paul asked me.

I saw the camera in Alison's father's hands. "They want to take our picture."

"Oh, yeah?" He nodded. "I guess I'm going to have to get used to that."

I sighed at his attempts to be humorous and got out. Paul followed. Who was more into themselves, I wondered, snobby rich girls or sports heroes? The only thing Paul had said about my gown when we had gotten into the car was "Nice."

"Nice?" Ryder had said, laughing at Paul's response. "We'll have to work on your vocabulary. We're not playing softball. She looks more than just nice."

"Huh? Oh, yeah. Very nice," he'd corrected himself.

Paul struck me as someone who couldn't easily be embarrassed, mainly because he didn't realize he was being kidded. He had simply shrugged. To be fair, I hadn't given him much of a compliment, either. I wouldn't say he was handsome in his tuxedo. He looked very uncomfortable, in fact, or, as Mrs. Marlene might say, like a fish out of water. On the way to Alison's, he'd said he wouldn't want to try to pitch wearing such a straitjacket. I'd looked at Ryder, who shook his head and smiled at me as if we both knew a secret.

As we approached the Reubens now, Alison stepped out to look at me in my dress. She was wearing a long prom dress with a shirred crisscross bodice and a sweetheart neckline. It had side cutouts and a wide strap that connected in the back. It had a natural waistline and cascaded loosely over her hips. I loved her chandelier earrings. I doubted any other girl would look as sexy.

"Oh, you look absolutely beautiful, Fern!" her mother cried. "That is a beautiful dress."

"Yes, you do," Alison said, with an expression I thought was a cross between surprise and disappointment.

"I love your dress," I said, still worried that Bea Davenport might be right. My dress was out of fashion, and the moment I entered the prom, everyone would look at me and think I was obviously wearing a hand-me-down.

Ryder stepped up quickly to pin Alison's corsage on her dress.

"Very pretty corsage," her mother said. "Yours, too, Fern."

"Thank you."

"C'mon, the four of you stop jabberin' and stand together here," her father ordered. "Boys on the outside, right, Tess?"

"Yes, that will be nice. We'll make copies for all of you," she promised.

Paul watched how Ryder put his arm around Alison's waist and did the same with me. Alison's father took a half dozen shots, and then Alison's mother hugged her and wished us all a great time.

"You drive carefully," Alison's father told Paul. Warned him sharply was more like it.

"I've got it under control," Paul said. "Just like any other game."

It was hard to contain the excitement in the air when Paul backed out of the driveway and we were on our way. Everyone was talking at once most of the time.

"You know, my hairdresser did me a favor and fit Fern in today," Alison told Paul. It was as if she wanted to absorb or take credit for every compliment.

"Great. I did my own," Paul said, laughing and missing the point.

Alison smirked. "Men always have it easier than women. Did you tell Ryder what the stylist called you?" Alison asked me.

A flutter of panic flew through my breasts.

"No."

"What did he call you?" Ryder asked.

Before I could respond, Alison blurted, "He called her the princess of Wyndemere."

"No kidding. What do you think of that, Paul?" Ryder asked him. "You might be with the prom queen tonight."

"Does that mean I'll be king?"

"Not necessarily, no," Ryder said. "Each is chosen independently."

"Who chooses them?"

"Traditionally, the band," Ryder replied.

"Okay. I'll offer them all tickets to the playoffs. They'll want to see that."

"Somehow I don't think that'll do it for you, Paul," Ryder joked.

The senior class prom committee had decorated the gym with hundreds of multicolored balloons and crepe paper. The basketball nets and backboards were collapsible and had been moved to the far corners. The bleachers were also folded up and away, making for more space. Tables and chairs had been rented, the tables also with multicolored paper tablecloths. At the end opposite to where refreshments had been set up, a stage had been put together for the live band, a local Hillsborough group simply called Flight, with a lead female singer who didn't look much older than us, two guitar players, a drummer, and a keyboard player. They had recorded their first album, and Ryder had negotiated a good deal for his class by giving them permission to sell their CDs tonight, which would also serve as mementos of the prom. A professional photographer had a backdrop set up for couples to have their photos snapped, printed, and framed before they left the prom. The backdrop made it look like the couples were standing on the edge of a cliff with the ocean behind them.

A half dozen of our teachers, some with their wives and husbands, were scattered around the gym to serve as chaperones. As soon as we arrived, the prom committee, headed by Grace Richards, practically attacked Ryder with their problems and questions regarding everything from the refreshments to the entertainment. Each was trying to impress Ryder with how important her problem was. Paul got into a conversation with some of his teammates, and Alison and I stood off to the side, where she soon attracted most of the girls in her class, who circled her with their excitement about her dress, giving me hardly a glance.

I looked for the half dozen girls in my class who also had been invited, but they were off with their escorts talking with girls from the tenth, eleventh, and twelfth grades. None of them was really a close friend of mine anyway. I began to feel foolish just standing there while Paul joked with his teammates about their tuxedos. Their girlfriends were all eleventh and twelfth graders and obviously hung around together.

Finally, Ryder broke free and returned. He took one look at me and shouted to Paul. "You're here to dance, idiot," he told him.

Paul looked stunned for a moment and then

nodded. "Hey," he said. "I'm not the best dancer, but no one seems to care. How about you?"

I shrugged. I wanted to enjoy dancing, but I was having a hard time getting into the mood. I knew the moment we stepped out there, we'd attract lots of attention. Paul's comical moves made me look foolish, too. When I glanced at some of the kids looking at us, I saw the grins and laughter. Off to our right, Ryder and Alison were dancing. They looked so graceful together; it was like they had been dancing together most of their lives.

Paul's friends began to kid him, which only made him more self-conscious and more awkward.

"Let's get something to eat," I suggested after an uncomfortable ten minutes or so. Anything to get off the dance floor with him.

He practically leaped at the idea and headed for the refreshment tables.

"You're a good dancer," he told me. "I just don't do it enough." He handed me a plate. "If you want to dance with someone else, too, that's all right," he said.

I looked at him in confusion. "Who would I want to dance with but you? You're taking me to the prom. The other boys have dates, too. What are you talking about?"

He shrugged. "I don't know," he said. "I don't mind sharing when there's plenty to share."

I smirked and concentrated on choosing what

to eat, but it wasn't long before something unpleasant came to mind. We sat at one of the tables,
and when I looked around, I saw two of Paul's
teammates looking our way and talking with wry
smiles. I knew they were looking at me. A familiar
alarm bell sounded in my heart. Were they all taking bets on whether Paul would score tonight in
something besides a baseball game?

Ryder and Alison made their way to our table.

"You guys that hungry?" Ryder asked.

"You knew I would be," I said.

I made it sound like something far more intimate than it was, but Alison didn't show the
slightest sign of suspicion. Nevertheless, Ryder explained to her how he found out from my mother
that I had been so nervous all day that I hardly ate.

"I don't get why you keep saying she's nervous," Paul said. "What's to be nervous about?
It's not the ninth inning with the top of the opposite team's batting order coming up." His wide
grin with food between his teeth made him look
clownish.

"Let's get something to eat and join them,"
Alison told Ryder. "I didn't eat that much today,
either," she added, as if that was something he
should acknowledge as well.

He shrugged and asked if we wanted anything
else, which put the idea in Paul's mind. He rose to
return to the refreshment tables with Ryder and

Alison. I nibbled on my food and stared down at the plate. I felt like I had gotten into a rocket anticipating a wonderful liftoff that had fizzled, and I hadn't been here a full hour yet. I was in such deep thought about it that I didn't realize Shane Cisco had slipped into Paul's chair.

"Hey, hey, hey," he said, grinning.

I didn't really know him. To me, he was just another junior who hovered around Ryder. I did know he was the school's best wrestler in the 163-pound weight class. Ryder had mentioned it a few times. I had little or no interest in the sport and had never attended a bout. What I did know about Shane was that his father owned one of the biggest lumberyards in the region, and the Ciscos had a very large, modern ranch-style home with a pool and tennis courts. He had a sister in the sixth grade.

What I did think about him whenever I did look at him in school was that his dark-brown eyes were too close together and his chin was too square. His head seemed too small for his wide, well-built shoulders. He was a good two or three inches shorter than Ryder and walked with his elbows out, like someone who expected to be tossed into a fight at any moment.

"You coming to my party after this?" he asked.

"I guess," I said. "We're with Ryder and Alison."

"My parents and sister are on a weekend trip to see my uncle, so we got the house to ourselves.

Six bedrooms," he added, grinning so hard that it tightened his lips into thin, pale red rubber bands.

I simply stared at him.

"Got the maid coming in the morning, so no one will know nothing."

"Hey," Ryder said, approaching with Alison right beside him. Paul was still at the refreshment tables. "What's happening?"

"Nothing. Fern and I were just talking about the after-party at my house." Shane stood up. "I was giving her the lay of the land. Or lay of the night," he added. "Better get back to my date. You know how demanding Babs Sanders can be. I might need help."

"A champion wrestler like you?" Alison said. "I'm sure you'll come up with the right moves." She glanced at me and winked.

"Yeah, well, I did develop a new hold," he replied, and sauntered off.

Alison sat quickly. "What did he say to you?" she asked.

Ryder sat, and Paul started toward our table.

If I complained too much, I would ruin everyone else's special night, I thought. "He just wanted me to know how great his party was going to be."

"He was born bragging," Ryder said. "He's the one member of the team Coach Primack doesn't have to work on developing the necessary self-confidence."

Paul sat with another full plate of food. Alison moaned jealously about how he could eat so much without gaining weight.

"Yeah, it drives my mother nuts," he said. "She says she just looks at food and gains five pounds."

Just as it was in the school cafeteria, Ryder and Alison's table became the center of attention. Couples drifted over to comment positively about the band, the food, and the decorations. Alison was once again involved with her classmates, and Paul got into a discussion with a couple of his teammates about the upcoming big baseball game. I must have looked very bored and alone. Suddenly, I felt someone grab my right hand. I looked up at Ryder.

"Let's have a dance," he said.

I looked at Alison. She narrowed her eyes and looked surprised. Paul didn't even notice I had gotten up.

Ryder and I walked onto the dance floor.

"Don't worry. He'll get into it as the night unfolds," Ryder told me.

"Not unless I get a catcher's mitt," I shouted over the music, the volume of which had been boosted.

Ryder laughed and we started to dance.

I realized we had never danced together. Except for when we were both very little, we had never even listened to music together. In my mind's eye, I kept envisioning how well he danced with Alison. Timidly, I began to improve my moves and get more into the rhythm. I saw how pleased and amused he was with my growing enthusiasm. It challenged him to do more than just go through the motions. Neither of us realized what was happening around us, but other couples had paused to watch us.

With my eyes down, I was moving in a familiar fantasy. There was no one else in the world but Ryder and me. I was so filled with happiness and pleasure that I couldn't prevent myself from being uninhibited. It wasn't until some of the boys around us began calling to Ryder and warning him he was taking on more than he could handle that I felt myself come back down to earth.

Shocked and embarrassed, I looked at Alison. She was smiling, but it was a different sort of smile, one filled with suspicion. Paul was simply sitting back and watching with his arms folded, looking like he had no idea why there was so much excitement and reaction to what Ryder and I were doing.

I glanced at Ryder. He nodded, signaling we should return to our table.

"Now, that was a workout I didn't expect," Ryder told Alison.

"You both looked amazing out there," Paul said.

"Yes," Alison followed. "Have you two been

practicing together or something?" she asked, that little note of jealousy ringing loudly enough for me to hear, if no one else had.

"Actually . . ." Ryder looked at me. "We've never danced together."

"I don't even know what music he likes," I told Alison.

"Do I like music?" he asked her.

She laughed. "Let's get our pictures taken before we forget," she suggested.

"Right. Paul?"

"Huh? Sure," he said, rising.

The four of us went over to the backdrop. Ryder and Alison went first. They looked so perfect together that the photographer had no suggestions for how they should stand. Just before he took the picture, however, I saw Ryder's eyes drift toward me. The photographer saw that, too, and suggested they take another. This time, he emphasized where their attention should be directed.

When Paul and I went to the backdrop, the photographer had to move Paul's body physically to get him to fit well into the photograph. I was afraid I would look terribly unhappy, so I concentrated my thoughts on Ryder's expression while we were dancing. It helped me smile, and the photographer was satisfied.

"I think that's harder than dancing," Paul said, which brought some laughter to the three of us.

Ryder insisted we all return to the dance floor, however. The music was getting good. "Just watch her and do what she does," he advised Paul.

"I'll try," Paul said. "I like what she does."

I decided it would be wise for me to concentrate on him and not Ryder now. I urged him to be more relaxed and not worry about what others might think. "Don't look at anyone else. Concentrate the way you would on the other team's batter," I added. He liked that, and I did think he began to do better.

The dance I had done with Ryder had given me a new shot of energy and passion for dancing. Like most of the girls I knew, when I danced now, I was in my own world. I could have been all alone out here on the dance floor. When we took breaks to get something to drink, some of the girls and even their dates complimented me.

Shane Cisco made a point of coming over to me to tell me that I was a very sexy dancer. "You look like you're having one orgasm after another out there," he whispered, then laughed and retreated before I could respond.

Ryder was paying all his attention to Alison now. I think he had sensed that same note of jealousy I had. I kept us away from them and got Paul back on the dance floor. At one point, there were only a half dozen couples dancing, us being one of them. I would never admit it, of course, but I did spend hours and hours dancing in my room. Music laid the pathway to fantasy, and growing up so isolated in Wyndemere, I depended perhaps more than most on the power of my imagination.

The music was interrupted, mercifully for Paul, who at times looked like he was in real pain. Grace Richards wanted to thank the members of her committee, the various teacher chaperones, and the rest of us for helping to make the prom a big success. I had no idea whether it was, never having been to one, but I didn't hear anyone challenging her review.

When the music began again, I agreed with Paul to take a break and get another cool drink. The chaperones had kept a very close eye on what everyone was drinking, so no one apparently tried anything, but then again, many were anticipating the after-party at Shane Cisco's house.

"You're having fun now with your date, right?" Alison asked me when she and Ryder joined us.

"My mother calls me a dancing fool," I said. "I could be doing that no matter whom I was with."

"Well, she was an entertainer. Fern inherited her rhythm," Ryder said.

"Maybe I did," I said, thinking about it. She had never told me much about the dances she had gone to when she was my age in England. Surely she had gone to some.

"Well, whatever, you put the devil in Ryder

tonight. He's never danced as much or as well," Alison said, eyeing him.

"I heard that," Ryder said, seizing her around the waist.

Alison laughed. He kissed her, and that flush of self-assurance she habitually possessed returned.

"The photographer is putting out the pictures," she declared. "Come on, Fern."

She took my hand, and we headed for the display table. I was afraid the photographer would have printed out the wrong one for her and Ryder, but he hadn't. Theirs looked perfect, and I told her so.

"Yes, we do. You look all right," she said, nodding at mine.

We took ours, showed them to the boys, and then put them with our things at our table, just as the music stopped again and Grace Richards stepped onto the band platform. The drummer beat out a lead-in, and everyone turned to watch, the chatter dying down.

"Now what?" Paul moaned. "More speeches?"

"It's time to announce this year's prom queen and king," Grace said. She conferred with the lead singer of Flight and then returned to the microphone. "First, the prom queen, the girl who showed the most poise, looked like she was having the best time, and was attractive enough in her gown to represent our school tonight."

There was another drumroll.

"And the prom queen is . . . Fern Corey."

I heard my name, but it didn't seem to register. I thought perhaps I had imagined it. I didn't move or react. There was applause, and then Alison reached over and literally shook me.

"It's you," she said, as surprised as I was.

"What?"

"You have to go up there, Fern. You're to be crowned prom queen," Ryder said.

I stood up, but I felt more like I was floating, being scooped along by a heavy wind. I didn't look at anyone on either side. Comments from the lips of surely jealous other girls followed me to the stage. Could I be eligible? I wondered. I wasn't a senior, and this was the senior prom. Maybe the band didn't know that. Someone would shout it out, and I would be terribly embarrassed, I thought, but Grace Richards was smiling and holding the crown, which was some sort of metal designed with gold leaves. As soon as I was close enough to her, she placed it on my head. There was applause, reluctant or otherwise.

"You can say something if you want," Grace told me.

I looked out at the crowd, all standing at their tables or on the dance floor.

"Thank you. I'm totally shocked," I said. That brought laughter and a few catcalls from some boys who said I was like the Energizer Bunny.

Grace indicated I should step back, which I did. I turned to smile at the band members, who were smiling at me and offering congratulations.

"And now the choice for this year's prom king," Grace declared. "He is someone who also has great poise and enthusiasm and is handsomely dressed. We all agree with the band. Our prom king is Ryder Davenport."

There was a great cheer. As Ryder stood and walked toward the stage, I looked at Alison. She seemed to dwindle in her seat. The empty smile on her face was frozen. I felt like rushing off the stage and placing my crown on her head. Ryder, however, didn't look a bit concerned. When Grace placed his crown on his head, he turned quickly to the microphone.

He began by thanking the committee again, and then, after giving me a quick glance, he said, "I wear the crown for myself and my date, Alison Reuben, who always makes me feel like a king."

The girls swooned, and the boys cheered. Alison's face lit up again. Traditionally, however, we had to dance together as the king and queen of the prom. We started it off, a slow dance.

"And you were worried how you would look and if you would enjoy yourself," Ryder said. "Your mother is going to be very proud of you, I'm sure. And Bea will have a minor heart attack."

I laughed, and then he nodded at Paul, turning

me toward him, and went to get Alison so everyone could join and finish the dance. The teacher chaperones all congratulated me. Paul finally looked like he was having a good time now. Every chance he got, he bragged to his teammates that he had the hottest girl at the prom.

"Everything's winding down," Alison told me. "Come on. Let's go to the girls' room and repair our makeup before we go to the after-party."

I followed her in. Other girls were there gossiping. Some grew very quiet when we entered, so it wasn't difficult to imagine they had been talking about either her or me. Probably me, I thought.

"Looks like Wyndemere won the night," Tara Morton told me, loudly enough for everyone to hear.

"I don't represent Wyndemere," I said. "But when I get home, I'll be sure to tell the house how pleased you are."

Some laughed.

Alison nudged me to walk away. "Ignore her," she told me. "She was born miserable."

Other girls gathered around us, paying more attention to me and far friendlier than ever. Alison was quiet about it. I was sure she was upset about my getting the crown and not her, especially since Ryder had been chosen to be prom king, but I didn't know what to say to her except how surprised I was.

She nodded and stepped back when more of her friends began to congratulate me. I joyfully soaked in their questions about my dress and how I had learned to dance so well. Some kidded me about Paul, warning me to be careful of his curveball.

What a roller coaster I'd been on, I thought, as we left the girls' room to meet the boys and head for the after-party. I just hoped that getting off would be as graceful as getting on had been.

Paul looked like Ryder had given him a pep talk. He stepped forward quickly to take my hand. "I thought this was going to be harder than pitching nine innings," he said as we started out, "but you sure made it easier for me. Now I hope I can make the rest of the night easy for you."

I smiled for him and thought maybe he wasn't very sophisticated, nowhere nearly as sophisticated as Ryder, but he was a nice enough boy, and for now, his simplicity seemed refreshing. Hopefully, he would distract me enough with his silly joking for the rest of the night to keep me from drooling over the vision of Ryder and me dancing closely for those special moments.

A few weeks ago, I was that impure girl stained by her mother's sin and destined to carry the word *illegitimate* to my grave. But for now, I really was the princess of Wyndemere, although I knew it wouldn't be for long and might make my life even more difficult in days to come, especially when Bea Davenport heard about it.

Ryder mentioned that again.

"Yes," Alison said, almost joyfully. "I'd avoid her if I were you."

Maybe she really meant I should avoid Ryder, I thought.

7

ALISON AND RYDER cuddled in the rear of Paul's car. Before we were thirty seconds away from the school, they were kissing and whispering and giggling. Paul, oblivious to it all, was babbling about the prom, relating some of what he thought were the dumb things his baseball buddies had to say about his dancing with me.

"I'm glad I'm in shape," he told me. "Because if I have to dance any more tonight, I'm going to have to dig out that second wind."

"If we do dance, I'll go easy on you," I said.

I didn't think Ryder had been listening, but he laughed.

A number of the couples had left for Shane Cisco's house before us. By the time we parked on the street, the music was booming. Fortunately, the Ciscos' house was a good acre or so from the nearest neighbor. It was located in a more affluent neighborhood of Hillsborough. Despite its distance from the city center, the street was well lit. Loud voices, laughter, and shrieks of delight were spilling out of the opened windows and the front door as we approached.

Ryder had advised that we leave our crowns in the car. "The wise guys will only kid us to death," he said.

I was more than happy to do so. Even though Alison didn't complain about how it had turned out, I was still uncomfortable.

Of course, despite the size of the Cisco house, it was nowhere near as large as Wyndemere. It did have wide open, flowing rooms and a full-length basement that had been designed for more entertaining. There was a long bar, a media center, sofas and chairs spaced well along the oak-paneled walls, and tightly woven cocoa-shaded carpeting. A portion had been cut around a light-beige marble floor that was great for dancing, and a dozen couples were doing so already. Everyone had to shout to be heard over the music.

Not all the prom attendees had been invited, but there were at least fifty now in the basement. When we came down the stairs, cheers sounded, and Ryder was immediately teased about being the prom king. While alcohol wasn't obvious, Shane's

parents having locked away the bottles behind the
bar, beer bottles began to appear, some boys dancing with them in their hands.

Before Ryder and Alison were dragged onto
the dance floor, he leaned toward me to whisper.
"Don't drink anything you didn't pour for yourself
or see it poured for you," he warned.

As the evening wore on, it became obvious that
some had smuggled in harder liquor, too. Shane
and some of his close friends were egging Paul on
to have a drink or do more. Babs Sanders pulled
me aside to tell me Shane had offered Paul his sister's bedroom. His friends were daring him to get
me upstairs.

"I think he's a virgin. Everyone told him not to
worry. You'd know what to do even if he doesn't,"
she said.

"Why?" I snapped back at her.

She widened her eyes and walked away. I
wanted to go after her and make her say aloud
what she was implying about me. It did seem like
everyone who was looking my way had expressions on their faces similar to Babs's and were
whispering and laughing.

I looked to Ryder, who never left Alison's side.
He glanced my way periodically and smiled, but
he soon seemed much more involved with Alison.
The lights had been turned down lower, and at one
point, I no longer saw him and Alison in the base-

ment. Paul and his friends kept teasing each other. If Ryder was my date, he wouldn't be leaving me alone like this, I thought.

Others, besides Paul and his buddies, were beginning to act wilder, too, talking louder, drinking beer and other things openly. Many on the dance floor resembled hospital patients suffering from Saint Vitus's dance, which made people with the brain disease move radically. They looked like they had globs of red ants crawling over their backs and biting them. Joey Dunsten tripped over his own feet and fell, knocking into others, who then screamed. Most were laughing.

I shook my head in disgust. This wasn't what I had anticipated the after-party to be. I thought only about leaving now. Where were Ryder and Alison?

"Hey," Barry Austin said, coming over to me. "You look like you're not having fun. I got something to loosen up the prom queen." He held out his hand, in which there were small white pills. "Go on. Take one for free."

"No, thanks," I said.

"Don't say I didn't offer."

"I won't say anything. You don't exist," I told him.

He smirked and walked off.

Paul returned to my side, and I told him what Barry was circulating.

"Yeah. I stay away from that crap. Might hurt my fastball," he said.

I looked at his drink. "What is that?"

"Just a little bit of vodka and soda," he said. "Joey Dunsten had a flask."

"I can see that. He can't even stand up straight."

"Yeah. Don't worry. I'm not getting drunk or anything. I'm not losing my license."

"Or your life," I said.

"Yeah." He looked at his drink and then put it on a table. "You want to get out of here for a while?"

"Yes, but more than for a while. Where?"

"Upstairs." He shrugged. "We could just talk and maybe even listen to some better music or something."

"Where are Ryder and Alison?" I asked, looking around.

"I think they're up in Shane's room. Whaddaya say? I'm getting a headache down here. You probably want to take a breather, too, huh?"

I considered it. When I looked around now, everyone was either with familiar friends or couples were into themselves. I realized also that the few girls from my class who had attended the prom were not here. It was mostly seniors and juniors with a few sophomores.

"Where do you want to go?" I asked him.

He looked at his watch. "We have Shane's sister's room for an hour."

"An hour? What's he doing, renting it out?"

Paul smiled but didn't reply.

Was he?

"C'mon. I've been here before. I know the house," Paul said.

I followed him up the stairs, hoping to run into Ryder and Alison, who I also hoped were ready to leave. They were nowhere in sight. Paul led me down a hallway and opened a door on our left. There was no question it was a young girl's room. The walls were pink with darker pink curtains. There were shelves with dolls and posters on the wall of young rock singers. The rug was a thick white looped carpet. Off to the right was a beautiful computer station and desk with shelves. The room had an en suite bathroom and a very large walk-in closet. There was a sweet fragrance in the air, but I saw no fresh flowers.

It was the bed that caught my attention, a king-size four-poster canopy bed in birch veneer with pink swirls through the frame and headboard. The oversize pillows and comforter were done in a light pink. It was the sort of room I always dreamed of having. What a contrast to my stark, dark-paneled walls and thin gray area rug over the dark floorboards. My bed wasn't even a queen-size; it was a double. My mother was always resistant when it came to my pinning anything on the walls. We couldn't use nails or make any significant changes to anything. I had two side tables, each with a lamp on it, but the main lighting came from a plain overhead fixture.

My desk was barely big enough for my books, notebooks, and laptop. If it hadn't been for Mr. Stark, I wouldn't have had the electrical outlets I needed, nor would I have Wi-Fi for my computer research.

"Hey!" Paul cried, and dove onto the bed. "This is comfortable."

"You should at least take off your shoes," I said.

"Sure. I'll take off everything if you want."

I glared at him, at his silly smile, and then looked at the books in the bookcase to my left. I saw the built-in audio equipment beside it. Attached to the wall to the right of the door was what I thought was at least a forty-inch television set.

"Hey, we can watch some television while we wait for Ryder and Alison," Paul said.

I didn't say anything. Paul pulled himself back and lay against one of the pillows, his hands behind his head, as he watched me continue to look around.

"What's your room like?" he asked.

"A dungeon compared to this."

He nodded. He wasn't really interested. "Ain't you tired? C'mon and lay down for a while," he said, patting the space beside him.

"If I do that, I'll probably fall asleep."

"Don't worry," he said, smiling. "I'll keep you awake."

He smiled licentiously now. I thought there was something different about him. He had lost that country-bumpkin look.

"Was there something else in that drink you had? Are you high on something?"

"I'm high on just you," he said. "I know I haven't paid enough attention to you, and I want to make up for it."

I pulled my lips back into an incredulous smile. He didn't sound like the Paul Gabriel I had gotten to know these past days or earlier tonight. "Where did you come up with that line, Paul?"

To me, it sounded like something someone had told him to say. Maybe his teammates had given him strategies to hook up with me.

"It doesn't sound like you," I said, pressing the point.

He shrugged. "A pitcher has to be able to adjust his technique on the mound."

"I'm not playing baseball."

"Me, neither." He patted the bed again. "C'mon. Relax."

"Ryder and Alison won't know where we are."

"Won't take long for them to figure it out, or Shane will tell them. Don't expect them to come out so fast. Besides, we'll hear them."

"Where are they?"

"Right across the hall. You don't want to interrupt them, do you?" He reached for the television remote. "We'll just see what's on and relax," he said.

I felt foolish just standing there. Reluctantly, I went to the bed, slipped off my shoes, and lay back against the other pillow.

"Comfy, huh?"

"It's a very nice room."

"You been out with anyone? I asked around, but no one knows if you have," he said. He turned to me, leaning on his left elbow.

"No. Why?" My suspicions about him were growing quickly. "Who's keeping tabs on me?"

"Nobody. So I'm your first date? I mean, your first real date?"

"Yes."

"You're very pretty," he said, more like recited.

Before I could say anything, he quickly kissed me and turned so that his chest was on my right arm and shoulder. Then he brought his right leg over my left and kissed me again, pressing his lips harder while he brought his right hand up over my breast. I squirmed to get out from under him. This wasn't the first real sexual experience I had envisioned for myself. There were other boys besides Ryder in school whom I had imagined dating.

"Stop," I said, pushing on his chest. He was too heavy for me to lift away.

"It's all right," he said. "Don't worry. I came prepared."

He dropped his hand to my thigh and then began to pull up my dress until he could get his hand under it. I turned and twisted to get free.

"C'mon," he urged. "What do you think Ryder and Alison are doing?"

"I don't care what they're doing. Whatever you think it is, I'm not doing it with you," I said, and tried to turn out from under him, but he wasn't moving. "Paul, stop," I said, as he continued moving his hand up my thigh, slipping his fingers under my panties.

"You wanted to go to the prom with me. Ryder said you would want to make out. Don't be shy now."

"That's a lie. Ryder never said that."

"That's what he meant," he said.

I looked at his eyes. The pupils seemed so large. "You lied. You took those pills from Barry Austin, didn't you? That's why you're like this."

"Like what?" he said.

His fingers crossed over my pelvic bone and began to move quickly, like some creepy-crawler insect, through my pubic hair. When his fingers began to enter me, I brought my left hand around and dug my nails into the side of his face, screaming, "Get off me! Stop!"

I had lived with a repeating nightmare frequently invading my sleep from the moment I was old enough to conceive of it, the moment I first learned what the concept of date rape meant. It was a deep fear of mine, not because I was terrified of it happening to me but because I suspected that was exactly what had happened to my mother. It made sense. Most young women who are attacked this way feel some responsibility. They had willingly placed themselves in the situation. Yes, they weren't expecting to be sexually attacked, but, like the unsuspecting mouse, they had willingly walked into the trap.

How complicated this made their claim of being violated. It was a classic "he said, she said" situation, especially if the woman didn't show any signs of violence, no trauma to her face or body. The only wounds were to her innocence, to her self-respect, and to her soul. The man even could get away with signs of violence on his body, claiming the woman had done it in the throes of her passion. That happened, didn't it? they could ask.

And who was deciding, judging this accusation, most of the time? Other men, that was who.

So perhaps my mother had let the violation of her go unreported and hoped nothing would come of it. Of course, anyone would logically ask why she had gone through with having a baby. Yes, it was becoming more difficult not to continue a pregnancy, but why didn't she get it done one way or another? Why let everyone in the world know what had happened?

Most important, who wanted to be faced with this horrible choice? It was so unfair. The man would walk off, unscathed, like some self-satisfied caveman. And in the end, the woman, no matter how clearly it was shown that she had been raped, would suffer not only because she had lost her own self-respect but also because everyone who knew her, although professing to be sympathetic, would always think of her as spoiled, ruined. How many men who knew her and what had happened to her would permit themselves to fall in love with her?

Surely this explained much of what had happened to my mother and why she was the woman she was now, living as she was.

The horror of this nightmare was what drove me to seek more romantic solutions to the mystery of my birth. She had the love affair with that handsome, charming married man. She couldn't get rid of his child. The child was part of him, and as long as she had this child, me, she had part of him. Was it really just a fairy tale?

What terrified me now was that I could have the same fate my mother had. All the terrible things

said about me because I was an illegitimate child
would be confirmed. People would whisper that,
like my mother, I, too, had been date-raped. *Go
complain. Go make an accusation against one of
the school's sports heroes, and see how many flock
to be at your side and support you.*

*Why did you agree to go up into the bedroom
if you didn't have this in mind? Who'd believe any
explanation you had?*

Finally, the pain of my fingernails digging into
his cheek triggered enough of a retreat in him
for me to turn more forcefully and slip out from
under him. I didn't realize that the entire time I was
struggling, I had been shouting. Of course, no one
below, with the music practically tearing down the
walls, would hear me.

But Ryder and Alison apparently had. Ryder
opened the door to see what was happening. Alison came up behind him. Ryder had his jacket off
and his bow tie loosened. For a moment, he just
stood there looking in at us. Paul didn't realize
they were there. He was moaning about his face
and cursing. I slipped off the bed, got into my
shoes, and ran past Ryder and out to the hallway.

"What the hell is going on here?" Ryder finally
asked.

"She wanted to come in here and get in the
bed," Paul claimed.

Ryder turned to me.

"He's on that Ecstasy crap!" I shouted.

Ryder turned back to him. "Are you? I told you not to do that, Paul. You said you wouldn't."

"I just took one. It was so damn boring down there," he claimed.

Ryder hesitated a moment and then backed up and closed the door. "Come on," he told Alison and me. He returned to the other bedroom and got his jacket. He had Alison's purse, too. He nodded toward the entryway and took his mobile out of his inside jacket pocket as we walked.

"Hey!" we heard Paul cry from the bedroom doorway. "Where the hell are you going?"

"Keep walking," Ryder said. He was talking on the phone.

Alison looked back at him for directions.

"Just walk out," he said. "We're meeting Parker at the corner of Hobly and Underwood."

The three of us headed out the front door and down the walkway to the street. He took my right hand in his and held Alison's with his left. We headed away from the house, no one speaking.

"How far did he get?" Alison asked after a few minutes.

"Far enough with those long fingers," I said.

I was feeling all right now. Ryder was holding my hand firmly. We found a large rock to sit on while we waited. I expected Paul to come running after us, but maybe he was afraid now.

"Did you take anything?" Alison asked.

"No."

"How come you went into the bedroom with him?"

"It was supposed to be just a rest from the racket downstairs."

"You believed that? You can't be that naive."

"Forget about it," Ryder told her. "It certainly isn't her fault."

She looked away. He had actually snapped at her to defend me.

Less than fifteen minutes later, Parker appeared, driving the Davenport limousine. He asked no questions. The three of us got into the rear, and he drove off.

"We're taking Miss Reuben home first, please, Parker."

"Absolutely," Parker said.

In silence, the three of us lay back, me cuddled against Ryder's right side and Alison against his left. He stared ahead. I closed my eyes. It was easy to imagine that it was only Ryder and me going home from the prom. When we reached Alison's house, Ryder got out to walk her to her front door.

"Great finish to what was to be a great night," she muttered to me.

What did she mean? Was she blaming me?

"Alison," Ryder called.

She closed the door. They walked to her front door and were there for a few minutes talking. He kissed her good night, but quickly on the cheek, and she went into the house.

I was hoping Ryder would embrace me again, but he sat a little farther away this time and stared angrily ahead.

"I'm sorry," he said after a minute or so. "I thought he was too straight to be any sort of problem. I really haven't gone out with him that much, but from what everyone else had to say about him . . ."

"It's definitely not your fault, Ryder."

"Yeah, well, I'm not finished with him yet. He spoiled Alison's and my night, too. I don't care how many shutouts he pitches. He's stupid."

"There were a lot more people into the drugs and alcohol down in the basement. It grew wilder after you left, so all I wanted to do was get out of there. I didn't mean for it to turn out like this." I hoped he believed me.

He was silent, thinking. Then he said, "Maybe it's best if we don't mention any of this part, Fern. My dad will be upset, and someone we know will be gleeful. As far as everyone knows, we had a great time at the prom. We were crowned king and queen—"

"Oh, our crowns! They're in his car. And the pictures—"

"Not important. We danced, had fun, went to the party, got bored, and left. End of story," he said. "Right?"

"Yes."

I looked toward Parker.

"Don't worry," Ryder said. "Besides, I'll get everything back from Paul tomorrow."

"Okay. I did have a good time, mostly," I said.

He reached for my hand. "You looked great, and you were definitely the best dancer out there. The band couldn't help themselves."

I didn't know if he expected it or not, but I leaned to my left and rested my head against his shoulder. I was forcing myself on him, but he put his arm around me anyway, and we were like that all the way back to Wyndemere.

When we arrived at the mansion, Parker opened our doors and woke us up. He reached in to help me out.

Ryder came around to my side and took my hand. "Thank you, Parker," he said. "I'm sorry we woke you so late, but it couldn't be helped."

"It's not a problem, Mr. Davenport," he said. He looked like his respect for Ryder had grown considerably. Ryder nodded, and we walked up to the front entrance.

"What time is it?" I asked.

"After three," he said. "I'm not getting up until at least noon."

He opened the door. Wyndemere, this late, seemed asleep to me. The shadows cast by the dimmed lights looked longer than ever. There were dark shapes on the walls I had never seen. Both of us walked softly.

"You okay?" Ryder asked in a loud whisper.

"Yes. Thank you. I did enjoy being with you . . . and Alison," I said.

He leaned over and kissed me on the cheek. "Night," he said. "I'll look for you sometime in the afternoon."

"Night."

He started for the stairway. I watched him for a moment, and then I made my way through the house to the hallway that led to our section. I didn't expect my mother to be awake, but as I turned toward my bedroom, she stepped into the doorway of hers. She was in her nightgown, her hair down.

"Enjoy yourself?" she asked.

"I was crowned prom queen," I said quickly, to cover up any sign of unhappiness.

"Really?" She smiled.

"And Ryder was crowned prom king."

Her smile froze and then re-formed. "How wonderful," she said. "I bet you're tired."

"Exhausted."

"You need any help with your clothes, anything?"

"No, I'm okay. Thanks, Mummy."

"I know you're probably very excited, but try to get some sleep," she said.

"I will."

She retreated, and I went into my bedroom. For a moment, I simply stood there, contemplating it, thinking how no matter how hard my mother and I tried, it was pathetic contrasted to Shane Cisco's sister's bedroom, but all the beauty in her bedroom and everything she had couldn't wipe away the bad feelings it would conjure up every time I thought of it.

Better to live with my own ghosts, I thought, and went about getting undressed and putting away my things. My mother need not have worried about my getting any sleep. The moment I crawled beneath my light blanket and laid my head on my pillow, I was asleep.

All I had to do was think about Ryder's arm around me as he and I rode alone in the limousine. I wished that ride would have never ended and we had been driven off to another world, a place where nobody knew who we were, a place where we could begin as if we had been reborn.

I slept as late as Ryder claimed he would, and my mother didn't wake me, although I was certain she had looked in on me a number of times. And then, suddenly, there was a knock on my door, a knock much harder and louder than my mother's.

I sat up quickly. When I heard my mother shout, "What is it?" I gasped. An electric feeling seemed to burn its way through my body and sizzle around my heart.

Bea Davenport opened the door. My mother was standing at her side.

"Get dressed," Bea ordered, "and come immediately to Dr. Davenport's office. Immediately, do you hear?" She turned to leave.

"What is it?" my mother asked her.

Bea looked at her. "You come, too," she said, and walked off.

My mother turned to me. I couldn't swallow. The dark shadows I had seen when we entered Wyndemere knew something we didn't.

And what could keep a secret better than a shadow?

8

I RUSHED TO get into a blouse and jeans and slip on some flats, while my mother stood there looking very worried.

"What is this about?" she asked.

My mind was filling quickly with possibilities, none good. "I don't know, Mummy."

"It has to be something very, very serious to bring Bea Davenport down here raging and the doctor demanding to see you, Fern. Could it be something to do with the prom? Did something happen last night?"

I paused. I suspected that someone had revealed all that had gone on at Shane Cisco's house concerning the drugs and alcohol, and that had gotten back to Dr. Davenport. Perhaps another parent had called him or even Shane's parents.

"Everything was great until we went to the after-party," I said, running a brush through my hair. "Many people were drinking beer and other things, and some were taking a party drug."

"Party drug? What drug?"

"Ecstasy. I didn't, of course, and neither did Ryder or Alison."

Her eyes narrowed with suspicion. "But the boy you were with?"

"He did," I said. "As soon as Ryder found out, he made us leave the party and had Parker pick us up and take us home."

"Oh. Parker must have told Dr. Davenport."

"Ryder didn't think he would."

"He didn't think he would? That's ridiculous. There is nothing Parker wouldn't tell Dr. Davenport. He's more devoted to him than he is to himself. Dr. Davenport operated on him and saved his life. Why didn't you tell me these things last night?"

"I thought it could wait until morning. I was tired; you were tired. Regardless, Dr. Davenport shouldn't be angry at Ryder. It wasn't his fault. He was as surprised as I was that Paul drank and took a pill."

"Drank, too?"

"He said just a little, but I don't know. It was very . . . chaotic at times."

"Were all your other friends at this party doing these things?"

"Not all, no."

She stared at me a moment and then nodded. "Let's go," she said. "This isn't going to be very pleasant."

With my head down and my heart thumping, I walked with her to the main house. The silence only made it more frightening to me. Not a maid, not Mrs. Marlene, no one seemed to be moving or doing anything. I didn't look at my mother until we reached Dr. Davenport's office. The door was open.

Bea Davenport was seated on the settee to our right, sitting up with her stiff, perfect posture, with her eyes looking forward like a judge ready to pronounce the death sentence. Ryder was in a chair in front of Dr. Davenport's desk. He was wearing a robe over his pajamas and was leaning forward, his hands pressed against his temples.

"Come in, please, Emma," Dr. Davenport said.

Ryder looked up quickly at us. We stopped beside him, I on his right and my mother on his left. The expression on his face told me this was far more serious than parents complaining.

"I don't know how much you know about all that happened last night," Dr. Davenport said.

"Fern slept late, but after Mrs. Davenport left just now, I asked Fern what this might be about, and she told me about some unpleasant things that occurred at the after-party," my mother said.

Dr. Davenport nodded. He was wearing his suit jacket and tie, but he looked very tired to me. His hair looked like he had been running his fingers through it. He nodded at the chair on his right. "Have a seat, Emma," he said. "This may take a while."

My mother sat, and then he turned to me. "I was called to the hospital about three thirty last night."

I looked at Ryder. He kept his gaze low now and seemed to be holding his breath.

"A young man was brought into the emergency room with some serious heart issues, an arrhythmia," Dr. Davenport said. He was looking directly at Ryder. Then he turned to my mother. "Arrhythmia in young people is often associated with a drug known as MDMA or better known to young people today as Ecstasy or just X."

My mother gasped and brought her right hand to the base of her throat.

"There was some concern about heart-valve damage, but fortunately, that didn't happen, and we were able to correct his heartbeat," Dr. Davenport continued. "The reason we're all meeting here right now is that the young man was the young man who took Fern to the prom and drove Ryder and his date, Alison Reuben, as well."

He looked back at Ryder.

"Ryder tells me that this young man came to

him first to inquire whether he should ask Fern to the prom. He admits that he convinced Fern to accept the young man's invitation. She apparently didn't know him well, and from what I'm gathering now, neither did Ryder, at least not as well as he should have."

"It was my decision to go with Paul," I said. "Ryder didn't have to convince me."

Dr. Davenport looked at me. "You knew the boy that well beforehand, did you?"

"No, not exactly. He's a senior and—"

Dr. Davenport turned back to my mother. "Ryder assures me he personally did not use any drugs." He turned his eyes on me. "Fern?"

I shook my head. "No, I didn't. Someone offered me one, but I didn't," I said. "I didn't drink anything alcoholic, either."

Bea Davenport blew some air through her closed lips and looked away.

"I swear," I said. "I didn't."

"She didn't," Ryder added, glaring angrily at Bea.

"Is Paul Gabriel going to be all right?" I asked Dr. Davenport.

"He'll recuperate, yes. He was lucky. A significant number don't. However, one tragedy is too much for those parents to bear."

I nodded and glanced at my mother, who looked now like she was about to cry.

"We had to involve the police, and they've

informed Mr. and Mrs. Cisco about what went on at their home. It's still an ongoing investigation. You two will probably be interviewed, as will Miss Reuben," Dr. Davenport said, looking at Ryder. "Expect the police to come here or perhaps have you go to the police station."

He let that set in for a moment and then sat forward.

"There's more. Apparently, someone else at that after-party drove into a ditch last night. He wasn't wearing his seat belt and sustained some head trauma. He has a concussion and will recuperate. No one else in his car was hurt, but he had a serious alcohol level and will face serious consequences."

Ryder looked up sharply. Apparently, all this was news to him, too. Dr. Davenport had saved it for this moment. "Who was it?" Ryder asked.

"Joey Dunsten," his father replied.

"Disgusting," Bea Davenport said. "This is what comes of this laissez-faire attitude when it comes to raising children these days, drugs and alcohol."

"You can't generalize about all children these days. Our children did not participate," my mother said.

"So they say," Bea responded.

"My daughter does not lie to me," my mother insisted.

"Yet she didn't tell you about what went on at the party, did she?" Bea countered.

"It was very late."

"Almost too late," Bea said sharply. "For all of us."

"She would have told me this morning," my mother insisted, but more under her breath.

Dr. Davenport looked at her and then sat back. "The would haves and could haves always pale in the light of tragedy or near tragedy," he said, looking at Ryder and me. "For the immediate future, I think it would be best if neither of you did much more than attend school and come home."

"What? Why? Why are we being punished for what other people did?" Ryder responded quickly. "When I saw what the situation had become, I called Parker to come get us, and we went right home."

"That's admirable. I'm not saying I don't commend you for it, but there's going to be a lot of commotion in the school and in the community for a while," Dr. Davenport said. "I'd like things to calm down. It's better that parties and dates be put off for a while. The full impact of all this hasn't been felt yet. Your friend might lose his privilege to play baseball. In fact, I'd say that's pretty likely."

"That's freaking unfair!" Ryder's face turned a shade of crimson I had never seen on him. "This party didn't involve the school. It was after the prom!"

"I believe your school has a strict policy about drug use, Ryder. MDMA is a class A drug. It's illegal to sell it or use it, and no doctor can prescribe it. You can be sure that when the police isolate who distributed the drug at the party, that person will face some serious legal issues. Paul Gabriel might as well."

He turned to me.

"If you're asked who offered the drug to you, Fern, and you refuse to answer, that could be construed as obstruction of justice. Same goes for you, Ryder. I think it's a good idea for both of you to take stock of the situation, be grateful you had the sense to make an exit, and, as I said, let things calm down here."

"For how long?" Ryder asked.

"A while," Dr. Davenport replied.

"A while? Is that the kind of answer you would give a patient?" Ryder said. "'You'll get better in a while?'"

I never had seen anger rise to the surface of Dr. Davenport's face or his eyes turn so steely and cold.

Bea Davenport leaped on the opportunity. "Just as I've been saying, Harrison, he's been quite insolent lately."

Dr. Davenport looked at her and then nodded. "I believe that is all for now," he said. "The conversation is over."

Ryder shot up out of his chair, turned, and stormed out of the office.

My mother rose slowly. "Let's go back, Fern," she said, a deep sadness weighing her down.

I felt the tears welling in my eyes. I had enough trouble saying hello to Dr. Davenport, much less challenging anything he said or did. The very thought of doing that would terrify me, but the shock and pain in Ryder's face had a greater impact.

"This is unfair, Dr. Davenport. Ryder took me out of an unpleasant situation immediately. I'm sure some of his friends will call him a goody-goody or something now. He should not be punished. And neither should I for things other people do," I said, this time not looking away.

"Fern!" my mother said.

"Not unexpected," Bea Davenport said.

"I hope not," I said, still flying high on my defiance. "I hope speaking the truth is always expected." I started to walk out.

"Just a minute, Fern," Dr. Davenport said. I turned back to him. "You and Ryder are ignoring a great lesson here. It is perhaps unfair to suffer because of the actions of others and not yourself, but understand that you will be judged by the company you keep. It is childishly naive to think otherwise. There are always consequences. When you settle down, be grateful you've learned this with little cost to yourself other than being grounded for a while."

I glanced at my mother, and then I walked out.

She stayed back for a few moments and then caught up with me. "We need to have a long talk," she said.

"Yes. We do. Finally," I replied.

I was crying. I was afraid, but I was quite satisfied with how I had stood by Ryder as well.

As we entered our section of Wyndemere, however, I realize that Bea Davenport could say all sorts of things about me now. She might convince Dr. Davenport that I was the bad influence he had referred to, that I was a bad influence on Ryder, and that I had somehow placed him and the family in this compromising situation. Maybe now she would persuade him to give my mother her walking papers. Where would we go? What would my mother do? Take a job as someone else's nanny? You needed references for that, and Bea Davenport would make sure my mother had no good ones.

Really, what would my mother do? She had devoted too much of her life to Wyndemere and the Davenport family and not developed any other work skills. People said to be careful what you wished for; you might get it. Was I about to get it? I had been wishing we would leave for years now, but on our own steam and not driven out.

When I glanced at my mother, I saw the pain in her eyes. She followed me into my room.

I sat on my bed, folded my arms under my breasts, and scowled at the floor.

"Dr. Davenport wasn't blaming either of you for what happened last night, Fern. He was merely suggesting everyone take a deep breath and let the dust settle."

"Bea Davenport was so damn happy about it," I said. "I hate her, and Ryder hates her, too. I think her own daughter hates her."

"Ryder's and your defiance of Dr. Davenport just now gave her the upper hand, Fern. You must learn when it's best to suck in your breath and wait. A branch that—"

"Bends doesn't break. I know, I know." I spun on her. "You hate that woman, too. I know you do."

"Let's just say I wouldn't rush to throw her a lifeline if she was in danger of drowning."

She sat beside me and stroked my hair.

"I think you understand now what I meant when I told you once that you grow up when you face challenges. Dr. Davenport was appealing to the potential adult in both of you. He wouldn't be doing it if he didn't care about you, both of you."

"Funny way to show it. Ryder was so upset," I said. "He did everything right. He basically rescued me, if you want to know. I wasn't going to get into details in front of Bea Davenport, but Paul was out of control. He had persuaded me to go to Shane

Cisco's sister's bedroom to get away from the rau-
cous party. Alison and Ryder were somewhere else
in the house, too. It was then that I realized Paul
had taken something besides just drinking some
vodka or something. It wasn't pleasant. He was
forcing himself on me."

"What?" She grimaced.

"I was screaming, and Ryder heard me. He
burst in, and I ran out."

"I see," she said. "Well, then, Dr. Davenport
was right. Maybe Ryder shouldn't have been so
eager to persuade you to go to the prom with Paul
Gabriel."

"He just wanted me to have a good time, have
a special night," I protested. "He wanted me to go
along with him and Alison. I'm sure he feels terrible about it now, and his father forbidding him,
forbidding both of us, to do anything fun because
of what others did is just . . . unfair. He makes it all
sound like a recuperation from an illness, too. Dr.
Davenport should try to be a father more and not
just a great doctor."

"That's exactly what he's trying to do. He's
looking out for both of you."

"He's looking out for the Davenport name
and reputation, especially because of what his
wife wants him to do. That's all she cares about.
She doesn't care about her own daughter enough,
either. They belong together. No wonder he mar-

ried her. I hate it here now. I hate it!" I cried. "Why didn't you just leave when you could? Why didn't you return to a singing career or at least return to trying? Then we wouldn't be stuck in this giant . . . dark . . . old mansion full of lies and ghosts."

She stared at me. The tears were streaking down my cheeks, but I didn't wipe one away. I took a deep breath.

"You said it was time to talk. Well, it is. I want to know everything now. I'm old enough. I feel like I'm living inside a cloud."

"Yes," she said. "You are old enough. But are you mature enough?"

"What's that mean?"

She rose, turned away, and, after a long moment, looked at me again. "I didn't tell you the whole truth concerning how I came to be at Wyndemere," she said. "Things for me were a lot worse in New York than I had described. It was as if my father's curses over my disobeying him and leaving England were coming true. When my first roommate left, I struggled. I was working as a waitress and living off tips mainly. I tried getting work singing in bars, but that was difficult when I tried to coordinate with auditioning for parts in Broadway shows and working at the restaurant. There were so many young girls like me in New York, all dreaming of beginning a career in show business. The competition was overwhelming. Two hundred and fifty girls would show up for a tiny part in a musical. They didn't even use your name. You were given a number. That's what I began to feel like, a number.

"Some girls my age were dancers going to every Broadway audition; some were trying to be actresses. When you went into a fast-food restaurant or one a little more like the one I had been working in, and you asked the young men or women what they were doing, pursuing, they all had similar answers. They were just working in service to make ends meet, but they were really pursuing a career in entertainment.

"Many were very, very talented. I was sure that in their hometowns, they were the bee's knees, but when they got to New York, they were competing, as I was, with even more talented people. Some of it might be luck, but in the end, you understood that the best of the best in a high school in Iowa or Nebraska, anywhere, or even a college drama program, would be lucky to get a job as an understudy in the chorus when it comes to Broadway."

She sat on my desk chair. I was mesmerized. It was as if she was opening the cover of a book of secrets kept buried for years.

"Eventually, I was at a very low point, much lower than I led you to believe. I had one roommate after another, some in worse financial condition than I was in. One got married and left me. I had fallen seriously behind on my rent without a roommate sharing. The extra jobs I would apply for wouldn't pay for my living expenses anyway, and many of these jobs wouldn't enable me to go to auditions. Why would I take one? I felt like . . . like I was being smothered by reality, and the worst thing I feared was having to return to England and beg my father's forgiveness.

"I had his pride, you see. Doing something like that would have been devastating." She paused as though she was deciding whether to continue. I was afraid she would decide not to.

"What happened?" I asked. I feared what her next confession would be. It was sounding more and more like one of the typical runaway-girl stories we read and heard about, a desperate girl who turned to prostitution to survive. And then one day discovered she was pregnant.

"I was behind three months on my rent at this point and down to my last few hundred dollars. I skipped lunch every day to still have that much. I wouldn't even have enough money to buy a ticket home if I gave up. I'd have to call to get my mother to persuade my father to send the money. Desperate people do desperate things," she said.

"What did you do?" I asked again. What could she have done that was a desperate thing? My skin felt like it had turned to ice. Did I really want to hear this? Wasn't I better off not knowing? Ignorance was bliss sometimes, and this felt like one of those times. Why did I push so hard for the truth?

"The landlord of my building, Leo Abbot, had a younger brother who had suffered a heart attack and had to have an emergency bypass. It was performed by Dr. Davenport. The family lived in Hillsborough, you see. At the time, I knew or cared to know nothing about Hillsborough.

"One night, Leo Abbot came to my apartment. I anticipated it, expecting him to give me my walking papers. He was a widower in his midfifties, who had two married daughters and five grandchildren. In the beginning, he was very pleasant and often teased me about my English accent and some of our expressions. He asked me about my family, and I told him how my father was furious at me for trying to develop a career in America. He said he couldn't imagine disowning one of his children the way my father had disowned me.

"To be honest, I exploited that to get him to be more patient about the rent. He liked me well enough to feel sorry for me and permit me to be in arrears for as much as three months, but I was sure his patience and sympathy had run their course. It was expected. He had a building with apartments in demand because it was in an ideal location. There was no question that he could rent the one I was in minutes after he had evicted me. I imagined he had a waiting list anyway.

"I had no more promises to make and no pending possibilities to offer with any plea for more time. When he asked to come in to speak to me, however, I sensed different vibes coming from him. Unexpectedly, he was as pleasant as he was when I had first moved in. He asked me what I was intending to do now. I cried and admitted that there was nothing left to do but return to England. I promised him that I would find a job there and send him money until my back rent was paid up. He nodded and listened, and I thought that was it. I was ready to contact my mother and throw myself on my father's mercy.

"'Well,' Mr. Abbot said, 'I guess you don't have a young man to help, no romances, yet?' I didn't. I had dates, but I had yet to get serious with anyone. I was so fixed on my career. I wouldn't permit myself to be distracted, and I knew how obligations to someone would conflict with potential opportunities. I had the ruthlessness to succeed. I was just . . . maybe not good enough."

"Or lucky enough," I offered. "You always said it was at least fifty percent luck, if not more."

She smiled. "Yes. You can tell yourself that. It helps relieve some of the pain of disappointment. Blame it on capricious luck, but you know I've told you many times that people who succeed simply have the persistence to accept defeat after defeat and still keep going. You can have all the talent in the world, but without that persistence, you won't make it. Maybe I didn't have it. Anyway, I told him I had no one like that. What difference did it make now, anyway?

"'Well,' he said, 'how would you like to make seventy-five thousand dollars?'

"'Seventy-five thousand?' I said.

"'Yes.' That seemed like all the money in the world to me. Then he added, 'Your back rent due will be paid for, and you will have no living expenses for some time. Everything will be tax-free. I can assure you. You'll actually have seventy-five thousand dollars after it's over.'

"'After what's over?' I asked him. What did I have to offer anyone who would willingly pay me seventy-five thousand dollars? Be his or her private singer?

"'Pregnancy,' he said.

"'What?' I replied. My indignation began to shoot through my blood."

"I don't blame you," I said. "I'd have thrown him out."

She smiled. "The fury of youth. Not something easy to hold on to when you're desperate, love. Hopefully, you never will be. Anyway, it wasn't what you're thinking. He wasn't pimping me out, at least not in that sense."

"Then what was it?"

"Surrogate conception," she said.

"Surrogate conception? I don't really know

what that is. I mean, I've heard something about it, but . . ."

"That's all right. At that time, I didn't know anything about it, either."

"But who wanted you to do that?"

"Dr. Davenport and his first wife, Samantha, were looking to employ a surrogate mother."

I felt the heat rise up my neck and into my face. What was she telling me? "You mean for Ryder?"

"Yes, but let me explain. There are two kinds of surrogate mothers, traditional and gestational. The traditional is artificially inseminated with the father's sperm. She carries the baby and delivers it and is the baby's biological mother. Gestational surrogates have the egg from the mother and the father's sperm from something known as in vitro fertilization. The egg and the sperm are combined in a laboratory. Once the embryo is formed, it's placed in the uterus of the surrogate mother. That was what I had done to me."

"But why? Why did they want to form Ryder in a laboratory?"

"It wasn't that they wanted him formed in a laboratory, exactly. It's not some Frankenstein experiment. At the time, it wasn't that unusual."

"But why do that? Why have a surrogate mother?"

"Samantha wanted a child, her own child, but she didn't want to go through pregnancy. I told you once that she was like a child herself. Everything in her life was easy, had been made easy for her. She was very beautiful, and she knew it. She didn't want to do anything that would threaten her beauty. The image of a pregnant woman and that woman being her terrified her. No, I should say it disgusted her. She simply couldn't do it. She was afraid of every aspect of it, the pain, discomfort, stretch marks. You name it, she was afraid of it. There are many women like that."

"But how did you know all this?"

"I didn't at the time. She told me all this months later. The why wasn't my business, and I wasn't thinking or caring about reasons. The money was overwhelming.

"So what I was offered was seventy-five thousand dollars to carry Samantha and Dr. Davenport's baby. Leo Abbot had convinced Dr. Davenport that I'd be an ideal surrogate mother. My age and my situation recommended me. Dr. Davenport had me brought to his office in the family limousine to be examined by an obstetrician and pediatrician, Dr. Bliskin, who was a good friend of his. He was a very nice, good-looking man. He put me through extensive tests to confirm my health and my ability to carry a child, and then Dr. Davenport had his attorney draw up a contract between me and himself and his wife. There would be no question the baby belonged to them. I thought I'd go through it, deliver the baby, get my money, and return to New York well financed to pursue my career. I even sent my mother and my sister Julia some expensive gifts just to annoy my father." She smiled.

"I lived in the main house then, one bedroom down from Dr. and Mrs. Davenport's bedroom. He had a nurse visit twice a week to check everything. I gave birth to Ryder in this house. Dr. Bliskin delivered Ryder. He remained Ryder's and, for a while, your doctor, but you were too young to remember him, I'm sure. He was married with triplet girls, all prematurely born. He had a lot to do with his own family, obviously, so this was something of what we called a busman's holiday."

"Why isn't he my doctor now? The last time I went to a doctor, it was Dr. Abrams."

"He's no longer working here. Years later, he went on to work in a big New York City hospital. How's that? He got to New York, but I didn't."

"Why didn't you leave immediately afterward?" I asked.

"I always intended I would. But I was talked into remaining to . . ." She paused.

I knew what she was going to say. "To breastfeed him?"

She nodded. "Dr. Davenport and his friend Dr. Bliskin believed that was the healthiest thing to do."

"And you were still going to leave when that was completed, weren't you?"

"Yes, but Dr. Davenport offered me an additional fifty thousand dollars to remain for a year as Ryder's nanny."

"And you had me eventually to care for, too."

"Something I'll never regret."

"What about my father, then?"

"What about him?"

"Does he even know I exist?"

"Yes, but he couldn't be your father or my husband."

"Who is he?" I asked.

"It's better if you don't know. Trust me about that, Fern."

"You'll never tell me?"

"Someday."

"He lives in this town?"

"Just leave it for now. Anyway, the reason I wanted you to know my history here is so you'll understand how deeply tied I am, we are, to Dr. Davenport. His wife can try to drive a wedge between us, but she won't succeed."

"How could he possibly love her?"

"She gave him Sam, and she fills a place he needs filled in his life. Why some women stay with the men they've married or vice versa is often more complicated than what you read in romance novels."

"Does Ryder know about you, what you did?"

"No!" she exclaimed. "And you must promise me, swear on everything sacred, that you will never tell him. That is something I promised Dr. Davenport, actually agreed to formally in the contract, never to reveal I carried and delivered his son. Will you promise me?"

"Yes," I said. "But someday he should know the truth."

"That's between Dr. Davenport and him, not us. Okay? Fern, you can hurt Ryder more than you know. He has a beautiful image of his mother. Just leave it at that."

"Okay." I thought a moment. "But how did she get away with people believing she gave birth to Ryder?"

"She claimed to be pregnant, and then in what were the latter months—some women don't show until the seventh month, actually—she left to supposedly give birth in a special maternity hospital in Switzerland. When she wanted people to know she was back and the baby was born, I was introduced as the baby's nanny, someone she had brought over from England. It made me sound very special, not that I was seen that much by her friends. It's not hard to hide things in Wyndemere," she added.

"The house of secrets," I said.

"Yes." She smiled. "That's right, love, the house of secrets."

When it came to secrets in Wyndemere, I was sure this wasn't the last one I would learn.

9

I WAS HOPING to see Ryder later in the day, but he didn't come around, and I didn't dare go into the main house with Bea Davenport on the warpath. Of course, I didn't see Sam. Ordinarily, I anticipated her sneaking over to see me, especially today to find out about my time at the prom. But now I imagined that she wouldn't try to come over even if Bea Davenport had gone to one of her lunches with her posh friends. Surely by now, Bea had poisoned Sam even more against me, claiming I was a very bad influence on both her and Ryder, maybe even dangerous.

A little after four, Alison called to see what I knew about the events that had occurred. She hadn't gotten up until nearly two and had a message on her phone to call Ryder. She said she had a half dozen other messages from her girlfriends, who had sounded frantic, but she called him first, and he told her all that had happened.

"He's so upset," she said. "And so am I. He was supposed to take me to lunch today. We had planned it."

"I think he's upset about more than just lunch."

"Paul Gabriel is just so stupid. He deserves whatever he gets, ruining it for everyone else. You must have been desperate for a date."

"I wasn't desperate."

"But I suppose you're feeling sorry for yourself more than anyone else now," she said.

"No. Why would I just feel sorry for myself?"

"This was your first prom, you got chosen to be queen, and now all everyone's talking about are the terrible things. I'm glad now I wasn't chosen prom queen. Not one I want to remember. My parents heard about it already. They know Paul drove us, of course, so they're very upset and . . ." She paused. I could sense that, as my mother often said, the second shoe was about to drop.

"What else, Alison?" I prodded.

"They asked all sorts of questions about you because you were his date. I tried to assure them you had nothing to do with any drugs or alcohol, but . . ."

"I should expect some people will think I did?"

"I can only tell people what I saw. Even the

smartest people generalize when something like this happens."

"You mean once our teachers find out, they'll assume the worst about me, too? Is that what you're saying?"

"Maybe. Maybe not," Alison said, but not with any conviction.

She wasn't telling me anything I didn't know. Gossip was gossip. Once it was spilled, it ran in all sorts of directions and stained everyone it touched. How could I go to the prom and to the party with Paul Gabriel and not be involved with the drug he took? I just got away with it, that was all.

It occurred to me that if, as Dr. Davenport had said, the police started their investigation seriously, I'd logically be the first one they questioned. What would Bea Davenport do next once her friends got wind of it all and her phone started to ring? Her precious reputation might be damaged.

"If you happen to see Ryder, tell him I said he should calm down," Alison said. "He'll only make more trouble for us all, especially me."

"I guess we should all calm down," I added.

"Yeah, right. I'm not looking forward to going to school on Monday. The chatter will be so loud I'll get a headache."

"I have one now."

"Don't worry. You have a doctor nearby. Any-way, hopefully this won't cause the school to cancel next year's prom or something, not that I'll care that much, but I imagine you might."

"Why wouldn't I? Why should so many innocent kids suffer?" I said.

"Right. But are you going to tell me you never used any X or drank booze at some party?" she said.

"I am going to tell you that, yes."

"Miss Perfect. I guess you really are a prom queen. See you at Headache Central."

After I hung up, I thought about Ryder sulking in his room. Alison was right, of course, even though she was thinking more about herself. He should calm down. What good did sitting around in a rage do now? On the other hand, who was I to talk? I had been sulking myself.

I had a little to eat. My appetite was subdued, but I thought I should have something and try to get my mind on other things. My mother was in the main house following up on some chores. It was like this every Sunday because most of the servants had the day off. So I sat alone at the table, hearing only my own thoughts.

Everything had happened so fast. One moment you're happier than you have ever been, and the next you're sadder than you've ever been, and all of it within the space of a few hours. I was still quite confused about Paul Gabriel. If anything, my impression of him had been that he was harmless and simple, hardly a threat. How easily he had been influenced. What made him want to take me, anyway? Did the other boys in school encourage him to ask me to the prom, assuring him he would have an easy sexual conquest? Now I was confident that all the wry smiles and whispers behind my back were not figments of my imagination.

A knock on the side entrance pulled me out of my troubled reverie. I hoped it was Ryder doing what he often did and coming around to our side from outside the house instead of having to go through it. But when I opened the door, it was Mr. Stark. From the smile on his face, I realized he knew nothing about the events that had occurred.

"How was the prom?" he asked.

It all seemed beside the point now. I felt silly telling him what a dance was like, but I did.

"And I was chosen prom queen."

"Wow. Someone has good taste," he said.

"They chose Ryder for prom king, too."

"Wyndemere wins it all, huh?"

"That's what I thought, until my mother and I were called to see Dr. Davenport earlier today."

"Oh?" He stepped in. "Why?"

I offered him something to drink or some of the egg salad my mother had made for me.

"No, I'm fine, thanks. So tell me what's up," he said, and sat at the table.

I described it all, leaving out some of the nasty

details involving Paul and me at the after-party. I did say he was out of control because he had drunk some alcohol, vodka, I thought, and took a party drug, which was why Ryder had called Parker to come get us. I imagined Parker would tell Mr. Stark anyway. I knew they were close friends.

"Only takes a few rotten apples to spoil the barrel," he said, his face darkening with anger. "You're all right, though? You weren't . . . hurt?"

I knew it was his way of asking if I had been sexually assaulted. "I'm okay. Just sad for everyone, especially Ryder, who only tried to do the right things."

"Your mother's in the main house?"

"Yes."

"How's she doing?"

"She's a little shaken up, too, although she will pretend she's not. Mrs. Davenport wasn't very nice to either of us. She wasn't even nice to Ryder."

"That right?" He thought a moment. "She doesn't know how lucky she is to have someone like your mother looking after her and this house. Okay," he said, slapping his knees and standing. "I'll see you later."

He started out, then stopped and came back to give me a kiss on the cheek.

"Prom queen. Mighty proud of you," he said, and left.

I went to the door and watched him march

around the house to check on my mother for sure. Who cared more about us than he did? I thought. If he was my father, why wouldn't my mother just tell me? What promises did she make? So much time had gone by. How could it matter now? It all got me thinking about what she had told me about her coming to Wyndemere, so instead of going to do homework, I returned to my room to read about surrogate mothers on the Internet.

One comment interested me more than the scientific facts. It was a discussion of whether in gestational surrogacy any DNA of the surrogate mother passed to the baby. The conclusion was no significant amount, because the placenta was like a screen separating the fetus from the mother. The embryo already had its DNA, half from the father and half from the biological mother.

Nevertheless, as I lay there thinking about my mother being pregnant with Ryder, breastfeeding him, and caring for him, it was impossible not to feel a closer bond with him. The same woman delivered us. However, thinking of him as first formed in a laboratory was off-putting. I was sure he wouldn't want to know that. Who would? My mother was right. I simply could never tell him what I knew.

However, I felt guilty knowing this secret about him without his knowing it. It seemed terribly unfair. Every time I looked at him, spoke to him,

I would think about everything she had told me. Would Dr. Davenport ever tell him? I was sure Bea Davenport would make him feel bad, feel strange, if she ever knew. She'd have a grand day with that. She'd even turn Sam against him, getting her to see Ryder as something strange and certainly not her half brother.

Of course, now I understood why Ryder had such affection for my mother. Surely he felt the secret bond between them without really understanding why. Her body had nourished him. She had stayed on as his nanny. She had held him and cared for him until he was more than an infant. When he got hurt and cried, she had been the one who comforted him. When he had done something funny or achieved something as a child, she had complimented him just as his real mother would have. She covered his face in kisses, washed and bathed him, dressed him, brushed his hair, looked after his health, until he was basically on his own, as she had done with me. Bea Davenport was here by then and slammed doors on my mother, even though my mother was something of a nanny for Sam, too. In her case, she was more of a glorified babysitter. And when that became unnecessary, the iron curtain fell.

Another thing that came to my mind when I was reading about surrogate motherhood was how the woman really felt about the baby she was delivering. How did my mother feel about Ryder? Could any woman really treat the entire thing as a simple business venture? Could she consider carrying a child to his or her birth as nothing more than carrying someone else's package? Was it possible to do this and not feel strange and empty when the child was taken? Was my mother okay with all that because she remained with Ryder, caring for him just the way his biological mother would and should? Now, of course, I understood why she had such love and concern for Ryder.

But no matter how into herself and distracted with her own life Samantha Avery Davenport had been, surely she had felt some jealousy about the way Ryder clung to my mother and not her when he was an infant. In the end, would she have been as cruel to us as Bea Davenport was? Would she have wanted my mother finally out of her and Dr. Davenport's lives? It seemed a natural way for a mother to act. What mother would want her child to be more devoted to his nanny than to her?

Despite how close and how tied my mother had felt to Ryder, she was, after all, expecting to be able to return to New York and pursue her career. She surely would have hated to say goodbye to him, but she had her money; she was still young. Now she could devote one hundred percent of her time and energy to developing her dream. The day Samantha died in the car accident must have been doubly terrible for my mother. She certainly couldn't have left Ryder abruptly after that. Perhaps Dr. Davenport had promised to find a replacement for her, or maybe he offered her more money than she revealed. Whatever the reason, the temporary position became permanent, and when it did, it determined who and what I would be as well.

I was beginning to understand how deep the darkness in Wyndemere really was. In ways neither of us fully understood, both Ryder and I were trapped in it, tied up in the mysteries and secrets woven by everyone who lived in this mansion. He would escape first by going to college in the fall. He would find new friends, a new girlfriend, maybe, and probably do all he could to stay away. I doubted he would even call me or send me email after a while. It would become much lonelier and much darker for me when that happened. There would be new ghosts. Bea would be sure to drive Sam further and further away from me. She'd have her own new friends, too, anyway.

I closed my eyes and imagined myself coming home from somewhere in the evening after Ryder had gone. The house loomed above me as it always did, only now it seemed darker, the shadow it cast in the moonlight spreading wider and farther. The eyes of the gargoyles glistened. The stone facing looked colder, and from a window Bea Davenport gazed down at me with a hateful smile, enjoying the way I trembled.

The images drifted, and I dozed off, not only because of the lateness of the evening before but also because of all the tension and turmoil twisting and turning in my body and mind. Later, my mother woke me to tell me she had invited Mr. Stark to dinner. She had prepared one of his favorites and mine, shepherd's pie. I knew Mrs. Marlene hadn't prepared it. Sunday was usually her day off. But I expected it would be delicious, and my appetite had returned, probably because I had eaten like a rabbit, only some salad. She even made my favorite vanilla cupcakes with chocolate icing, something Mr. Stark loved, too.

She had done all this to help cheer me up, cheer both of us up. At dinner, no one talked about the earlier events. Mr. Stark asked more about my being prom queen and wanted more details of the dance. I knew he was asking all these questions to keep me from thinking about the bad things, but while I was describing everything, I recalled that both Ryder's and my crowns were in Paul Gabriel's car, as were our pictures. When I mentioned it, Mr. Stark offered to look into it.

"Let's wait on that," my mother told him. "Everything will find its way here in proper time, I'm sure. It's best to let the hornets return to their nest for a while."

It was clear now that she was on Dr. Davenport's side when it came to how we should all react to what had happened. Take a pause. Let the sparks drift to earth and lose their fire. We were practically to behave as if there hadn't been a prom, and my being crowned queen was some dream that had popped like a cork from a bottle.

I helped clean up. Mr. Stark remained talking to my mother after I went to my room. I knew that despite how tired I felt, I would have trouble falling asleep. I couldn't get Ryder out of my mind and decided to call him. His phone rang and then went right to voice mail.

"Hi," I said. "I've been thinking about you all day. I hope you're all right. I know you're disappointed in your father, but maybe he's right. We should let things calm down. At least, my mother thinks he might be. I just want you to know I'm not sorry I went to the prom. You surely wouldn't have had me go with Paul if you knew he would behave the way he did. I'll see you in school. Night."

I hung up and prepared for bed. My mother and Mr. Stark were still talking, their voices a low murmur. I was sure they were talking about me, but I didn't want to spy on them. I slipped under my light blanket and turned off the lights. It was a warm night, so I left my one bedroom window open. It was just to the left of the bed, the curtains not completely drawn.

There was an owl close by. Its mournful hoot was like a lullaby. As I lay there, I tried to resurrect the wonderful memories of dancing with Ryder, being crowned queen, and enjoying the compliments from girls and boys who never gave me a second glance at school, some surely thinking I was not good enough. For a few hours, at least, I had felt accepted and envied.

Now that the boy who had taken me was in big trouble, what would it be like at school? As Alison had suggested, would everyone assume I had been on Ecstasy as well but had gotten away with it? Would someone even spread the rumor that I had convinced Paul Gabriel to take it? Would I be blamed for his being thrown off the baseball team, a boy who had a possible professional career ahead of him?

The big thing, of course, was what to do if and when the police called me in and asked who had offered me a pill. Dr. Davenport wanted me to tell the truth. But he didn't have to live with these kids in school. What would Ryder do? Maybe he wasn't offered any. He wouldn't have to snitch on anyone. But me, I would look like someone who cared only for herself. Every nasty thing said about me or thought about me because I had no father would grow branches. *She's everything we'd expect her to be*, mothers would tell their daughters. *Stay away from her.*

I woke in the morning and felt the terror ahead of me instantly. I was actually trembling a little when I showered and dressed. When I came out to have some breakfast, my mother looked at me with concern.

"Maybe I should stay home today," I said, before she could ask how I was feeling.

She shook her head. "Staying home today will only make it more difficult to go tomorrow, Fern. You did nothing wrong. Just carry on as usual, and ignore any nasty comments."

I plopped into a chair. She put my glass of juice in front of me.

"What did you do with all the money you earned as a surrogate mother?" I asked.

She smiled and brought her coffee to the table. "Why?"

"If you have enough left, maybe we could go somewhere else. I'm old enough now to get a good summer job, too. Maybe I could even work somewhere on weekends."

To my surprise, she didn't protest or tell me I was being ridiculous. She nodded softly and stirred her coffee. "I thought about doing just that many times. Once the children no longer needed a nanny, I even considered taking you back to England with me. It would really have been a new start."

"Why didn't you do it?"

She kept that soft, *Mona Lisa* smile and then looked up at me. "As silly as it might sound to you right now, Wyndemere became my home. For the past almost eighteen years, these people have been the only family I've had. I don't mean solely the Davenports. Mrs. Marlene, Mr. Stark, some of the maids, many of the local merchants—this small and independent world replaced a lot of unhappiness. Living and working here, caring for the grand old house, replaced a dream—or a fantasy, which might be a more realistic description—but I began to enjoy the responsibilities and feel something for the venerated mansion.

"I know every crack and crevice in the house. It reeks of history, which, yes, has much unpleasantness attached to it, but in the early years, even the earlier years of Dr. Davenport's first marriage, there were grand dinner parties. A man as highly respected and as important as he is attracts the most distinguished and powerful people. After I arrived, I met a senator and a governor here.

"I felt a growing importance. I was in charge of so much and still am. Dr. Davenport grew dependent on me, not only because of his children but also because of how orderly I could keep his domestic life. I like to think I've had something to do with his being the great success he is.

"Yes, Bea Davenport is a pain in the arse most

of the time, but with all her bluster, she is nothing more than a minor annoyance to me most of the time. She gets what she wants, or at least she thinks she does, by ordering the help about like Captain Bligh in *Mutiny on the Bounty*, changing things in the house to suit her, but—I don't know if you'll understand—she hasn't altered the essence of Wyndemere. It's too big and powerful for her to overcome. Oh, she might change the color of this or that, a piece of furniture here and there, some curtains, whatever, but she'll never alter its soul."

"You talk about it like it's a living thing."

"Oh, it is. To me, it is." She smiled, obviously at a memory. "When I was younger and everyone was asleep, I'd sit in the grand room and listen to the tinkle of a chandelier or the creak in a floorboard and think, *Wyndemere likes me, wants me, needs me.* A house absorbs so much, you see. All the laughter, yes, but also all the crying, the moans and groans, slammed doors, tiny feet scurrying over carpets and up and down stairs, doorbells, dishes and glasses rattling, a toast to this, a toast to that, vows and promises, the aromas of the food, the fresh flowers, perfumes and colognes, all of it.

"Previous owners and both of Dr. Davenport's parents uttered their final words and took their final breaths here. Ryder, as I told you, had his first cry here, and so did you.

"Yes, it might sound funny to you, but I do

think of it as a living thing. It had something magical about it. It held me. It held me more firmly than my own family had held me."

She paused, thought a moment, and then looked at me as if she had just realized she had been talking to me.

"You have to eat something, Fern. I'm making you scrambled eggs."

I didn't say anything. I had never heard her talk that way when she described Wyndemere. It was as if she had been talking in her sleep. I was actually afraid to break the moment. She had some eggs with me and told me that, yes, she still had a lot of her money, our money.

"It was Dr. Davenport who got his business manager to help me with my investments. We have a living trust now. I have your college education set aside." She leaned in toward me to speak low, as if there were other people in the room. "From time to time, I received a bonus. I still do, although high and mighty Bea Davenport doesn't know. I doubt she knows anything about the finances of this place. Anyway, when you think of it, we don't have any living expenses. That includes medical care. No, love, a woman like me doesn't just get on her high horse and leave all this in a huff."

"But you really don't have any fun, Mummy."

"Oh, I do now and then. When you were all very little, Dr. Davenport would take us in his motorboat on the lake. And there were grand picnics for all of us. Do you remember any of that?"

"Vaguely. Yes, but he hasn't since Bea came into his life, and I'm not talking about only picnics and rides in a boat. You have little or no social life."

"I have what I need."

"Dr. Davenport must have changed a lot since you started."

"After Samantha's death, he became a workaholic and is even more so now. Maybe," she said, smiling and doing that lean-in-to-whisper thing again, "to get away from you-know-who. I'd work longer hours in a coal mine to stay away from a wife like that. My father used to look at some women in the town and say that. Regardless of how we parted, he left me with some choice words. And don't you go repeating them," she warned, with a feigned look of reprimand before smiling.

I laughed. How easily and wonderfully my mother could ease me out of a bad mood or a sad thought. I looked at the clock. "Gotta go," I said, and gathered my books.

"You hold your head high, Fern. I know you'll be fine," she told me.

As I walked around to the front of the house to where the school bus stopped for me, I felt uplifted by her words and by the beauty of the spring morning. There wasn't a cloud in the sky. The grass had been mowed the day before, and the aroma was sweet and sharp. I paused to look back at the enormous property of Wyndemere and the lakefront. Today the lake looked as still and as shiny as ice. A flock of sparrows turned toward the front of the house and flew over the sprawling maple and hickory trees. I could understand why my mother thought Wyndemere was a living thing.

I made the turn to the front and started toward the bus stop, but I paused instantly. Ryder was standing there with his book bag strapped onto his back. I hurried across the lawn to him. To my right in front of the mansion was the limousine with Parker, as always.

"What are you doing?" I asked.

"Going to school. What are you doing?"

"No, really, why are you standing here?"

"I told Bea this morning that if you're not permitted to be taken to school in the limousine, I'm not going in it, either."

"Why?"

"If we're being punished together, we're together. Simple as that," he said.

I turned because I heard Sam crying. Bea was taking her out, actually dragging her toward the limousine. She was moaning to go to school on the school bus, too. Bea stopped when she saw us and came marching toward us. She was in one of her more expensive-looking cream-pink silk robes. Her hair was wrapped in a scarf. Without her usual makeup, she looked pale, her eyes deeper and her lips the color of sour grapes.

"I have a call in to your father!" she screamed at Ryder as she drew closer. "If you know what's good for you, you'll get into that limousine."

"I do know what's good for me. That's why I'm getting on the bus with Fern. Unless you've decided to permit her to be driven to school every morning and brought home every afternoon, too."

"Insolent." She looked at me with fury in her eyes. "You won't drag this family into the gutter," she said. "I can assure you of that."

"What did I do?" I asked.

"You were born," Ryder said. He meant it to be sarcastic and demonstrate how arrogant and disgusting Bea was, but she smiled.

"Exactly," she said. She spun in her slippers and marched back to Sam, who was standing there with her head down, her shoulders lifting and falling with her sobs. After practically shoving her into the limousine, Bea slammed the door closed and glared at us.

Parker drove off, and she started back to the front door.

"I didn't mean that the way she made it sound," Ryder said.

"I know. I hate to see you get into trouble because of me."

"It's not because of you. It's because of her."

We heard the school bus coming.

"I feel sorry for Sam," I said.

"She'll survive. The limousine isn't that uncomfortable."

"Yes, but will we?"

He laughed and let me get on the bus first. The looks of surprise on the faces of the other students were precious. Ryder stopped at an empty seat and let me get in first. Then he took off his book bag and put it on his lap.

"You can put it above, too," I said.

"Oh. Right." He stood up and did so. "So this is how the poor people live," he added when the bus started away.

"Alison called me last night. She's worried about everything, everyone," I said, and left out that she was really more worried about herself.

"I know. We'll be fine. But prepare yourself for a lot of questions from those who were at the after-party and at the prom. Oh, Paul's mother is bringing our crowns and pictures to school today when she and her husband meet with the dean and Coach Allen about Paul. He's still in the hospital. My father wanted him kept there another day for observation."

"He's lucky they called your father."

"Yeah, but not lucky for us. Look," he said, turning to me. "You will surely be questioned about who passed around the Ecstasy. Did anyone see Barry offer it to you?"

"I don't know, Ryder. Maybe. He wasn't exactly hiding it."

"Well . . . too bad for him, then," he said. "My father is right about keeping information from the police. Don't worry about who hates you for it. Barry put himself in trouble. You didn't do it, and besides, someone else might reveal it, too. Maybe Barry will even confess to get some sort of probation deal or something."

"People won't believe I didn't take it, too."

"There are some people who still believe the world is flat," he said.

The bus made more pickups. Some of the kids who attended the prom and the party got on, and everyone was talking about Paul and Joey, some shouting questions at Ryder.

"My attorney has advised me not to say anything," he replied. Most believed him. "See?" he said to me. "Say anything with a straight face, and most will believe it. Although . . ."

"What?"

"Maybe we will need an attorney."

"Are you serious?"

"A little, but don't worry. My father pisses me off right now, but there's no question he'll look out for us. You can be sure of that."

I smiled and sat back. Ryder pressed his hand over mine for a few moments, and suddenly the fear I felt flew off like a frightened sparrow. The bus turned into the school drive and came to a stop.

"And so it begins," Ryder said. He ran his forefinger across his throat and laughed.

"Damn the torpedoes. Full speed ahead," I replied, stealing another line from my mother's repertoire.

He let me out first and followed, holding my hand and walking right beside me into the building.

10

ALISON WAS WAITING for Ryder in the school lobby. She looked very annoyed, leaning on her right foot, her books pressed hard against her breasts and her lips turned inward.

"Hi," Ryder said as we approached. "What's up?"

"I was worried about you when the limousine pulled up earlier and I saw only Sam got out," she said. "You came on the school bus?" She made it sound like we had come on a garbage truck or something.

She looked at me curiously. I didn't think Ryder realized it, but he was still holding my hand.

"My stepmother has thrown us into the wicked corner together, so I decided if Fern can't ride in the limousine to school and back, neither can I."

"Are you terrified or something?" she asked me, her eyes on our hands.

I let go of Ryder's quickly. "Yes, I am," I said. "But I'll be okay. Ryder and I had a good talk about it on the way to school."

"Oh? Well, maybe you can have a nice talk about it with me, too, Ryder," she said. "My parents were bonkers last night as friends called with more details. I hadn't told them about Joey's accident and arrest for a DUI. They wanted to know every detail about the party and how close we came to being in the car with Paul. And guess how it ended," she said. "Just like your father, they now want me to take a break on dates and definitely no parties for the next few weeks. Before I can go to anyone else's house, they'll be in there with mine sweepers. Thank you, Joey and Paul, especially idiot Paul. It was really stupid to double-date with him. What were you thinking?" She rattled it all off without pausing for a breath.

"It'll blow over. Don't worry," Ryder told her. He looked at me. "Look for me between classes if you need anything," he told me. "Stay cool." He reached for Alison's hand. She just turned instead, and they started for their homeroom with Ryder continually reassuring her.

I sucked in, gulping air as if I was going under

water and, as Mr. Stark might say, girded my loins as my classmates began to converge on me excitedly from all directions, practically drooling with questions. Most didn't know, of course, that Ryder had sent for Parker to rescue us from Shane Cisco's party and that I had left without Paul. They fired their questions with AK-47 speed.

Was I at the hospital, too? Did I take any Ecstasy? How was Paul? How much drinking went on? What did my mother have to say? Was I in trouble? Was there a lot of wild sex?

I didn't answer anything. I just walked to homeroom, shaking my head. They followed like bees hovering over a hive. There was such a mixture of chatter that my head did seem to be spinning even before the bell rang for homeroom and everyone had to take his or her seat.

When the bell rang to go to our first class, they were all over me again. Along with the questions about Paul and Joey Dunsten were questions about how it felt to be prom queen. For a while, I felt like I was two different people, the one who attended the prom and enjoyed herself and the one who had been part of an alcohol and drug orgy. Regardless, I had suddenly been thrust into the spot reserved for the class's most popular girl. Everyone, even girls who wouldn't ordinarily give me the time of day, was hanging close, hoping to hear something they could spread. I was a notorious new celebrity, but did I want to be? I wanted to run out of the building.

When I had made it through my first-period class, I thought perhaps the concern about a real police investigation and what could follow was exaggerated, but I wasn't seated in my second class for five minutes before the class was interrupted by a student messenger from Mr. McDermott, the dean of students, requesting that I come to his office. Everyone watched me rise, gather my things, and leave the room. My heart didn't feel like it was pounding or thumping this time. It felt like it was buzzing, resembling a warning signal on a fire alarm that had gotten stuck.

The dean's secretary looked up from her paperwork quickly when I entered the administrators' offices. From the look on her face, it was easy to see that everyone in my school was lit up with the news about the weekend's events. The sleepy community of Hillsborough had been awakened and shocked into the realization that we weren't special, we weren't immune to the insidious problems plaguing many communities. Every terrible thing that was happening elsewhere with young people could happen here and did. Heads were being pulled out of the sand.

"Go right in. Dean McDermott is waiting for

you," she said, the condemnation darkening her eyes and tightening her lips.

I moved with the tiny steps of a geisha and entered his office. My eyes went immediately to the man sitting on the right in front of his desk. He wore a dark-gray suit and a black tie and had a face chiseled from granite, looking like a man who was incapable of smiling without shattering his cheeks and jaw. His dark eyes focused so sharply on me that I had to turn away quickly, even though that made me look very guilty of something.

"Fern," the dean said. "Have a seat." He nodded at the chair directly in front of his desk.

Dean McDermott was the school's varsity basketball coach as well as the school's disciplinarian. The boys on his team were consequently the best behaved in the school, and despite the nasty job he had, he was very popular. He was just under six feet tall, with dark-brown, slightly graying hair and kelly-green eyes like Alison's. No matter how bad the student had been, he always approached him or her with a soft, understanding smile, putting whomever it was at some ease, sometimes warmly enough to elicit a confession at the start. He was smiling like that at me now.

"So you were chosen prom queen," he said, which put me off-balance immediately. It was the last thing I expected him to mention.

"Yes. It was a big surprise."

"But I'm sure well deserved. My wife was chosen queen of her high school prom," he said. "I didn't know her then, but I was jealous of her prom date anyway."

He looked at the man seated to his left, but the man, as I anticipated, didn't smile. He straightened up and pulled his firm-looking shoulders back. He had no time or patience for small talk.

"This is Detective Beck from the Hillsborough Police Department," Dean McDermott said. He folded his hands and leaned forward. "Paul Gabriel's serious health episode has everyone quite alarmed. My phone's been ringing all morning with parents who are very concerned. Of course, everyone wants to know how widespread this is and what we're doing about it. Now, I . . ."

He paused when we heard a knock on his office door.

His secretary opened it slightly and peered in. "Miss Corey is here," she said. I instantly felt like I had swallowed a small icicle.

My mother, wearing one of her nicer light-blue dresses and lipstick, which she rarely did, stepped in.

The dean stood. "Miss Corey. Thanks for coming."

"Of course I would come. I should have been called as soon as the police told you they would conduct interviews in the school today and they would involve my daughter."

"Absolutely," the dean said. "You were on our list. You just beat us to it."

He went around his desk to pull another chair out from the corner of his office and place it right beside mine. My mother looked at me with a comforting smile. When she sat, he introduced her to Detective Beck, who this time smiled slightly and nodded, proving he wasn't a sculptured block of stone after all.

"Dr. Davenport assured me you weren't going to begin questioning my daughter until I had arrived," my mother said.

Dr. Davenport? He had alerted my mother? He had called the school on my behalf?

"Oh. We've just introduced everyone here," the dean said when he returned to his seat. "I was, in fact, congratulating Fern on being chosen prom queen. No specific questions about the issues were asked."

My mother didn't change expression. She wasn't someone easily sold on anything less than the complete truth.

The dean tried a smile but then nodded at Detective Beck when my mother replied with one of her piercing glares. "Why don't I turn this over to Detective Beck now?" the dean said. "He works narcotics especially."

My mother barely nodded. Detective Beck leaned toward us. I saw his badge was pinned to his belt, and a little farther back on his hip was his holstered pistol. Even with my mother at my side, I was frightened. This had become very serious, way beyond any ordinary school violation. Detentions and reprimands were left outside the door. Our school had a no-tolerance policy when it came to drug use. Students involved didn't simply get suspended for a few days; they went to jail, or they could be expelled.

"We've been tracking the flow of what kids call 'party drugs' into our community, Miss Corey," Detective Beck said. "People don't know it in general, but we've had a few incidents in the grade school."

"Grade school?" She looked at me. We were both surprised at that.

"Apparently, some older kids have either made it possible for their younger brothers and sisters to get to the crap or actually gave them some. That's another investigation, but right now, we want to center in on this prom party and what went on. Your daughter, from what we understand, was the date for the boy who nearly died. Is that correct?" he asked, turning to me.

"Yes," I said.

"Were these drugs circulated at the actual prom in the school, or did he bring his own?"

"I didn't see him bring anything or anyone distributing any at the actual prom, so I couldn't say for sure. We had teacher chaperones, too," I added, thinking *Why not ask them?*

"Later, however, they were at the Ciscos' home, correct? And widely used?"

"I can't say widely. I don't know how many took the drug," I said.

From the way his eyes grew even more steely and the corners of his mouth collapsed, it was clear he didn't like the way I used exact language, probably sounding more like an attorney. "Did you see Paul Gabriel, your date, take the drugs?"

"No."

He started to smirk more with disbelief. "Are you going to tell us that you were oblivious to all this going on around you? You didn't even know there were drugs present?"

"No. It was offered to me," I said.

"Before she says anything more, I want it understood that she will not be the sole witness to this," my mother quickly said. "The worst thing you can do is pit one student against all the others. If it comes to that—"

"It won't. We already have most of the information we were seeking. We simply want more confirmation, as you suggest," Detective Beck said. He looked at me. "Who offered you the drug?"

So here it goes, I thought. I had begun my school life with a serious disadvantage, like an Olympic swimmer with a lead weight on her ankle. I was the illegitimate child who couldn't even identify her father. Having only one parent at home wasn't all that unusual, but it was one thing to be the child living in the home of a divorced parent and another to be like me. There were a number of students in divorced homes at Hillsborough, as there were everywhere. Someone once told me nearly one-third of the marriages in America ended up in divorce. And then there were the many couples who didn't even bother getting married but lived as though they were, and somehow all this was okay because there was someone who could serve as a mother and a father.

On what level everyone's behavior was located on the totem pole of disapproval changed almost daily these days. You could live in sin, but you couldn't sin and go on with a normal life or be a child resulting from that sin. How was I really different from a girl my age who lived with a man and a woman who had never taken an oath of marriage, religious or civil? Why was that fair? And when you were little, only in the first few grades of public school, you had no idea why adults looked at you and whispered. Why wasn't that cruel?

Nevertheless, lately I thought I was holding my own. I had friends, went to their birthday parties, and hung out with them whenever I could. It seemed to me that the stain that gossip had put on my forehead was fading. Parents were permitting their daughters to be friends with me. No nasty remarks were being cast in my direction, and fewer were being whispered behind my back.

For a while on prom night, I was even a star. Everything negative and unholy about me was certainly completely forgotten. I felt finally fully accepted by everyone, but in a moment, I would, as far as most of the kids in the school believed, probably as most of the kids in every school would believe, become a traitor, a deserter who cared only about herself. It would mean I'd never again be trusted with anyone's secret. Worse, how could I be invited to anything? If someone did something his or her parents would disapprove of, I might reveal it. If someone tried to defend me, he or she would be quickly reminded about what I had done after the prom. *Fern Corey? Didn't she turn on her friends and help get someone into very serious trouble recently? How could you trust her?*

I might as well be homeschooled now, I thought. The choice about how to answer the detective's question was mine to make, but I must make it now. Refusing to answer would only put me in deeper trouble. It was basically what Dr. Davenport had said and what Ryder had confirmed.

Ryder's advice actually was more important to me. I knew he was just angry about everything and everyone at the moment because of the way his father had reacted to everything, but I think he meant what he had said on the school bus. At least he would stand by me.

Seeing a man with a badge and a pistol underlined Dr. Davenport's words, too, *obstruction of justice*. I could be led out of the dean's office in handcuffs. My mother would be devastated, and perhaps then Bea Davenport would get her way and have us thrown out, even deported.

No, I really had no choice.

"Barry Austin," I said.

"He's a senior," Mr. McDermott told Detective Beck. "And he has a younger brother in the fifth grade."

The implication of that rang doom bells. Maybe he was getting it to the grade-school kids, too, through his younger brother. He would surely go to jail. This was going to be a very big scandal in this community.

Detective Beck nodded and came close to smiling, confirming what I suspected: he was eyeing a promotion.

"What did you do when you were offered the drug?" Detective Beck asked.

"I told him I wasn't interested, and he walked off. I didn't know that Paul Gabriel had taken something from him," I emphasized.

"Did he take it after you had left the party?"

"No, before."

"When did you know he had? Did he tell you? Did he try to get you to join him? Did he help Barry Austin distribute it?"

"No!" I said sharply. "I mean, I didn't see him do that."

"But you knew he had taken it. When? How?"

I felt the heat rise into my face. Why did I have to tell everything? "Later," I said. "We left the basement to get away for a while."

"Get away? Did you leave the house?"

"No. We went to a quiet room."

"A bedroom?"

I glanced at my mother. "Yes."

"And then?"

"He began to act weird."

"Threatening?"

Tears were coming into my eyes.

"Why is this important?" my mother asked. "She's told you who distributed the drug. She's not here to make a claim against the boy."

"Okay. So what happened? You didn't go off with Gabriel, apparently."

"When Ryder realized things were bad, he told me to leave the house with him and Alison."

"And Ryder is . . . ?"

"He's Dr. Davenport's son," my mother said. "Alison Reuben was his date. The family chauffeur took them all home. His name is Parker Thompson. I'm sure he'll confirm what she's saying."

Detective Beck scribbled something in his small notepad. "Was this the first time this Barry Austin offered you drugs?"

"Yes."

"He never offered any to you in school?"

"No."

"Did you see him offer it to anyone in school?"

"No."

"Did anyone tell you that Barry was the go-to guy if you want drugs?"

"No."

"So this all came as a complete surprise?"

I just stared at him. What was he hoping I would do, start reading off the names of every student who had told me he or she had done X or something?

"I think she's told you all she knows," my mother said.

"You'd be surprised at how many parents around here are shocked at how much their children know and don't know about all this," he said.

"I wouldn't. My daughter and I have a special

relationship. We trust each other," she shot back sharply.

He sat back and nodded at Mr. McDermott.

"I think that will be all for now," Mr. McDermott said. "We'd appreciate your not talking about this interview," he added.

"If this goes further and you're involving my daughter in it any more, we'd like enough warning to have an attorney present," my mother said, mostly for Detective Beck's benefit.

He didn't say anything.

"Of course," Mr. McDermott said. "Unfortunate situation for us all, but these are the times we live in, I'm afraid."

"Yes," my mother said. "These are the times." She rose.

"Ask Mrs. Blumberg to give you a pass back to class," Mr. McDermott told me. "I know it seems beside the point right now, Fern, but congratulations again on being chosen prom queen."

"Thank you," I said.

I left with my mother.

"Why didn't you tell me this morning you were coming to school, Mummy?"

"I didn't know there would be a police detective here to interview you so quickly. From the way Dr. Davenport had spoken in his office, I thought it would be a more formal thing at the police station, or they'd come to Wyndemere to see you. Dr.

Davenport informed me an hour ago and told me to come. I called and told Mrs. Blumberg I was on my way."

"Does Dr. Davenport now believe I took drugs, too?"

"No. If he did, he'd have you examined, I'm sure." She sighed deeply. The tension seemed to age her years in moments.

"I'm sorry, Mummy."

"I know. Just do your work, Fern, and obey Mr. McDermott's and the detective's wishes and don't discuss any of this. Tell anyone who asks that the police asked you not to talk about it."

"That will go over like one of Mr. Stark's lead balloons," I said.

"The point is, it will go over." She kissed me and left.

I turned to Mrs. Blumberg, who had been watching us with great interest. "I need a pass, please," I said. She had it written already and handed it to me. I started to turn away.

"Just a minute," she said. She reached beside her chair and came up with my prom queen crown and an envelope with my prom pictures in it. "I believe this belongs to you. It was brought here a little while ago."

I took it slowly. The dazzling fake jewels almost brought me to tears. How could I walk around with this?

"Thank you," I said, and hurried out, stopping at my locker first to put away the crown and the pictures.

I took my time walking back to class. Before I opened the door, I breathed in deeply, as deeply as someone about to go diving in a pool, someone who had no idea what it would be like when she came up.

All heads turned my way as soon as I entered. I went right up to Mr. Albert and gave him my pass. He nodded, and I returned to my seat, keeping my eyes forward.

"We're on page forty-one of the textbook, Fern," Mr. Albert said.

I turned right to it and avoided looking at anyone looking at me, but when the bell rang to end class, they practically smothered me, closing in to find out what had happened in the dean's office.

"I'm not permitted to say anything," I said, hurrying away from everyone.

That became my stock answer until lunch hour, when I entered the cafeteria alone and looked for Ryder and Alison. To my surprise, every seat at their table was taken, mostly by Alison's girlfriends. Ryder nodded at me. I went to get my lunch and then looked for a place to sit. Everyone who had been friends with me was urging me to sit at their table. They all believed

I would finally talk to them and tell them everything.

I stood there, undecided and feeling stupid, when suddenly Ryder approached me. He was carrying his tray.

"We'll sit over there," he said, nodding at an empty table on our right that was as far from other students as we could get.

I looked back at his table. Alison did not look very happy. I expected she would join us, but she didn't.

"I was called to the dean's office shortly after you left," he said. "Everyone knows we both were. What did you tell them?"

"The truth, just as you and your father advised me to do."

He nodded.

"My mother was there."

"I heard."

"Your father called her and told her to be sure to call the school and be here when I was going to be interviewed. I was surprised he did that."

"He's really fond of your mother. I've heard him give her credit for lots at Wyndemere, especially when Bea complains and mentions her. Anyway, at least you had your mother there. My father left me to the wolves. It's his way of teaching me a lesson."

"What did you tell them?" I asked him.

"That Barry offered me some X, too, and Alison. Of course, we both refused." He took a breath and in a lower voice added, "She might not have refused if I wasn't there. Anyway, they wanted to know if it was the first time. I didn't lie. I've never used it. My father would kill me, but I've been to other parties where Barry either sold it or gave it away. Then I described everything I could remember from the time I heard you scream. I made sure to emphasize that you hadn't taken any, nor did you drink anything alcoholic. I admitted to drinking a few beers." He shook his head. "It ain't good," he said.

"Paul's mother or someone brought my crown and pictures to the school. The dean's secretary had it all for me when I came out of his office."

"Me, too."

"I put mine in my locker."

"Me, too," he said. "Uh-oh, here it goes," he added.

We both paused to look across the cafeteria, where Barry Austin, sitting with some of his closer friends, was approached by Dean McDermott himself. The entire cafeteria grew silent, but we couldn't hear what he said to him. Whatever he said was enough to get Barry up. He followed the dean out, and the chatter resumed, only at a greater volume.

Shane Cisco and Billy Wilcox rose from their table immediately and hurried over to us.

"You guys told on Barry?" Shane asked.

Billy Wilcox, another member of the baseball team, had his arms at his sides, his hands clenched. He was almost Paul Gabriel's height but better built because he was also a member of the school's wrestling team.

"Whatever trouble Barry's in is Barry's own fault, Shane. And you should have thought of your parents when you let all that go on at your house."

"At the end of my last class, I heard for sure that Paul's being thrown off the team," Billy said. "He's screwed."

"Whose fault is that? Maybe Barry's for bringing the drugs to your house, Shane. You shouldn't have let him," Ryder said. "You should have laid down some rules."

"Oh, so I'm to blame? This is the first time you've seen people take X? What are you, the doctor's perfect little patient?"

"You'd better shut your mouth, Shane. You're just digging a deeper hole for yourself."

Shane looked at me. "There was a cop here, and you were called in to see him, too. You told him about Barry, didn't you? Did you tell him about anyone else, too?"

"I was told not to discuss it," I said.

"She didn't have to tell him anything. They knew everything. Maybe *you* told him to get yourself out of big trouble," Ryder cleverly inserted. "Otherwise, why wouldn't the dean have taken you out of here along with Barry Austin?"

Billy's eyebrows lifted with the oncoming cloud of new suspicions. He looked at Shane.

"That's crap," Shane said.

"Is it? It all happened in your house. Your parents could have legal issues, too, and they know it. Maybe they had their attorney talk to the police yesterday, and everything's been arranged to save you rear end."

"Bullshit."

Ryder shrugged. "If I were you, I'd keep my mouth shut, then. Spreading stories about Fern and me isn't going to help. It's only going to add gasoline to the fire."

"Fern and you," Shane said, practically spitting our names at us. He turned to Billy. "Let's leave the stoolie birds alone."

Billy looked at Ryder and me and hesitated a moment. He didn't look as confident as he had when he first approached us. "Why'd you leave Paul behind, Ryder?" he asked. "You saw how he was."

"He was bad, Billy. He went wild on Fern. You weren't upstairs to see it. I was hoping he'd just sleep it off there, but he had a bad physical reaction and had to be in the hospital. No matter what I would have done, he would have been discovered or died, maybe. Of course, I'm sorry he's off our team, but he's still alive, thanks to my father."

Billy nodded slightly and caught up with Shane.

"You really think that's true? That Shane told first, that his parents made some sort of deal?" I asked.

"We'll see. You can see how they are, eager to blame someone else for everything. Just suggest the possibility of what I suggested if anyone really bothers you. The best defense is an offense anyway." He smiled.

I looked across at Alison. She looked even angrier than before. Shane's words echoed in my mind: *Fern and you.*

It was crazy, but in the midst of all this trouble, something made me happy.

When the bell rang to end lunch, Ryder waited for Alison. I saw him arguing with her as they left.

Tara Morton caught up with me first. "What was that all about? Is Barry going to be arrested?"

"I don't know. I'm not supposed to talk about it, but I can tell you the police knew a lot," I said, "and not because of me or Ryder. There's been a lot going on. You know some of it yourself. What happened to Paul just brought it to a head."

"Are you saying that any of us who used X could be in trouble?"

I knew what she was searching to discover. Had I turned in anyone else? "I don't know anyone specifically who used it, Tara. Do you? Because if you keep talking about it, one of the teachers might hear you and report you, and then you'll be called in to meet with a detective."

Her face went from red to yellow like a traffic light. She nodded and faded back to relay what I had said to the others. Maybe it got the claws off my back for the rest of the day, but I was certainly not the star I had been on prom night.

When the bell rang ending the last class, I hurried to leave the building. Then I hesitated, deciding whether to get my crown and pictures out of the locker, but decided it would only create more curiosity. I just wanted to get home and into my room as quickly as I could.

The air of doom had settled in every room in the school and was darkening every corner. Before the seventh period had begun, word was spread with lightning speed that Barry Austin had been taken out of the building in handcuffs and might be expelled, even if he didn't go to jail. Of course, I knew there was more to it than merely a bunch of kids using Ecstasy at a house party. I didn't want to hear about it and feel everyone's accusing eyes on me.

Ryder had baseball practice today. I wondered how that was going to go. If his teammates listened to Shane Cisco and blamed Ryder for what had happened to Paul, he was sure to be in for a bad time. I hurried toward the school bus and then stopped halfway there when I saw Ryder waiting for me.

"Why aren't you going to practice?" I asked.

"I need a day," he said. He looked very unhappy. "Alison and I had a fight. C'mon." He nodded to the steps on the bus, and I got in and sat quickly.

"What happened?" I asked as soon as he sat beside me.

"She thinks I ruined her prom because I wanted you to be happier than she was. That was why I arranged for Paul to take you. She went on again about your wearing my mother's dress. What's really bothering her is now she's grounded for a while. It didn't do any good to point out that so were we."

"I know she would have rather you had taken her in the limousine. She told me so. The double-dating had never really excited her. She wasn't really excited about helping to pick out your mother's dress. I'm sorry. I feel like this was all my fault."

"It wasn't all your fault. Forget about it. Get ready for my stepmother. She'll be worse than the detective. She's in a rage about my not going in the limousine this morning and Sam's hysterics."

I knew he was right. The worst was yet to come.

11

RYDER AND I were happy that no one on the bus had asked us anything about the day's events, but we were aware that everyone had been watching us and whispering our whole trip home. When we reached our stop at Wyndemere, we got off the bus and stood there a moment, silently contemplating the mansion as the bus pulled away.

Dr. Davenport's car was parked right behind the limousine.

Ryder looked at me and reached for my hand. What a shocking picture we would make for Bea Davenport, I thought. We walked like two people on their way to their own funeral.

Before we reached the steps, however, Ryder stopped. "My dad's rarely home this early," he said.

"I can only imagine the hysterics she performed on the phone. You'd better go around to your entrance."

"Don't argue with him, Ryder. Riding the school bus with me is not that important. I'll be fine by myself."

"Yeah, well, I'd rather be on the bus to make sure of that," he said, and headed for the front entrance. I watched him go in and then started down the walkway toward the rear of the mansion.

The spring blue sky had been battling streaks of gray clouds all day. Pulling reinforcements from a storm in the Midwest, the clouds were overtaking the more welcoming azure and now looked more like forecasts of rain. Above, on the mansion, the gargoyles looked down angrily at me for bringing grief to Wyndemere. Down to my right, across the lawn and between the patches of woods, Lake Wyndemere was a darker gray, the surface looking more like the shade of an aged and well-worn quarter. There were no boats out. The wind strengthened, and the newly sprung leaves on trees young and old looked like they were struggling to remain attached.

I opened the door and entered the kitchen. All was quiet. I was sure my mother was somewhere in the main house overseeing some work or helping with dinner preparations. I dropped my books on my desk in my room and practically dove onto my bed, facedown. For a while, I lay there feeling stunned and helpless. It had been a horrible day, a day that should have been wonderful for me as the reigning prom queen. What a joke. My crown was stuffed in a hall locker. I quickly put an end to my self-pity and thought about Ryder and what he must be facing at the moment. How could I let him face this all by himself?

I got up, hesitated, and then hurried out of my room.

The hallway from our living quarters to the main house was not very long, but it was always poorly illuminated with some simple low-wattage wall fixtures, as if the original owners and now the Davenports always wanted to impress everyone with the fact that the help lived in a place so different from Wyndemere's interior that it was truly like leaving the property, even going beneath it to some dark, unpleasant world. I hated walking through it. Whenever we were invited to something in the main house, something usually all the servants were welcomed to attend, I'd go around to the front of the house, even though my mother wouldn't.

Occasionally, when I was much younger but old enough to be left on my own, I would sneak down the hallway, especially when my mother was working in the main house, and then snuggle in a nook that housed a large black Egyptian pot that the original owners, the Jamesons, had brought back from one of their world trips. I could easily fit in between it and the wall and remain fairly well hidden. From there, I would look out at the comings and goings of the servants, Bea Davenport, her friends, my mother, and often Ryder and Sam. The nook was only around a half dozen feet from Dr. Davenport's office doorway.

Once as he was entering it, I thought he had seen me, but he had said nothing. I liked to think that he had smiled to himself, thinking I was cute or amusing, but it could just as well have been a grimace of annoyance. At least he hadn't yelled at me or chased me away.

Older and taller now, I was less dependent on the black pot to hide my presence and more dependent on the shadows. I saw two maids chatting in subdued voices as they crossed the hallway and went into the dining room. Neither looked my way. A moment later, my mother hurried along and went toward the stairway. She was carrying a vase of red and white roses. Sam was following her just the way I would when I was her age, talking incessantly and probably asking one question after another.

All was quiet again, and then I heard what was

definitely Bea's high-pitched, whiny voice coming from inside Dr. Davenport's office. Considering all the trouble that had occurred today, it was very risky for me to step out of the shadows and quietly approach the office doorway. Anyone seeing me eavesdropping there would surely cry out, and I'd be in bigger trouble, certainly with Bea. Nevertheless, my curiosity and concern for Ryder were too great for me to succumb to fear.

I approached the door.

Now inches away, I stood, practically holding my breath, and listened.

"Your stepmother is right, Ryder," I heard Dr. Davenport say. "I have seen a dramatic change in your behavior. You should have been more concerned with your sister Samantha's feelings. The talk about this disastrous past weekend spreads into the middle school, too, and her classmates might be teasing her or asking her embarrassing questions. You have to be a big brother and let her feel you're there to protect her. Now, Bea is the mistress of Wyndemere, but, more important, she is my wife and your legal guardian. Her orders and instructions are to be obeyed as if they came directly from me. Is that understood?"

I heard nothing but imagined Ryder had nodded or perhaps simply stared at the floor stone-faced, the rage in him swelling his shoulders. He'd never cry, but I had seen his eyes glaze over with

trapped tears whenever his father reprimanded
him. I felt like rushing in and throwing my arms
around him. *Let him alone!* I'd scream. *Stop hurt-
ing him!*

"You will accompany Samantha in the limousine to school every morning," Dr. Davenport
continued. "It's admirable that you have been a
friend to Fern, but you're both young adults now,
and I agree with your stepmother that in light of all
that's happened, anything more than that is inappropriate."

"What do you mean?" Ryder asked. "What's
inappropriate? What did she tell you?"

I could easily imagine him glaring hatefully at
Bea, who surely had a self-satisfied smile smeared
over her face.

"I don't want you sneaking off to spend time
with her in her room, and I don't want you encouraging her to come into the main house unless either
your stepmother or I have a specific reason for it,"
Dr. Davenport said quickly and sternly.

"Why not? What did she do? She's the victim
here. Her prom evening was ruined, and she's had
to deal with all the questions and comments some
of the bitches made."

"She hasn't done anything I know of, but we
both think it's wrong for you to encourage too
much familiarity," Dr. Davenport said in a more
reasonable tone of voice. "It was unquestionably

a mistake to arrange this double date for the prom in the first place. Your stepmother is already fielding too many inquiries from important people in Hillsborough. We have to be concerned about the family's reputation."

"The family's reputation? That's the first time I can recall when you've sounded like a snob, Dad. I guess she's rubbing off on you after all."

"Ryder! I can't tolerate your being so insolent to your stepmother. I'm not going to warn you about it again. Until you show proper respect and decorum, we'll be putting the idea of your getting your own car on your next birthday on hold."

"That was something you promised me. Now she has you breaking your promises," Ryder said. "I'll say it the way you like to say it, Dad. Let me be perfectly clear. She will never be my mother. I will never treat her like I would my mother."

"Then treat her like my wife!" Dr. Davenport responded, his voice raised unlike I had ever heard it. "Until I believe you are doing that, confine yourself to this property every weekend. Parker will be instructed not to drive you anywhere but to school and back. I want you to spend your time thinking about all this and what you can do to tone it down. Is that perfectly clear enough for you?"

Ryder did not respond. I turned away quickly, my heart pounding, my heart breaking for him. I started to cry on my way back to my room, and when I got there, I closed the door and sat on my bed and stared at the wall. Who was more loyal to Dr. Davenport than my mother, and yet look how he thought of me, her daughter. I was like an untouchable in this house. If I never said another word to him again, it would be too soon.

Lying on my side, I closed my eyes. I felt hollow inside. My sobbing put an ache in my chest. The strain of this terrible day and what I had just heard exhausted me. In moments, I was asleep and grateful for that. My mother didn't wake me until she had our dinner ready. I was sure she had looked in on me and left me sleeping. When I finally did open my eyes, I saw her standing there, looking down at me.

She immediately felt my forehead. "You're a little warm, Fern. I'd like to take your temperature."

"If there's anything wrong with me," I said, sitting up, "don't call on Dr. Davenport."

"What? Why?"

"I overheard him tell Ryder basically to stay away from me. According to Bea, I'm dirtying the Davenport name. I don't want to live here anymore. I don't!" I shouted, hopefully loud enough to be heard in the main house.

"Calm yourself. How did you overhear this?"

"I went out and listened just outside Dr. Davenport's office door."

"But why would he say such a thing?"

"Ryder went to school with me on the school bus this morning, and Bea had a meltdown."

"He did?"

"And rode back on it as well. Sam was upset about having to ride alone in the limousine."

"I see."

"He's confined to Wyndemere on weekends until further notice, and Dr. Davenport might not buy him the car he promised for his birthday. I don't care how many people he has saved. Ryder's right. He's a snob and very unfair."

She nodded. "We have to let things calm down, Fern. People say things they really don't mean when they're upset."

"Like your father said to you? Get out? Get out of his and your mother's and your sister's life?"

"Yes. I think there were many nights when he regretted it, but it had gone too far, and he didn't know the way back. Neither did I, but that doesn't have to happen here. You know Bea Davenport almost as well as I do, as well as all of us who work here do. She doesn't like looking foolish or being the object of unpleasant gossip, especially in the circles where she dwells. The weekend brought unpleasant attention to Wyndemere, and she's just flailing about like some overwrought spoiled brat. As I've said many times, ignoring people like that is the best defense."

"Ryder can't. He's being punished because of her and because he's helping me."

"Dr. Davenport will ease up as soon as the fire dwindles," she said. "Now. Let's take your temperature. When people get so upset, their immune systems suffer, and they get ill."

She went for the thermometer, and I lay back on my pillow.

I really did want us to leave now, leave at all costs. I even considered running away if she wouldn't leave. Maybe I would go to England and find her sister. All sorts of fantasies began to play in my imagination.

She returned with the thermometer. I didn't have any fever, but I was burning up inside with rage.

"Let's just get some good, hot food into you, and then you know what? We'll take a nice walk down to the lake. How's that?"

"Maybe I'll jump in and drown myself," I said.

"Take a shower and change your clothes," she ordered. "Stop this tantrum." She smiled. "I'm making one of your favorites, one Mrs. Marlene taught me well, chicken piccata."

I did smell the aroma, and despite my fury, my stomach churned with hunger. I had barely eaten anything at lunch. I nodded and did what she asked.

After a shower and a good dinner, I did feel

better. My mother had tried to change the topic while we ate, but I didn't think she was doing that solely to get me to stop thinking about it all. She was genuinely excited about what she was telling me. She had received a note in the mail from the doctor who had delivered both Ryder and me, Dr. Bliskin. It was like she had won the lottery or something.

"He wanted to know how we were and said he was doing some traveling involving a medical convention and just might take a short detour on the way home and stop at Wyndemere. Wouldn't that be nice?"

"Probably mainly to visit Dr. Davenport and kneel at the throne."

"Oh, Fern, that's not nice. Of course he wants to see Dr. Davenport, but he specifically wanted to be sure we'd be around, too."

"Oh, we'll be around." I thought a moment. "Where would we have gone?" I asked. "Well?"

Was there somewhere we could go, somewhere she had kept secret? Had she been thinking of returning to England to what remained of her family? A new start in life might have been just the right thing for both of us.

"We wouldn't have gone anywhere special, Fern. He simply meant he wanted to be sure we were still here when he visits," she said.

When she told me about this, she held the note as if it was a precious historical document or something. Then she put it back in her purse. Why was she saving it in her purse? Was she going to take it out and reread it as if it was a beautiful poem or something? Whatever pleasure it had brought her was meaningless to me.

"I don't remember him," I said petulantly. It was certainly not anywhere nearly exciting enough news for me to forget the misery I felt for myself and for Ryder.

"Well, he remembers you and me, of course, very well. C'mon. We'll take that walk now before it gets too late. You need some fresh air. Put on a light sweater, love."

My mother and I rarely took walks together on the Wyndemere property, but I refused to get happy about it. I didn't want to do what she suggested and ignore what was happening by distracting myself. Dr. Davenport's words still circled my head like annoying flies.

Folding my arms under my breasts, I left the house with her and walked the pathway that led over the grounds and down to the Davenports' boat dock.

"Dr. Bliskin occasionally took time out when he made a house call for us or for Sam and walked down to the lake," my mother said. "Most of those times, Dr. Davenport was at work and couldn't accompany him, so I did. He was always very envious of Dr. Davenport, you know. Men always accuse women of being very competitive, but the truth is, they are far more vulnerable to suffer envy than we are. They're so concerned about their manliness, proving it.

"There isn't that much of an age difference between them, either. Dr. Davenport is only three years older, but because he is this highly respected and regarded cardiac specialist, Dr. Bliskin talked about him as if he were some venerable old man. I teased him about that," she said.

I didn't know if she was rattling on like this as a way to get me out of my funk or because she was really remembering some happier moments in her life here. Obviously, Dr. Bliskin was someone she had liked very much. She wasn't even looking at me when she spoke. She was gazing ahead at the lake and walking. I could have stopped yards back, and she wouldn't have noticed.

"'You have to remember,' I told him. 'It's true, Dr. Davenport is an exceptional man, brilliant and skilled, but he was someone born with a silver spoon in his mouth. Like Americans say, he was born on third base and thought he hit a home run, whereas you came from a far, far more modest background. In some ways,' I pointed out, 'you have accomplished more.'"

I was impressed that she remembered her conversation with him word for word.

"I mean, Dr. Bliskin had to work and win scholarships, and his parents sacrificed so much so he could have a medical degree. Why, he was still paying off loans until the day he left Hillsborough, you know. I think that was what made him a compassionate man. Too many doctors treat the disease or the illness and not the patient."

"Like Dr. Davenport," I said.

"What?" She paused as though she had just realized I had been walking with her. "Oh. Well, not exactly. I mean, Dr. Davenport cares for his patients. He just views them as more of a . . . a challenge. That's not a bad thing, either, Fern. He takes his failures very personally, not that he fails that much, but when he does, when he loses a patient, he's very difficult to live with, I'm sure."

"I doubt Bea even notices or cares," I said.

We had reached the dock. The Davenports' motorboat bobbed in the water next to a pair of rowboats as the strong early-evening breeze stirred the lake. It wasn't overcast any longer, however. The winds had blown the storm farther north. Mr. Stark was always giving us weather reports. I think it rubbed off on me.

"Dr. Davenport had given Dr. Bliskin permission to use his boat anytime he could. The Davenports didn't have as elaborate a boat back then, but it was quite nice."

"Did you go on it with Dr. Bliskin?"

"Once. I brought you along, too. You were only six months old. You were quite fascinated, even at that young age," she said, and looked out at the lake.

The breeze toyed with her hair. She brushed some strands from her eyes and kept that soft smile, what Mr. Stark called her "clotted-cream English smile," on her face. At the moment, her jewel eyes sparkled.

My mother was very beautiful, I thought, far more beautiful than Bea Davenport or any of her posh friends, for that matter. Why hadn't Dr. Davenport seen that and, instead of having himself fixed up with the hospital administrator's daughter, probably to continue his meteoric climb to the head of cardiology, married my mother instead? To me, his marrying Bea was the same as selling your soul to the devil.

"Everything's going to be all right, Fern," my mother said, as if she had just heard the lake whisper it in the breeze. "Just let a little time pass. The amount of harm done to us in this life is proportional to how we accept it. That was the one lesson I permitted my father to teach me."

"What does that mean?"

"When you're young, everything is far more

dramatic. A pimple on your face is as bad as a scar. If age does anything worthwhile, it certainly is the way it thickens your skin, hardens your resolve, and helps you endure disappointments and defeats. That's the conundrum, our riddle we have to solve as human beings. Would you rather remain young and vulnerable or grow older and wiser and calmer?"

"What's your choice, Mummy?"

She widened her smile and nodded at the lake, at some memory, for sure. "It's a common tragedy we share, I guess. We'd rather be young and suffer emotional pains. What's that quote? ''Tis better to have loved and lost than never to have loved at all.'"

Why was she talking about love?

She put her arm around me, but I was thinking she was doing it for herself more than for me. She was suddenly more vulnerable than I had ever seen her. I wondered if this was the moment when I could get her to reveal who my father was. It was on my lips to ask, but I had a terrible sense of guilt taking advantage of her, too. I couldn't do it.

"Let's go back," she said. "You probably have homework to do."

We walked like that for a while, slowly, her arm still around my shoulders. Wyndemere loomed ahead of us. It always seemed to be looking down at me. It was never just there. It was always towering, impressive, and demanding respect. It was the only world I had known. I wanted to hate it. I often did, but now more than ever.

And yet I couldn't deny the power it held over me, over us all. It gave us a special sense of security. It was like a fortress, full of secrets, yes, and visited daily by the winds of family turmoil. But I recalled when I was very little and was permitted to follow my mother about that the chandeliers drove back the darkness, and the halls were filled with the laughter and conversations of the important political and social guests, all dressed in tuxedos and gowns, glittering with expensive jewelry. To me, it was more like a castle, a house of fantasies. It was no wonder that invitations to a Davenport event were highly prized and sought. It was no wonder that my classmates and people I met in the community wanted to know more about Wyndemere. Maybe that was why it was no wonder that my mother hadn't left or still didn't talk of doing so.

Back in my room, I did my homework but occasionally paused and thought about Ryder, surely sulking in his room. I was afraid to reveal that I knew what he was suffering, that I had eavesdropped on Dr. Davenport reprimanding him. I thought he might be embarrassed, and I would only bring him more pain. In the end, I decided it was better that he tell me anything he thought I should know.

I dreaded tomorrow, beginning with him sullenly getting into the limousine with Sam and then later at school, when surely the famous second shoe would be dropped, and we'd all know more about what was going to happen to Paul and Barry and anyone else tied to the prom-night events. How many would resent me—and Ryder, for that matter? What would our teachers have learned, and how would they act toward us? What would Alison be like? Would she spread stories about me now? Those who had been envious of me would bask in the nasty comments. I would read that forever dreaded question on the faces of many. *Why expect anything better from an illegitimate child who couldn't be sure who among all her mother's lovers was her father?*

My mother came in to check on me, and then she went to bed. Slowly, I did the same, trying to hold back time. The faster I went to sleep, the faster morning would come. Maybe I would pretend I was sick and not go to school, but then I thought it would be worse to stay home. Nothing would change by skipping a day.

I slipped under my blanket and stared up at the dark ceiling, where some of the full moonlight was streaking along it and down the wall to my right. If there really were ghosts in Wyndemere, tonight was going to be a party night for them for sure.

I closed my eyes and began to drift into a welcoming sleep. I didn't know how long I was asleep before I heard something that snapped my eyes open again. The shadow I saw moving toward me did look ghostly. I was about to scream just before it moved into a slight glow of the starlight, and I saw it was Ryder.

I knew that, especially now, this visit was strictly forbidden, that he was defying his father and Bea and risking getting himself into even more trouble, but I didn't want to say it.

I sat up quickly. He was in his robe and slippers. He didn't say anything at first. He simply sat near my legs and leaned forward, taking the posture of Rodin's famous sculpture *The Thinker*. I reached for his left hand, lying on his knee. He turned to me slowly, his face pale in the starlight coming through my open window.

"I won't be riding with you on the bus," he said.

"I told you that would be all right, Ryder. I won't let anyone bother me."

"You tell me who does," he said. "I'll deal with them."

"Right. I get you into more trouble and give Bea more ammunition."

I was still holding his hand. He looked down at our hands and put his right hand over mine. "I'll tell you what my mistake was, Fern. My mistake was not taking you to the prom myself."

I couldn't speak. Had I heard correctly?

He lowered himself beside me. I moved over slightly. He pulled himself up so he was able to share part of my pillow, and he turned fully on his back.

"I always wondered what it would be like sleeping here. Did your mother ever tell you that I often cried to have a sleepover night when I was about six and you were about four?"

"No."

"It always seemed like an adventure to follow your mother into this section of Wyndemere. I think I thought I was going to another country or something."

"You were; you are."

"I'd probably be better off," he said. "I had a bad fight with my father and Bea. He's forbidden me to go anywhere on weekends and is telling Parker not to take me anywhere until I basically kowtow to Bea. He's rescinded his promise to buy me a car on my birthday until he's confident I'll be obedient and respect whatever Bea tells me."

"Do whatever you have to, Ryder. Don't defy her just for me."

He turned. "That's the best reason to defy her," he said. He raised himself a bit and suddenly kissed me on the neck. The warm electric feeling shot through my breast to the pit of my stomach so quickly that it took my breath away.

When I turned slightly to him, he brought his lips to mine. It wasn't a kiss so much as a soft brush of his lips, and then he lowered his head and brought his mouth to my chest, nudging the buttons of my pajama top open with his fingers, his lips traveling between my breasts first and then to my nipples. He turned his face so the fullness of my breast was against his cheek. Then he rose again and kissed me on the lips, this time a long kiss.

I hadn't moaned; I hadn't spoken. It seemed more like one of my fantasies. The moment I uttered a sound, it would go away. He wouldn't be in my room. I would realize I had dreamed it all.

But he didn't disappear when I said his name. Instead, he twisted himself around, slipping under my blanket, and embraced me. When he pressed himself against me now, I felt his hardness and shuddered. His hands were on my waist. I was excited, happy, but frightened, too. He lay like that for a while, his head now resting on my shoulder.

"I guess I've shocked you," he whispered.

"Yes."

"I'm sorry."

"No, it's all right. I'm glad you kissed me, touched me."

He lifted his head and kissed me on the tip of my nose. "I'm angry and frustrated," he said. "I almost wish Bea would come walking through that door and find us together."

A frightening thought came to me. "You're not doing this for that reason, are you?"

"I don't know," he said. "Maybe." He pulled back. "Maybe not. I don't know. I was thinking about you, imagining myself here beside you. I didn't hesitate to go down the stairs and come here."

He sat up when we both heard what sounded like my mother going into the kitchen. Neither of us spoke; both of us were holding our breath. I could hear her footsteps. Would she look in on me to see how I was?

Ryder moved very, very slowly, lifting the blanket away. Then he slipped off my bed and lowered himself to the floor just as my mother opened my door. I had pulled my blanket up and turned on my side. I didn't move. She was standing there watching me. Seconds felt like minutes, but finally she closed the door softly and returned to her bedroom.

Ryder rose. "That was close," he whispered. "I'd better get back. I'll be waiting for you in the school lobby when the bus arrives tomorrow."

"Okay," I said.

He started for the door.

"Ryder," I whispered.

He turned back. "What?"

"I'm glad you came here tonight. For whatever reason."

"Me, too," he said, and quietly opened the door and slipped away.

Go on, Fern, I challenged myself. *Just try to fall asleep.*

12

I DID FALL asleep quicker than I imagined I would. The tension and fear I brought to bed with me had been swept away by Ryder's kisses and caresses. It was a fantasy realized, but what did it mean? How could we ever care for each other in this house, in the Davenport world? Would every moment have to be stolen and hidden? Would I have to lie to my mother?

What a wonder Wyndemere was, I thought. It not only housed many secrets, it created new ones. It was as if the deep shadows, the moans and creaks in the walls, and antiques full of memories encouraged additional mystery. It welcomed more whispers and clandestine activities. It was a garden ripe for lies. Black roses grew everywhere, and now Ryder and I were about to plant a new one.

Suddenly, Bea Davenport's forbidding me to enter the main house for any purpose other than something that was absolutely necessary was welcomed, for how could I be in the same room with Ryder and not have my deeper, loving, sexual affection for him unmasked? Bea's ever suspicious and condemning eyes would pounce on a look, a smile, a surreptitious touch. Now that I thought about that, I did have new nightmares.

There! she cried, loudly enough to bring Dr. Davenport out of his office or down the stairway. She was pointing her long right forefinger at us. The fingernail looked like a razor. *Didn't I warn you? Didn't I have good reason to prohibit her from socializing with your son, whether it was something as seemingly innocent as riding along with him and our daughter in the limousine or as dangerous as having her at dates and parties with him?*

In my horrible dream, Dr. Davenport's handsome face then became disfigured. His beautiful silvery eyes reddened with rage, and his lips contorted as his teeth grew more like vampire fangs.

No! he cried, and slammed his fist against the wall. Every chandelier shook, some paintings fell off walls, and a trembling expensive antique vase tumbled and smashed on the floor.

Of course, I woke up with that sound. It was nearly morning and useless to try to return to sleep. I lay there with my eyes open, thinking and planning, with panic stinging my spine. Ryder had to beware of this show of affection toward me. He should be especially careful when he looked at me, even when he gazed my way while I was waiting for the school bus. Bea must never see his face at those moments. And when we were in school, we had to be even more careful. For all I knew, Alison had sensed something in Ryder as well as in me, and that was the real reason she was so angry and wanted to break up with him. She would be the first to point out how close Ryder and I were now. Hopefully, he would understand when I would avoid sitting with him in the cafeteria or walking with him in the hallways between classes.

It wouldn't be easy. I had no confidence in being able to quiet my demanding heart. I would surely long for his hand, his touch, and a soft loving word. Could I avert my gaze, pay attention to anyone else's conversations, and keep my distance, especially today, when everything about prom night had come to a loud crash for Ryder and myself at Wyndemere? Somehow I had to be measured enough in my exchanges with him to keep even the most suspicious and envious of my classmates unaware.

As usual, I heard my mother up ahead of me, preparing some breakfast. I washed, brushed my hair, and dressed. I'd wear no makeup today, not even a touch of lipstick. I wanted to be more like a nun in my appearance so I could assume that demeanor and keep the lid on my new boiling, raging desires. My mind was full of expectations. Ryder would return to my bedroom, maybe not tonight or tomorrow night, but he would return, and our kisses would be longer, his caresses more demanding, exploring, driving away my fragile virgin resistance. He'd be prepared for that. It would happen, and whatever we did in our lives, wherever we were, even if we were with someone else, we would never be able to forget those loving, erotic moments.

Of course, I could not say that for him it would be a first as well. Whenever I fantasized about making love for the first time and imagined the boy doing it for the first time, I envisioned us both fumbling and stumbling, like two people blindly walking on the deck of a rocking boat on the darkest night. When some of my more revealing girlfriends described their first times, a few made it sound so terrible that they were seriously considering abstinence until marriage. For them, it had been painful and unsatisfying. The boy had his orgasm, his initiation, but they hadn't come close.

"I don't fancy myself being someone's training ground," I told them, which made them widen their eyes.

"Fancy?" Carla Sheldon said. "What's that mean?"

"Don't forget her mother's English," Kim Green reminded everyone. "English people always fancy this or fancy that."

I had grown so accustomed to my mother's expressions that I didn't think twice about repeating them, but I was always sensitive to any allusions to my mother, for fear that the next statement would pave the way for a comment about her getting pregnant with me and my never knowing who my father was.

All this played in my mind in a twisted ball of rubber-band thoughts entangling with each other. My mother immediately saw how distracted I was, but she blamed it entirely on my fear of what awaited me at school regarding the infamous second shoe. There would be more collateral damage. Others who were in the vicinity of the illegal activity or tied to it would suffer anything from relatively minor reprimands to suspension from school. Families would be tainted. There would be an avalanche of rage in our community, perhaps aimed not solely at the ones who brought it about but also at those who revealed it.

Paul was obviously at the top of that list. Other students who took the drug would complain about him. Why didn't he just wait until it had worn off or sought the help of someone who would have covered up for him? They wouldn't believe his health was in such danger. His extreme reaction was so rare. Everything could have been avoided. I couldn't believe that I was actually feeling a bit sorry for him, but I was.

Another thought popped into my head. Maybe they would spread the rumor that Dr. Davenport, embarrassed that his son, Ryder, was in some way tied to all this, exaggerated Paul's health issues and blew them up far more than necessary. And by cooperating with the police and the school administration, all Ryder Davenport and Fern Corey did was enable this terrible blot on our community to happen. How could I not be distracted and afraid?

"Whatever happens to other students because of all this is not your fault, Fern. You must not act as though you have done something wrong," my mother said, pouring my juice. "You go to school just like you always have, and you do your work and ignore any nasty remarks, just the way I told you yesterday.

"If the dean calls you to his office to talk about any of this because of something new they've learned, you are to ask him or his secretary to call me immediately, and you are to say nothing more. I know that makes you look guilty to other people, but things said are often twisted or exaggerated."

She sat with her coffee. She had made me a soft-boiled egg and toast.

"I haven't lied about any of it," I said.

She nodded. "I know. I believe you."

She sat there, watching me eat.

"Last night, Dr. Davenport asked to see me," she revealed after a long and obviously thoughtful silence, during which she had debated whether to tell me.

"How?" I asked, probably too quickly. Had he come to our part of the house?

"How? The usual way, through the intercom."

"What time was this?"

"Not long after you had gone to sleep," she said.

My mind spun with a myriad of frightening questions. On her way to Dr. Davenport's office, had she seen Ryder go into my room but kept it to herself? Did Dr. Davenport anticipate all this? Was that why he had called her to his office? Did he threaten her? Was Bea present? Afterward, did she come to my door to signal to Ryder that he should leave?

There was more than one second shoe dropping today. There were three, maybe four.

"Why?" I asked, in a voice so low that I wasn't sure I had said it out loud. "I had no idea you went there."

"I didn't stay in the office long," she said. "He simply wanted to tell me what I'm telling you now. He's concerned that no one hold you and, for that

matter, Ryder to blame. He said police and pros-
ecutors are often overly anxious when it comes to
prosecuting a case and winning accolades. It's why,
he says, we all need attorneys most of the time. He
has one of his standing by in case we need him, and
he said he would pay any expenses. I was not to
worry. That's very kind of him, don't you think?"

I released my trapped hot breath. "Yes."

"Perhaps, then, you were a little too quick in
your condemnation of him. As I've said, let things
settle."

"If they ever will," I said, and nibbled on my
eggs and toast.

"They will." She smiled. "Remember what I
told you about blowing things out of proportion.
Now, I will be available all day should you need
me, but you'll have to have your dinner alone tonight. Don't worry. Mrs. Marlene is sending over a
nice plate of her special lasagna. She's serving that
to the Davenports."

"But why? Where will you be?"

She smiled. "Not long after you and I had our
walk last night, Dr. Bliskin called. He's invited me
to dinner. I haven't been to a restaurant in so long
that I practically had forgotten they existed. I almost panicked and refused. That would have been
silly, of course. He's come so far."

"Is his wife with him?"

"No. He's on that medical convention trip,

remember? He'll be stopping by here tomorrow night. Dr. Davenport has invited him to dinner. You know Bea Davenport would never approve of my being at the table, so tonight's my best opportunity to spend some time with him, catching up."

"Catching up?"

"Yes. He was very fond of us, and I was very fond of him."

Fond? What did that mean? I wondered.

She finished her coffee and stood. "Eat your breakfast, Fern. You need to be strong today."

I nodded and ate what I could. After I finished getting ready for school, I looked in at her. She was standing before her full-length mirror in her bedroom, toying with her hair. I saw she had a few dresses out on her bed. It had been a long time since I had seen her so concerned about how she would look. She became aware that I was standing in her doorway.

"Oh. I have a lot to do today," she said quickly. "I thought I would decide what to wear tonight now and get that worry out of the way."

"It's a worry?"

"You know what I mean," she said, smiling. I nodded and started to turn away. "Wait," she called.

I turned back, and she held up two of her best dresses.

"Which one doesn't look terribly out of fashion?"

The one on her right, a unique shade of ruby, was always the dress that I thought complemented her complexion and brought out the colors in her eyes and hair the best. It had a deep scoop neck and sheer beaded sleeves. The waist was tightly encased in heavy-duty beaded chiffon. When I was much younger and had seen her wearing it, I had felt a little embarrassed because my mother looked so sexy. I rarely thought of her as being sexy then and especially now. It seemed so out of character for her.

For most of my life, in fact, my mother was almost asexual. She avoided makeup, did little to make her hair more attractive, and kept to clothes that deemphasized her still quite alluring figure. Somewhere it was written in her book of destiny that all that feminine energy was to be reserved for me, given to me. She had long since passed the time when that mattered to her, despite the way Mr. Stark would look at her, especially when she was unaware of it.

The ruby dress was the most expensive piece in her relatively modest wardrobe. She never told me how she had gotten it or who had bought it for her. I suspected Mr. Stark. There were times recently when I caught her putting it on just to gaze at herself in it, probably wondering if it still fit well and if she still looked pretty wearing it. If she saw me watching, she would quickly take it off, wondering aloud why she even had kept it in her closet and had not given it to some charity.

"There's no choice to make," I said. "The ruby, of course."

"Yes." She nodded and tossed the other dress onto the bed. "I thought so, too. I was just worried it might be too tight on me now."

"Like you've gained any weight," I said. "You don't sit still for a moment."

She nodded. "We'll see."

"Do you know where he's taking you?"

"Yes. He made a reservation at Le Coeur de la Rose."

"I never heard of that place," I said.

"It's an old French restaurant in Gardner, just outside of Hillsborough. I was surprised it was still there myself."

"When did you last go there?"

"Oh, years ago." She laughed. "I wore the same dress. Anyway, I'll leave the telephone number and address on the table."

"You mean you'll be gone that early?"

"Oh. Yes. It's actually my day off. Coincidence," she said. "Early cocktails somewhere else first."

"Where?"

"I don't know. It's up to Dr. Bliskin. But you can reach me on my mobile if you need me."

"You always forget to keep it charged," I reminded her. "You hardly ever use it except to be more accessible to Bea, which is why I think you let the battery die."

She laughed. "She does hate that, but today I'll make sure. Don't worry." She held the ruby dress in front of her and turned back to her mirror. "Yes," she said to her own image, as if she was looking at someone else through a window and not herself in a mirror.

I shook my head with amazement at the sudden feminine flutter of excitement in my mother. I wished I could remember more about Dr. Bliskin. Was he very handsome? Was he more concerned about us than any of his other patients? Why? Suspicions were blossoming, but I didn't want to be thinking about that all day, not today.

I said good-bye, but I don't think she heard me. Smiling to myself because she was behaving more like a teenage girl than I was, I walked out and around to the front and down to the school bus stop. The thin wisps of clouds promised a beautiful day. It was warmer. Summer was sending out messages of its impending arrival. Leaves were greener, bushes were blossoming, flocks of more birds were arriving, and the cool breezes rushing up from the lake were more welcomed. It was difficult to be sad or even afraid on days like this. Gloom was out of place, something to tuck in a corner and forget. Everyone on the school bus would be talking louder, with more excitement. Maybe they would stop thinking about me, I thought, which was certainly wishful thinking.

I glanced at the limousine. Parker was facing forward, waiting for Ryder and Sam. Most mornings, either he would be standing outside the vehicle with a rag to wipe away the slightest splotch of mud and would nod, wave, and say good morning to me or, if he wasn't outside the car, he would stick his head out the window and call good morning to me. However, this morning, he looked like he was afraid even to glance at me in his rearview mirror.

I hurried along, but I did hear the sounds of the front entrance opening, some footsteps, and then the limousine doors being opened and closed. I didn't look back. Instead, I looked anxiously for the school bus to arrive. The limousine drove off. I watched it disappear, and then I looked back at the house.

Bea Davenport was still there, standing at the entrance and gazing at me. Even from this distance, I could see the look of satisfaction splashed like a broken egg yolk all over her face. I turned away quickly, and when the school bus approached, I practically lunged for the steps, lowered my eyes, and found an empty seat, the seat Ryder and I had sat in the day before, actually. That was some comfort. I looked at no one and didn't have a single conversation.

When we arrived at school and entered the building, two of my classmates, Carol Sue Fisher and Cindy Stevens, were waiting for me like hawks swooping down on a mouse. I didn't see Ryder.

"Did you hear?" Cindy asked first. Before I could ask, *Hear what?* she said, "Paul Gabriel has transferred to another school."

"A private school," Carol Sue added. "That'll cost his parents lots of money."

"But he probably can play baseball there," Cindy said.

"I'm happy for him," I said. "I don't want him to ruin his life."

"But no one knows what Barry will do. He was arrested, and he's been expelled. He can't go to school here, no matter what," Carol Sue said.

"And we don't know for sure yet, but everyone's saying Russel Jones was arrested last night. He was selling drugs with Barry."

"He'll probably be expelled, too!" Carol Sue said. "Shane is also in trouble with the police, besides his parents, but we don't know how much yet."

"Are you and Ryder and Alison all right?" Cindy asked.

I started walking toward my homeroom, a little dazed. I hadn't even had a chance to take a breath. They followed me, repeating questions. I looked for Ryder, but he was nowhere in sight. Good thing, too, I thought.

"So?" Carol pursued when we reached the classroom door. "How are you?"

I turned to them and smiled. "I feel fine," I said. "Just a little tired. That math homework was just too much, don't you think?"

They both looked at me, stunned. Maybe they thought I had gone crazy. I was smiling like someone who had won the lottery.

"But I got it done," I said, and walked into homeroom. Both of them remained behind, as if I had turned them to stone.

The chatter in homeroom and throughout the school all morning was about Paul, Barry, and some others who were in very serious trouble. I fielded questions constantly and relied solely on the statement "I was told not to talk about any of it. Sorry." Disappointment quickly became anger. Why couldn't I talk now? Was there someone else being investigated? Did I or Ryder turn someone else's name over to the police?

I didn't see Ryder until lunch hour. Either he was embarrassed by his show of affection last night, he was embarrassed that he had revealed how angry and hurt he was, or he had thought of the same things I had this morning and cleverly avoided talking to me so our newly blossomed relationship wouldn't get back to Bea and his father. He sat with some of his classmates and only gave me a glance or two.

Alison was with other girls in her class, but she was also exchanging remarks with John Shepherd, another senior who was on the baseball team with Ryder. I could see she was flirting with him, and before the lunch hour ended, she rose and sat beside him at his table. When the bell rang, they went out together. I looked at Ryder to see his reaction, and this time, he looked at me and smiled. Guiltily, I checked to see who was noticing, but no one seemed to care. Maybe I was being too careful.

As we all left, he walked up to me and whispered, "Go to the bathroom ten minutes into your last-period class."

Before I could respond, he walked off with his friends. I wasn't surprised that Ryder had won most, if not all, of them back. Someone as popular as he was would have an easier time getting his classmates to see his side of the story. That pleased me. The more forgiven he was, the more I should be. Nevertheless, I was very nervous when I asked to go to the bathroom exactly ten minutes into my last-period class. I felt like everything I did and said aroused new suspicions in both my teachers and my classmates.

Ryder was waiting for me near the girls' room. Without speaking, he led me toward the stairway for the second floor and hovered between it and the wall.

"I'm sorry I haven't spoken to you more. How are you doing?" he asked.

"Okay. I was sorry to hear about Paul, of course, but not so much about Barry."

"It seems he's involved with someone from the community college who's selling X and harder drugs to classmates. It's pretty serious, but don't you worry about it. You don't know anything more. Listen . . . about last night."

"I'm not sorry," I said quickly.

He smiled. "Me, neither, but for now . . ."

"I understand."

"Except," he said, "if I'm confined to Wyndemere on the weekend and it's nice, why don't we go for a row on the lake? Bea will be occupied with one of her social clubs, and I know my father works this Saturday."

"Sure."

"I'm staying for baseball practice now, and we have a game away on Thursday, so I won't see you at the end of the day. I'll call tonight."

"Call whenever you can. My mother's going on a dinner date with a doctor who took care of us years and years ago, Dr. Bliskin."

"Really?" He thought a moment and nodded. "I remember him, but I remember him married with triplets or something."

"Yes, that's the one. He's just in the area for a conference, but he's coming to dinner with you and your father and Bea tomorrow night."

"Is he? I guess I have to go to you to learn about my own life and what's happening next in Wyndemere," he said. He looked around and then kissed me quickly. We heard footsteps. "Go," he said, and I hurried away and back to my class. My feet felt like they were winged.

Just that little conversation with him made me feel so much better. I had no trouble talking to other students on the bus ride home. When I arrived at Wyndemere, my mother was gone, just as she had said she would be. I went right to my homework. Just before Mrs. Marlene arrived with my dinner, my mother called to see how things were. I told her about Paul, Barry, and the other boy and how no one had called me in for any more questioning.

"I'm sure they have enough now without you. Or Ryder, for that matter. Dr. Davenport's influence is important."

"Where are you?"

"We're on our way to the restaurant," she said. "Don't wait up for me. I'll look in on you when I get home. Oh, and Dr. Bliskin will stop in before he attends the Davenports' dinner tomorrow. He's looking forward to seeing you."

It was on the tip of my tongue to blurt out,

Why? Is he my father? I didn't, of course. Mrs. Marlene was calling for me.

"Eat it while it's hot," she told me. She looked about. "Why haven't you set your table?"

"I lost track of time," I said, and hurried to do it. She stood there watching me. I knew that by now, my mother had told her everything that had happened.

"I'm sorry your special night was ruined, Fern," she said. "Just remember that every tide has its ebb. I'm sure it will all turn out well, especially if Dr. Davenport's taken some interest."

I sat. "I'm fine," I said. Then I looked at her sharply. "You know my mother went to dinner with the doctor who took care of both Ryder and me years ago."

"Yes. A very nice man," she said. "I'm making dinner for him tomorrow night. It'll be one of his favorite recipes, too, osso buco."

"How did you know what was his favorite?"

"Oh, your mother told me," she said. "She knows all the important details about everyone who comes in and out of Wyndemere. Enjoy, and let me know if you need anything else."

"Thank you, Mrs. Marlene," I called as she started away.

She cast one of her bright, motherly smiles my way and left.

While I was eating, Mr. Stark stopped by. I

was surprised my mother hadn't told him she was going out to dinner.

"Oh, Dr. Bliskin," he said, nodding. "I didn't know he was back here."

"For a medical conference. He'll be at dinner here tomorrow night. Did you know him well?"

"Oh, sure. Fine doctor. Cathy always liked him. Where'd they go?"

I told him, and he nodded again.

He looked lost in thought and suddenly realized it. "How are you doing?"

"I'm fine, Mr. Stark."

"As you should be. You call if you need anything," he said. I had the feeling he was disappointed in hearing about my mother's dinner date. He nodded, smiled, and left.

Between Mrs. Marlene and him, I had a set of surrogate grandparents, I thought. They were probably better than any of the actual ones my friends had.

I cleaned up the kitchen and returned to my homework. None of the girls who usually would call me at night to deliver some new gossip called. Most were probably mad at me for not confiding solely in them so they'd know something ahead of the others. So many acted as if their friendship was a special gift for me. I should show more gratitude, kiss their feet.

As the night grew later, I listened more keenly

for my mother's return. Ryder called after he had gone to his room. He told me the dining room had been more like a funeral parlor, but he hadn't given in and apologized to Bea. In fact, he had avoided looking at her.

"Maybe you're only tossing more wood on the fire, Ryder. Can't you pretend a little?"

"Not when it comes to her. Don't worry about me. I'll survive. How about you?"

"My mother's not home yet," I said. I wondered if he knew anything, if he had overheard Bea say something or ask something of his father, or if he had overheard some gossip in the house. "How much catching up do she and Dr. Bliskin need to do?" I asked, fishing to see if Dr. Davenport had mentioned him at dinner and said something I should know.

"It's been a long time, I guess. I'm happy she's enjoying a night out. She works very hard here, chasing after Bea's stupid requests." If he knew something, he was obviously not going to say.

"Are we really going rowing this Saturday?"

"Absolutely, rain or shine," he said. "I'm kissing you good night. Feel it?"

"Yes," I said, laughing.

"It's a new app on my phone called Kiss and Tell."

"Ha ha."

"Night, Fern. Sweet dreams," he said.

After we hung up, I lay back and stared up at the ceiling. Above me and a few thousand feet or so to my right, he was lying in his bed. One night, I thought, I would sneak through the house and float up those stairs. I would very quietly enter his bedroom. He'd be asleep, and I'd slip so softly in beside him that he wouldn't wake up.

And I wouldn't wake him, either. After a while, I'd slip out and float back down the stairs, walking in the shadows, and then hurrying through the hall to crawl back into my own bed.

I'd be like one of the Wyndemere ghosts. The next day, when I told him I had lain beside him for twenty or so minutes in his own bed, he'd not believe it.

I thought it was a dream, he'd say. *And then I found a strand of your hair and inhaled the pillow beside me. It was your shampoo, for sure. I thought I was going mad.*

But we are, I would say. *Mad for each other.*

The dream scenario was so pleasing I could put out my lights and turn on my side to hug the pillow and welcome my new fantasy.

I never heard my mother come home.

But when I saw her in the morning, rushing past my bedroom door to get breakfast started, she was still wearing the ruby dress. I didn't let her know I had seen her.

My body trembled.

Something that rarely happened was happening.

One of the great secrets of Wyndemere was unfolding right before my eyes.

Finally, perhaps, it had decided it was time to emerge from the shadows.

13

I DELIBERATELY MADE more noise than usual getting up and ready for breakfast. Before I came
out of my bedroom, my mother rushed into hers
and changed clothes quickly. I felt as if I was *her*
mother catching her doing something deceitful.
I was at the table when she emerged, now in her
dark-blue denim pullover dress that basically had
become her uniform. She had four nearly identical
ones, none very flattering to her figure, all making
her look more matronly. She wore a pair of black
shoes that always looked very masculine to me.
And of course, she had washed off any makeup she
had worn and pinned back her hair in that severe
bun. What a contrast she was to the attractive
woman who had prepared so enthusiastically for a
dinner date yesterday.

"Everything go all right last night?" she asked me.

"I was about to ask you," I replied.

She went for her coffee. "Oh, it was very pleasant, and the food was as good as I remembered."

"What about Dr. Bliskin?"

"He's doing very well in his practice, and his children are all starting their first year in college, each going to a different one. I imagine they wanted to have a sense of independence. It must have been hard for each one to grow up with two identical sisters. It was only natural for everyone to continually contrast and compare them."

"What's he like? Is he how you remembered him?"

"He looks like he's not aged a day, and that's not easy for a doctor, with all the responsibility and stress," she quickly added. "So, tell me quickly. What happened in school?" She sat with her coffee.

I told her what I had learned about Paul and Barry.

"Were the other students understanding or resentful?" she asked pointedly.

"More resentful, I'd say. They all expected me to give them great detail, but I refused to talk about it. I think I might have lost the half dozen or so friends I've made at Hillsborough. We'll see," I said.

"Anyone who resents you for not doing what you were told is not really a friend anyway," she said. "You'll make new ones, I'm sure."

"Here? I doubt it," I said. "But right now, I'm not worried about it." I looked at the clock and then at her. "Maybe when I come home today, you'll tell me more about our Dr. Bliskin," I said. "You haven't even told me what he looks like, just that he looks the same."

"Oh, as I said, you'll meet him yourself before he attends the Davenport dinner."

She rose to make herself some breakfast. I knew when my mother was avoiding me. She actually looked a little frightened of how I was studying her and the questions I was asking. She certainly avoided my eyes. I was tired of what she would call "skirting the issue."

"So . . . am I going to finally meet my father?" I asked.

She spun around. "What?"

"It would help to know that ahead of time."

"No."

"No it wouldn't help, or no I'm not meeting my father?"

"You're not meeting your father," she said. "He's a father to triplets. That's enough fathering for him, maybe for any man," she added, and turned back to scrambling herself an egg.

I didn't believe her, but my mother had a way of not telling me the truth or the whole truth and yet not sounding like she was telling a lie. She was too careful about how she composed her words. I hadn't meant that I wanted him to assume the role of my father, and she knew that, but she wasn't going to talk to me about any of this right now.

"Okay, then," I said, rising. "I'll get my things and go meet the bus."

"Well, I do hope you'll have a better day," she said, then kissed me on the forehead, brushed back my hair, and went off through the tunnel of Wyndemere to work.

This time, when I went out to the bus stop, Bea Davenport did not escort Ryder and Sam to the limousine. Parker was standing at the car and waiting for them. He smiled and nodded at me, and I smiled back. When I reached the bus stop, I did not turn when Ryder and Sam came out, until I heard them get into the vehicle. I watched it pull away. For a moment, it felt like nothing different had occurred. I had never gone to the prom, Paul Gabriel had not gotten us all into trouble, there was no gossip at school with police investigating, and most of all, Ryder had not come to my bedroom and been loving the way a real boyfriend would be. It was all some fantasy, and now it was gone as quickly as a dream usually flees when you open your eyes in the morning. You might remember this or that, but by the time you're into your day, it's dwindled to an image or two. Reality has thrown cold water on it all.

When I arrived at school, this feeling was reinforced. Little was being said about the prom or the incidents after it. Everyone was talking more about the coming end of the school year, summer plans, and, of course, the dreaded finals we'd all face. The baseball season was going to conclude soon, too. The boys were talking about their usual subjects. I heard no mention of Paul or Barry. In fact, by lunch, I hadn't heard one word about the prom, and certainly no one talked about my being chosen prom queen now. My girlfriends and others were not even whispering behind my back. I was truly yesterday's news.

At times, I felt invisible, forgotten. I almost wished someone would ask me something about the investigation, but the truth was that the scandal was apparently over. The police had arrested whom they wanted. Some of the others who had taken Barry's X were now breathing sighs of relief and probably didn't want the subject mentioned. They were incidental. They were given a warning, a warning they shrugged off. I wondered if anyone had learned anything at all from what had happened. It was almost as if it had happened at some other school. Certainly, Alison Reuben no longer shared anything with me. None of my girlfriends was even slightly envious of my relationship with one of the prettiest and most popular girls in the school anymore. That relationship had been short-lived, and, frankly, now I didn't care.

It was as if the clock had been turned back, not by an hour as it was during Daylight Savings Time in the fall but by days, if not weeks. But there were subtle changes around me. When I asked a question of someone, she answered in one or two words, and it didn't lead to any other conversation. I felt like I was looking in on the world and not part of it. Maybe everyone's desire to forget the bad things that had occurred meant they had to ignore me. I was too much of a reminder.

There was one dramatic and obvious change. Alison Reuben looked like she was developing a serious relationship with John Shepherd and was no longer spending time with him only to annoy Ryder. Ryder wasn't paying much attention to her anyway, nor was he paying any additional attention to me. Although I knew it was how we had planned we should behave for now, it still saddened me. Why couldn't we take a big leap forward together? Why couldn't we be defiant? Why couldn't I be his girlfriend and be with him every opportunity we had to be together in school? Why couldn't we be open about the new and more mature way we felt about each other?

Of course, I knew the answer, knew how quickly Bea Davenport would pounce and make life miserable for us both and my mother as well. It would be selfish of me to cause her any more trouble, and whatever poor opinion Dr. Davenport had of me would only be reinforced. The "Berlin Wall" between Ryder and me at Wyndemere would grow ten feet higher.

Of course, it was something Ryder realized as well, and that was why he was being careful, but he was too good at it, good at ignoring me, I thought sadly. Why was I having so much more trouble keeping my eyes off him? He had yet to throw a smile my way, let alone say anything to me. Maybe he had woken up this morning and had decided he'd be better off letting things return to the way they were. Once we had shared some of our youth, but afterward we were forced to be strangers living far apart in the area's biggest mansion, a mansion big enough to house two different worlds, one for the privileged posh and one for my mother and me. For all I knew, his father had given him another lecture this morning, and he had made promises, promises that didn't include me or, more to the point, excluded me.

Weighed down with these depressing thoughts, I was dragging myself through the day and barely paying attention in class. When the bell rang to end the day, I gathered my things lethargically and drifted out like someone hypnotized to get on the school bus. The usual pattern to our lives had returned. I was back in the allotted groove carved for me the day I was born to an unwed woman.

Ryder was heading for one of his final baseball

practices, but he paused ahead of me and waited for me to reach him. I didn't rush to join him. I was afraid of what he was about to tell me: that he had made a mistake coming to my room and encouraging my affections for him. He would say he didn't know what he had been thinking. A loving relationship between us was really impossible. *Sorry*.

"Hey." He looked around to be sure no one was within hearing range. Then he smiled. "I'll call you after dinner tonight and tell you about Dr. Bliskin," he said instead. "And don't forget about Saturday," he added. "Rain or shine."

I was speechless. The smile hidden all day inside of me burst out. I trembled with glee and watched him rush off. Buoyed by his words, I hurried out to the bus with renewed energy.

I remembered that Dr. Bliskin supposedly was coming to see me. I was very eager to see him, to hear what he had to say. Maybe he would confess, despite what my mother had said. So much darkness could be washed away in moments. I wondered what was happening now between him and my mother. Had they spent any more private time together during the day? Had they made promises to each other, maybe planned a new life for us? She had been out all night with him. It had to have meant something.

When the school bus pulled up to my stop, I saw a car I had never seen before parked in front of the mansion. Now that it was possible that I would meet the man who obviously had excited my mother in ways I had not seen before, I was quite nervous. I walked slowly to our entrance. The sky was mostly clear, with only a puff of a cloud here and there, something when I was a little girl my mother told me was God's breath. It felt even warmer than it had been yesterday. It was a good day to be happy. Would I be?

Just as I was about to open the door, I saw them.

They were walking side by side, my mother and this man, obviously coming back from the lake. They walked with their heads down, my mother's arms folded under her breasts and him keeping his arms behind his back, sauntering along like a college professor or something. My mother stopped when she raised her head and saw me looking their way. She waved. I went into the house, dropped my books on my desk, and then checked the way I looked. My hair, once captured in a beautiful style for the prom, looked scruffy. I ran a brush through it and then decided to put on some lipstick. I heard them enter the house. My mother called to me.

I came out of my room slowly. Dr. Bliskin and my mother were standing in the kitchen waiting for me. He wore a light-gray sports jacket and a pair of jeans with black sneakers. My mother must have been right about him not changing much, because he looked younger than I had anticipated. His dark-brown hair was a little longer and more styled than Dr. Davenport's hair. There were no gray strands, either. He looked to be about six feet tall and fit, with broad shoulders.

I scanned his face, searching for any features that resembled my own. He had a darker complexion and hazel-brown eyes. Unlike Dr. Davenport's, his face was not as well chiseled. His cheeks were fuller and his forehead wider, but he had a strong-looking mouth and a firm jaw. The bridge of his nose resembled mine, just a trifle wide. I liked his smile. It looked authentic, like the smile of someone who was really happy to see me.

"Wow," he said. "How beautiful she turned out to be."

"Fern, this is Dr. Bliskin, the man who brought you into this world," my mother said.

I looked at her, surprised. Was she telling me this was indeed my father?

He laughed. "I assisted, but your mother had most to do with it," he said.

"Can you say hello? You're usually so talkative that we have to raise our hands to get to speak," my mother teased.

"I am not. Sorry," I said, turning to him. "Hi."

"All right, no small talk," he said firmly. "I want to hear all about you. Your mother was telling me you were chosen prom queen this year."

I looked at her, surprised again. How much did she tell him?

"Yes. I never expected it."

"Modesty in a woman is quite unusual," he joked.

"Say men," my mother responded.

It was easy to see there was more than merely a friendship between them. Their story was surely fascinating, I thought. After years and years, they were together as if they never had parted.

"How about a cool drink?" my mother offered him.

"Just some water, please. So, Fern," he said, sitting at the table and nodding at the seat across from him, "tell me a little about yourself."

"What do you want to know?"

I sat. My mother gave him his water and offered me some. I shook my head, and she sat, too.

"For starters, what interests you? In school, that is. What subject?"

"I like English, literature. Some things in science fascinate me. I'm not blown away by math, but I like it when I solve a particularly difficult problem."

He nodded, his eyes reflecting his surprise and appreciation. Maybe I was wishing so hard for it that I made it appear, but I was sure I saw a deeper warmth in those eyes.

"Your mother said you were a very good student. What besides subjects do you like at school? Any extracurricular activities?" he asked. He had a strong, resonant, deep voice, a voice that, like Dr. Davenport's, expressed authority.

"I was in a play last year. And I enjoy field hockey."

"At least you don't have her into cricket," he told my mother.

She laughed. "I doubt she'd even know how it's played. I was never a big fan. My father was, and my older sister likes it more than I do. Fern has a very good singing voice. She's in chorus. She forgot to mention that."

"Makes sense, knowing who her mother is."

"Was," my mother said.

"You like the idea of becoming a singer?" he asked me.

"My mother's scared me away from it," I said, and he laughed.

"I never did any such thing," she protested. "I simply described how difficult it was and my failed efforts."

"You have to test things for yourself, Fern. Life is full of trials and errors. Discouragement is too easy to swallow," Dr. Bliskin said. I was sure he was being as serious as he was when he prescribed treatments or behavior to help his patients heal. "Never let someone else's successes or defeats determine your own. People your age are always comparing themselves to each other. Look for what's different in you, whatever sets you aside."

" 'To thine own self be true,' " my mother said. "She can recite it better than Helen Mirren."

"That so?" He sat back, looking more relaxed and informal now. "Are you sweet on the boy who took you to the prom?"

I looked at my mother. She hadn't told him the grisly details? "No," I said. I turned back to my mother. Did she expect me to tell him everything? "You didn't tell him about after the prom?"

"I thought you should," she said. "Dr. Bliskin might have some good advice for you going forward. As I told you, he's one of those rare doctors who treats patients, not illnesses."

"Your mother should work for a public relations firm." He leaned forward. "Fill me in," he said. "What happened after the prom?"

I began. The thing about talking to him was that it felt easy. It was truly as though I had known him and he had known me for some time. I didn't know whether it was his doctor's training and experience or what, but he seemed very sincere.

"I'm sorry this happened on what your mother tells me was your first really serious date. Drug overdoses are a major problem. I've even had experiences like that with my own friends," he said, "and at medical school."

"Really?"

"Yes, there were some who thought it cool to get high. They had that foolish self-confidence. Everyone's body reacts differently to drugs. One or two got into serious trouble and were thrown out of school. They wouldn't have made good doctors anyway. I think you're handling the situation well. You did what you had to do, and it's out of your hands now. Your mother's right. Let things settle down, and eventually put it behind you. There are brighter days ahead."

"I think things have already settled down," I said. "At least, it seemed that way today."

"Good."

"Where do you live now?" I asked. I thought it was my turn to be inquisitive.

He told me, and he told me about his daughters and where they were going to college and what they each thought they would pursue.

"Pamela is the dramatic one. She's been on a stage since she was two, so I'm not surprised she's going into the dramatic arts." He looked at my mother. "You predicted that, Emma, remember?"

"Yes, you could see the way she rolled her eyes and postured even at four. She was also a good mimic, as I recall, second nature to a good actor."

"Oh, she wanted your accent in the worst way," he said. "She'd go around the house saying things like 'Cheers' and 'Brilliant.' She does concentrate on her speech. She'd love talking to you, Fern.

Your mother's rubbed off, quite clearly. In every way," he added, glancing at her. Then he looked at his watch. "Oh, I guess Harrison's home by now. There was no one in Wyndemere when I arrived. Bea was somewhere. I'd better go make my presence known," he said, rising.

"Go around to the front," my mother said. "I'll walk you to the entrance."

"Okay. Well, I'm staying overnight," he told me, "so maybe I'll catch you tomorrow before you head for school."

"Then where are you going?"

"I'm going home," he said. He looked at my mother. She averted his glance and took his empty water glass to the sink. "It's really been a pleasure to meet you, Fern. I hope I can see you once more before I go."

"I'm here all night," I said deliberately.

"Yes, well, I have to catch up with the Davenports. Morning is more possible, perhaps. You'll be asleep for sure when dinner and after-dinner drinks are over."

I shrugged. "Nothing's for sure," I said. "Nice meeting you, too," I added, doing a terrible job of hiding my disappointment.

I returned to my bedroom and heard them leave. I flopped onto my bed.

If he was my father, why couldn't he just come out and say it, say he was sorry or something? Was he waiting for me to come right out and ask. *Excuse me, but I was wondering, are you my father?*

Don't show me how interested you are in what I've become and what I want to do with my life and then just get in your car tomorrow and return to your family. Was this a guilt trip? Did he feel better about himself now? He'd shown some interest in me so everything was all right?

Forget about growing up in a shadow, Fern. Forget about how you've been viewed and treated and how hard it's been for you to find acceptance. Forget that you live with your mother in the "dungeon" portion of this mansion, socked away to be forgotten or, as your mother would say, "out from under anyone's feet."

Thank you for your visit and your burning desire to say good-bye in the morning, Dr. Bliskin. I'll stay up all night in anticipation.

I lay there sulking around with these thoughts until I heard my mother return, and then I leaped up. Time to kill a secret, I thought. I was in the mood for it.

"Why did you give me that answer when I asked if he was my father? Why don't you tell me the truth now? I'm old enough. I think I've heard worse things lately and survived. Well?" I said.

She stood there looking at me as if I had gone mad. Instead of answering, she began to fiddle with things in the kitchen, taking out a pan. "I have a very nice piece of salmon to prepare for you tonight."

"Are you kidding? I know you were out all night, Mummy. I saw that you were still in your dress this morning. Where were you? You're not just friends. You were his lover, weren't you? I'd have to be deaf, dumb, and blind not to see there's something between you."

She paused. "Yes, we were lovers," she confessed. She thought a moment and then sat at the table. "It happened after Ryder was born. He was coming here to check on him more than usual, certainly more than necessary, and we simply began to spend more time with each other."

"He was married, though."

"Yes, he was married and had his children, but there was something missing in his life."

"What?"

"Passion," she said, looking up at me. "Very often, people have it for a short period with each other and mistake it for something that will last. They get married too quickly, perhaps. Children come, work takes up more and more of your life, and pretty soon you forget what you're missing. Then something rekindles it, and you realize this is what you need, what you've missed, and you take the leap.

"It wasn't only him, however. I missed it, too. Truthfully, I never was lucky enough to experience it the way it should be, and so when he came along and we began to read each other's feelings accurately, it happened.

"But the responsibilities and burdens were planted in his life, and I wasn't going to ask him to hurt so many just to please myself. In some ways, it was more difficult a parting than the parting I had with my family," she said.

"Is he my father?"

"It doesn't do you any good to hear that he is, Fern. He's as much of a stranger to you as anyone who comes into your life for a few minutes and goes away forever. A father is someone who accepts responsibilities. Any healthy man can impregnate a woman, but I've never thought of such a man in terms of being a father. I guess I've felt that way ever since I was a surrogate mother. Biology is not parenthood. Sperm doesn't make someone a father. Not in my book," she said firmly.

I stared at her a moment and then turned and went to my room. Maybe she was right. Darkness was too strong in Wyndemere. It would not be defeated easily. People are too easily forgotten here. The shadows overtake them, even the memory of them. Look at what happened to the little girl Holly, Dr. Davenport's sister. How cruel her parents were to erase her existence entirely, simply to ease their own sorrow. Dr. Davenport's first wife was reduced to a framed picture in his office and some clothing in the attic. Ryder knew little more about her than I did about my real father. When I gave it deeper thought, I realized that everyone was lonely in Wyndemere. My mother had me, but she was still lonely. She had lost someone, someone perhaps she never really had, but still, it was the idea of him that was gone. His short visit only intensified the pain for her. That was really why I walked away from her just now and didn't keep demanding an answer. I couldn't look at what she was feeling. I could see it in her eyes, and it was like a sword through the heart.

Dr. Bliskin was seated at the kitchen table when I came out for breakfast in the morning. I had fallen asleep early and slept through the night. If he had visited my mother after the Davenport dinner, I hadn't heard anything, certainly not enough to wake me. When I saw him sitting there in his light-blue shirt and jeans, the shirt collar open, he looked relaxed but like someone who had been there a while. Had he sneaked into her bedroom the way Ryder had sneaked into mine?

My mother sat beside him. She didn't look upset about his leaving. If anything, she looked younger, energetic, as though whatever there was deep inside her to brighten her day, her view of the world and herself had been lit again, if only for a little while. I felt both happy and sad for her. When you had something as precious as this, wasn't it more difficult to visit with the feelings and then put them back to sleep? But she did love quoting Alfred Lord Tennyson's "'Tis better to have loved and lost than never to have loved at all."

"Morning," Dr. Bliskin said. "I see you're one of those young ladies who look good regardless of the time of day."

My mother smiled at what I imagined was a comical look on my face. The last thing I thought about myself in the morning was that I looked good. It took a while for sleep to evaporate from my eyes, and I had yet to brush my hair. Who expected someone besides Mr. Stark to be sitting here this early?

"I thought doctors were supposed to tell the truth," I said, and took out some juice.

He laughed. "Yes, she's your daughter, Emma."

"I'm a regular clone," I said dryly.

"Would you like some porridge today, Fern? It's still hot. I made some for Dr. Bliskin and myself."

"I'm not that hungry. I'll just have some toast and cheese," I said, and went to make it.

Both were quiet, watching me. Had they talked it over? Was this the moment?

"Well, I'd better get myself moving," Dr. Bliskin said. He rose. "Long trip ahead."

"I'll walk you out," my mother said.

"It's been a real pleasure meeting you, Fern,

and seeing what a beautiful and intelligent young lady you've become. I wish you well, and I'm confident you're going to do great things. Your mother is very proud of you and for good reason."

"Thank you," I said, and turned my back on him. I held my breath, anticipating something, anything. Instead, I heard the door opening and then closing. The silence was thunderous. I didn't even realize that I had started to cry.

By the time my mother returned, I had eaten what I could and gotten ready for school.

"Is he ever coming here again?" I asked her while she cleared the table.

"I don't think so," she said.

I felt like saying a lot of things, but I said nothing and left.

The rest of our week was uneventful. Some of the girls began to talk to me as much as they had previously, but no one invited me to do anything socially with her. I planted my face in my books and did my homework. I even began to create some study guides for my finals. My mother worked as hard as ever, too. Ryder kept his distance, especially in Wyndemere. We spoke on the phone at night. He was holding his ground, even though his getting a car of his own was slipping away. He said his dinners with his father, Bea, and Sam were worse than ever, the only bright spot being when Bea complained more vigorously and he could see his father losing patience, even snapping back at her occasionally.

"Wyndemere has become a minefield," he said. "I come out of my room only to eat dinner. Bea refuses to talk to me, which is great. She even avoids looking at me. I feel sorry for Sam, though. Her mother has threatened her with severe punishment if she merely turns toward the hall to your rooms. Fortunately, she's going to an overnight birthday party Saturday. Last night after dinner, my father asked me if I had anything to say. I knew he meant for me to apologize to Bea. She sat there looking so satisfied with herself. I felt like puking up what I ate."

"What did you say?"

"I said I thought the meat loaf was better than usual. You could have cut through steel with my father's glare. He rose and left the table without speaking, and Bea said she had never met a more ungrateful person than me. I introduced her to herself, and she rushed out, probably to tell my father. Sam looked terrified. I had to help her with her homework to make her feel better."

"Are you sure you're handling it the right way, Ryder?"

"The only way," he replied. "Saturday, meet me at the dock at two. It's better if we go there separately, just in case."

"Okay," I said.

At the moment, it was the only thing I had to look forward to, but I couldn't smother the feeling that somehow it would make things worse for both of us.

14

FOR A WHILE Saturday morning, I thought it was going to rain and rain hard, but winds swirled the clouds, and by midday, there were some patches of blue. My mother told me the Davenports were having a dinner party and she would have a lot to do all day. We hadn't done much with each other during the remainder of the week except eat dinner. I wasn't very talkative at the table. I did my chores and immediately went into my room and closed the door. I knew I was being a sullen brat, but I couldn't help it. I supposed that in some ways, I was doing just what Ryder was doing, alienating the one person who cared the most about me, but, like him, I couldn't help myself. I felt like I had a half dozen Bunsen burners inside me, each boiling another mixture of anger and frustration.

Time moved so slowly through Saturday morning. I tried to distract myself by doing as much of my homework as I could, but by lunchtime, my mother could see I was quite fidgety. I was looking at the clock more than I was looking at her.

"What are you going to do with the rest of your day?" she asked.

Of course, I didn't want to mention Ryder. "Just relax, take a walk."

"Oh, if I can break away, maybe—"

"That's all right. I want to be alone," I said quickly, maybe too quickly.

She fixed her gaze on me. I could throw up walls of stone, and my mother could still see through to my heart. Her eyes darkened with suspicion. I looked away.

"Be careful, Fern," she said. "Don't get yourself in between Ryder and his parents."

"He'll never call Bea his parent, Mummy."

She shook her head. "His father will never approve of his disrespecting her. He'd better find a middle ground."

After she returned to the main house, I felt bad about lying, but right now there was nothing more important to me than being with Ryder. I put on a pair of blue denim shorts and a white tank top and looked at myself. In a burst of daring, I pulled off the top, took off my bra, and put the top on again. My breasts were perky, my nipples erect and clearly outlined against the light cotton material. My mother would be, as she would say, "gob-smacked" if she saw me go out like this. I reached into my closet and took out my floral kimono. It would work to hide my daring look if she happened to see me leave.

When I stepped out, I realized it was a little cooler than I had anticipated. The patches of blue I had seen this morning were shrinking, some no more than the size of a basketball. Nevertheless, I didn't go back inside to get something warmer to wear. There was a ray of sunshine on the lake. To me, it was an invitation, an assurance all would be well. I was wearing a pair of running shoes without socks. I wanted to jog down to the dock, but I was afraid someone was watching, perhaps my mother gazing out a window, and would wonder why I was hurrying there. Instead, I tried to look pensive, my head down, walking slowly and looking more like I was drifting with my thoughts and not planning anything specific.

When I reached the dock, I turned back to the house. No one was following. Relieved, I sat on the side where one of the two rowboats was tied and dangled my legs over the water. The lake was a bit more active than usual, tiny waves slapping the dock posts and making the rowboats bob. I checked my watch. It was a little after two, yet when I looked back, I did not see Ryder coming.

Something had stopped him, I thought. We were not going to have the afternoon together that we had hoped to have after all. Maybe his father didn't go to work and was home giving him another lecture. Maybe he was afraid of the not-so-promising weather, even though he had said, "Rain or shine." I knew that if he didn't come, I'd be miserable for the rest of the day and especially the night. No one had invited me to anything; no one was even calling.

I fell into such deep despondent thought that I didn't know how much time had passed. Suddenly, I heard Ryder say, "Be careful you don't fall in."

I spun around. It was as if the sun had washed away every dark cloud above us. He was standing there in a pair of black shorts, a Hillsborough T-shirt, and sneakers. He wore one of his baseball caps. I leaped to my feet, and he laughed at my enthusiasm.

"I thought you might not be coming," I said.

"My father came home for something in his office. I wanted to wait until he left again, just in case he called for me to be sure I hadn't gone anywhere. Bea's been hovering around me more than usual, too. She's like a happy jailer now, and Sam was looking to see what I was doing. I had to sneak away from her as well."

He went to the first rowboat and stepped in.

"This one has a blanket in it," he said, and

pulled it out from under the middle bench seat. He reached up for me. I took his hand and gingerly stepped down, losing my balance almost immediately and falling completely into his arms. We both wobbled.

"Sorry."

He held me closely and smiled. "You've lost your sea legs. When we were little, we had no problem in the rowboats or my father's speedboat." He kissed the tip of my nose and then helped me sit.

I watched him untie the boat and then attach the oars and push off from the dock. I looked back at the mansion. No one had come out and seen us.

"We're fine," he said, seeing my concern. "They're preparing the house for some sort of big dinner party with members of the hospital committee and some heavy donors. Bea wants every smudge on every wall and every floor wiped away. She had your mother rushing about and checking every corner and making sure the silverware is polished. It's as if the president was coming or something. Actually, she just likes ordering everyone to do things. Wait until she gets to hell and tries to tell the devil what to do."

He fell into a smooth, regular rhythm of rowing, the muscles straining in his shoulders and neck.

"I'll help row if you want."

"What? And ruin my chance of getting blisters? No way."

"Where are we going?"

He looked behind him. "I thought it would be fun to go to Dead Man's Hole. Remember that cavelike indentation on the Massachusetts far shore where the land rises sharply?"

"Yes. Dead Man's Hole. How did it get that name?"

"I had read a pirate story and got the name from it. It's just wide and high enough for a rowboat to go half in, but it always looked bigger and more scary. Once when you were in the boat, too, and I asked to go there, you started to cry."

"You remember that?"

"Vaguely. No, vividly. You're not going to be scared today, are you?"

"Not if you're with me."

"I'm not exactly going anywhere else," he said.

The sun broke out between two large, gray clouds and immediately warmed us. It felt very special; it felt like we had been spotted and blessed. I sat back, opening my kimono.

Ryder's eyes seem to feast on what he saw. "Maybe we're both a little underdressed now that we're out here."

"I'm okay."

"If you get cold, use that blanket," he said. "I'll get warm rowing."

He looked back and adjusted our direction a bit and then rowed harder. I closed my eyes to bask in what sunshine we had. For the first time in days, I felt relaxed and very, very happy. I knew he was staring at me.

"So what did you think of Dr. Bliskin?" he asked.

I sat up. "I found out for sure that he was my mother's lover."

"Really? He did mention her name often during our dinner. He cheated on his wife?"

"Apparently."

"Why didn't he divorce her and marry your mother?"

"Not in his DNA."

"What?" He smiled.

"He couldn't deny his obligations, responsibilities. He's like your father. He buries his unhappiness in his work. At least, that's what my mother thinks."

"She said that?"

"In so many words, yes."

"She's certainly right about my father. I don't know if I could smother true love with hard work. Seems to me it has to affect your abilities somehow. People can get pretty messed up, no matter how intelligent they are."

"Yes," I said. "They can."

He paused.

"Do you want me to row a little?" I asked.

"No. I just want you to sit there and let me look at you," he said.

The boat bobbed. He rose and carefully sat at my feet. Then he pulled up the blanket and cast it out so he could drop it over both of us. I slipped down beside him. He kissed me softly on the lips and brushed back some strands of my hair.

"Where have you been all my life?" he joked.

"Downstairs in the dungeon section."

He laughed and stretched out so he could look up. I did the same. We watched a flock of sparrows maneuver with perfect precision and go west. Then he turned, leaned over, and kissed me softly.

"Can you imagine Bea's face if she saw us?"

"You're not doing it just to get back at her, are you?" I asked.

"Hell, no. But I won't deny that the possibility of her having enough heart palpitations to require my father to perform an immediate bypass would be quite neat."

"Forget about her. Forget about everyone," I said.

He smiled. "Easily." He looked away and then at me again. "I can tell you this. I'm not going to continue sneaking around to see you whenever I want to see you."

"Why not?"

"Because I'm going to come right in to see you whenever I want to, and you're coming to see me as well. You're coming to eat dinners and lunches with me and Sam, and you're coming to my room whenever you want to, and if she doesn't like it, too bad. My father can take away all my privileges. I know. I'll refuse to go to school. I'll even refuse to eat."

"You would do all that?"

"Not that I would. I will. It's a promise," he said. "Get used to it."

I smiled. "I'm used to it already."

He kissed me again and this time reached under my tank top to caress my breast. I lifted myself enough for him to pull it up and over my head and arms. Then he kissed and licked my nipples and lowered his head to kiss down to my stomach.

"Are you cold?"

"No," I said.

I wasn't. The heat from my heart was traveling over every nerve in my body, enveloping me in a delightful warmth and stirring me in ways unlike any fantasy I ever had. I pressed his shoulders, holding him tightly, and opened my legs for him to move between them. He unbuttoned the top button of my shorts and then brought his lips to every newly exposed inch of my body. I could hear his heavy breath. I could hear my heart pounding. When he drew down even closer, I leaned back, my hands relaxing, every iota of resistance crumbling.

Good-bye, virgin Fern, I thought. Good-bye

to wondering and dreaming, to questioning and doubting. Good-bye to childhood and innocence. Good-bye to silly little looks and giggles, dramatic shocked expressions, and terrifying possibilities making you gasp and retreat. Good riddance to those girls who were condescending and irritating with their worldly knowledge of sex and femininity, trying to keep you like a child in a pen of adolescence, warning you that you couldn't understand, that you might never understand what they knew.

Hello to love like I imagined it, welcoming what would be my lifelong memory, my moments to return to whenever I was alone, even when I was old and gray. I would always be here. And what made it more special for me than it was for the so-called worldly girls who had treated it as no big thing, more of an initiation into some club of arrogance that they believed put them on an equal footing with any boy, was that I was entering this maturity through a portal of love and not simply lust.

"Are you okay?" he whispered, probably because I was so quiet.

"Yes," I said. *Oh, yes,* I thought. *I'm more than okay.*

He was lowering my shorts.

And then he stopped.

At first, I thought the wind simply had lifted the surface of the lake and splashed us, but it didn't stop. I opened my eyes, and we both turned. We could see the rainfall coming toward us, hard and heavy. The wind gusted and wrapped us in the cold drops, colder than the lake itself. I pulled up my shorts, and Ryder rushed back to the bench to grab the oars. He started to row hard and fast. I quickly put on my tank top and wrapped my kimono around myself.

"Shove the blanket under the bench," he ordered. "So it stays dry. We might need it later."

I did so quickly. He rowed harder. I looked back. We were well past halfway from the dock.

"Where are you going?" I called, thinking maybe we should turn around.

"Your favorite spot. Dead Man's Hole. We can wait it out."

He turned the boat a little, and we lurched forward. The rain was like sheets of water now. It actually created small puddles on the bottom of the boat. I embraced myself. It was colder and colder. Minutes later, Ryder expertly turned and maneuvered us into the rise at the beachside and almost three-fourths of the rowboat was in shelter. I moved closer to him, and we embraced.

He got up quickly then and pulled out the blanket. It was damp but not soaked. He wrapped it around us, and we sat there watching the rain swirl, drops still reaching us because of the wind. The far end of the boat was filling with them.

"One of our famous summer downpours, a month or so early. I didn't think it would get this bad. Stupid," Ryder said.

"It happened so fast."

"Usually does. Speaking of being smart and stupid, we weren't exactly brilliantly prepared for it," he said. "Look at how we dressed."

The boat rocked. He reached out to grab some wild bushes to keep the boat from slipping out from under our feeble protection. The sky grew darker as gray clouds took on the look of anger, charcoaled and burnt. We saw some lightning and heard the thunder getting closer.

"We'll be all right," Ryder said. It sounded more like a prayer.

With his right hand, he held me tighter.

What really brought us to this place? I wondered. Was it really a desire to be loving, or was it a desire to escape from who we were?

"Take the oar on your left, and just push it up against the top of the cave to help keep the boat from slipping out. Think you can do that?"

"Yes."

I hurried to. The oar was heavier than I had thought, however, and it was not easy lifting it and holding it firmly against the dark earth above. The rocking of the boat made it even more difficult, and a few times I almost lost my balance and had to put the oar on the boat before trying again.

"Let's switch jobs," Ryder said, seeing how I was struggling. "You sit over here, and just hold on to the branch. Careful, though," he said, showing me his palm. He had been holding a rough area on the bush, and it had cut through his skin.

"Oh, Ryder."

He dipped it into the water quickly and shook his palm. "I'll be fine."

I handed him the oar and moved forward to take hold of the bush. It hurt, but I didn't let go. He pushed hard on the oar. Maybe it was the humidity and the rain being swept in by the wind, but some of the earth above crumbled beneath the oar and the pressure he was exerting. It dropped into the boat, and he had to pull the oar farther back.

"Maybe we should just try to row back, Ryder!" I shouted. The rain was echoing around us. It felt more as if we were in a tunnel than in a cave.

He looked out and shook his head. "Coming down too hard yet. We'll be bailing out water with our hands all the way, and I'd hate to think what would happen if we turned over or something."

I didn't know if I was crying out of fear or if it was the rain on my face.

"I guess for A-plus students, we are pretty stupid," he said, smiling. "Love blinds you."

I smiled. At the moment, I thought it was all worth it to hear him say that, even if he was only trying to be funny to make me feel better.

There was no letup in the rainfall for what seemed like hours. At one point, it did lessen, and we both relaxed a bit.

"Should we try now?" I asked.

There was another streak of lightning and a louder boom.

"It will take us a half hour, probably closer to an hour at this part of the lake with the wind blowing against us. I think we should wait a little longer, Fern. Maybe it will become a steady but much lighter rainfall. Not pleasant but safer," he said. "Try to hold on."

I nodded. Another piece of the cave roof crumbled, and again he had to adjust the oar. The boat slipped a little farther forward. The water in it was a good inch deep. He reached down with his other hand and began scooping some out, but it was very ineffective and awkward for him. The rain that was blowing in on us had soaked our blanket, too. Now I was shivering.

"Stupid," he said, visibly angry at himself. "I'm simply stupid."

"What time is it?"

He leaned over to read his watch. It was on the

arm he was using to hold the oar against the inside of the cave. "Four twenty."

"My mother might be looking for me," I said. "I told her I was going for a walk."

He nodded. "I'm sure Sam's reported me gone, too." He looked out and nodded. "Okay. I think we'd better risk it. It's getting darker with this cloud cover. Use my shoes. I have a bigger foot," he said, taking them off, "to scoop out water as we go. These rowboats aren't exactly new."

I nodded. I couldn't remember being more terrified, but there was no time to think about it now.

He lowered the oar and quickly put it into the oarlock on the boat. "Ready?"

"No, but I'll never be," I said.

He laughed at that, and then he pushed gently on the oars, and we were back out on the lake, fully exposed to the rain.

As we pulled away, the rain seemed to lighten. I began to scoop out as much water as I could, using both my hands, with one of his shoes in each. He rowed hard, so hard that the rowboat bounced on the water. Then the rain increased again. There was more lightning and thunder, and the wind grew stronger. He was right about its direction. It was blowing against us, obviously making the rowing harder and harder for Ryder. At one point, with the water rising in the boat, I thought we should stop and turn back to the little cave. Ryder shook his head and rowed. When we were about halfway across, I looked toward the dock.

"Mr. Stark and Parker are on the dock!" I shouted.

Ryder turned to look. They were both holding umbrellas and waving at us.

"Good. They have umbrellas. I'd hate to get wet," Ryder joked.

He rowed harder, but I could see he was weakening. The strain in his neck and shoulders was showing as his strokes became slower, an oar sometimes completely missing the water. I could feel his panic.

"I can row!" I cried. "I'll take a turn."

He shook his head. "You just keep bailing out."

A bolt of lightning seemed to hit the lake. We both jumped on our seats. The boom was so loud, too. Ryder paused. He looked back at the dock and shook his head.

"Why don't they get your father's boat going and come get us?" I asked.

"I think something's wrong with it. He hasn't used it for so long. He's neglected repairs."

"Parker and Mr. Stark are getting into the other rowboat!" I shouted.

Ryder looked back. "Good. Let's keep getting closer and make it faster for them to reach us."

He rowed and rowed. He was so tired. I could see the panic now in his face. When he had paused,

I saw the blisters on his palms. I began to shout at Mr. Stark and Parker, urging them to get to us faster, but I didn't think they could hear us. Ryder put another surge of energy into his oars, and then, for some reason, the one on the left came out of its oarlock. Something had broken on it. The thrust he had created with his extra effort carried him forward, and he fell on his left knee.

"Ryder!"

He looked at me and then stood and began to see what he could do about the oar. The boat rocked harder, and holding up the oar made him lose his balance. He fell to his left. I lunged to grab him, but he went over the side of the boat, still holding the oar. When he hit the water, it washed over him quickly. I could see he had lost his breath. I screamed and screamed when he went under. When he came up, he was choking and gasping. The oar was too far away for him to grab. Instead, he reached for the side of the boat. I was leaning over, too, holding out my hand, but he was too far, and the boat, moved by the wind, was drifting away from him.

I looked up desperately toward Parker and Mr. Stark.

"Help!" I screamed.

Parker dove into the lake and began to swim toward us. Ryder bobbed and reached out. The rain was pounding, and the wind was relentless. I could barely see him. The boat rocked again, and I nearly fell over, too. Instead, I fell back hard. It knocked the breath out of me, and I scraped my back on the bench. When I struggled to my feet again, I no longer saw Ryder. The panic I felt turned my whole body to ice. I kept screaming and screaming.

Mr. Stark finally drew close enough, but it wasn't easy for him to get his boat close enough to ours. There was nothing else for me to do but leap into the lake. He held out an oar for me to grasp. I did, and he pulled me close enough to lift me out of the water and into his bobbing boat. I was crying so hard that my tears were competing with the rain running down my cheeks. Before I could ask anything, I saw Ryder rise at the side of the boat. His eyes were closed, and Parker had him around his waist. Mr. Stark moved quickly to hold him and pull him onto the boat. Then Parker boosted himself up and over the edge.

They had Ryder on his back. Parker immediately began trying to resuscitate him. With both hands on Ryder's chest, he began to push down, rest, push down. He kept doing it and then checking to see if Ryder was breathing. I was frozen on the bench. Mr. Stark had put his jacket over me. We both watched as Parker started again and again and then tilted Ryder's head back, lifted his chin, pinched his nose closed, and covered Ryder's mouth with his. He breathed into him and continued the chest compressions. There was a desperate and terrified look on Parker's face.

I think I was screaming. I'd never remember exactly.

Suddenly, Ryder coughed. Parker turned his head a bit, and Ryder vomited water. He was gasping. Parker turned and nodded at Mr. Stark, who immediately returned to the oars and began to turn the boat. Parker sat beside Ryder, keeping his head on his lap. I went to my knees and then tipped over onto my side, unconscious. When I awoke, I was in Mr. Stark's arms being carried toward the house like a baby.

"Ryder?" I said.

"There's an ambulance on the way," he said. "Let's get you inside and dry. Here comes your mother."

I turned slightly and saw her running toward us. Then I closed my eyes, too tired to cry, too tired to speak.

15

AFTER MR. STARK carried me into the house, my mother got me into a hot bath as quickly as she could. I was so exhausted that I felt as helpless as a baby. She left me there to soak for a while. I heard other people talking outside the bathroom. It sounded like Mr. Stark and Mrs. Marlene, but I couldn't make out any words. I kept my eyes closed and just lay there enjoying the feeling of warmth reaching deep into me and driving away the horrible shivers.

When she returned, she helped me out of the tub and began to dry me, rubbing so vigorously I thought she would peel off my skin. I didn't complain or offer any resistance. Talking seemed to require strength I had yet to regain. She was mumbling, though quite incoherently, under her breath. Maybe she was saying a prayer, or maybe she was expressing her anger. I kept my eyes closed and waited for her to finish. I felt her turn my hands over.

"Got to treat these bruise burns," she said. "And this scrape on your back. Anything else hurt?"

"No. Not hurt. Just aches."

"Where?"

"My legs, everywhere, I guess."

"What were you thinking? What were you both thinking?"

She opened the cabinet and took out the antiseptics, still mumbling. When she was finished, she helped me get into one of my warmer nightgowns. Then she helped me stand and guided me to my bedroom. Mr. Stark was standing in the kitchen sipping on a cup of tea.

"How's she doing?" he asked my mother.

"She's doing," she replied.

She helped me into my bed.

"How's Ryder?" I asked. She didn't answer me. "How is he?"

"They took him to the hospital. I don't know any more than that," she said.

She went out and minutes later returned with what I knew to be Mrs. Marlene's famous Irish hot toddy. It had tea and cinnamon, with a good dose of rum as well as some other secret ingredient

Mrs. Marlene would never reveal to anyone but my mother.

"Can we call the hospital and see how he is?"

"We'll call. We'll call. Sip this, now. Go on," my mother ordered.

I drank as much as I could, and she took the cup and placed it on my night table. She fixed my blankets firmly around me.

"Let me know how Ryder is," I said.

"I'll let you know. I'll let you know. Now, you get some rest," she told me.

"But Ryder," I said.

"You just rest," she said, the concern in her voice replaced with a sternness I wasn't used to hearing.

She left, and probably because of the hot toddy more than anything, I fell asleep quickly. I slept for hours and hours, and when I woke, I woke with a start and cried out. I immediately felt my mother's hand on my arm. I had no idea how long she had been sitting there watching me sleep, but it seemed like quite a while.

"There, now," she said. "It's all right."

It took me a moment to gather my thoughts. "What time is it?"

"It's late, Fern."

"How long have I been asleep?"

"Hours. It won't be long before morning."

"Morning? How's Ryder?" I asked.

"He's okay, but they are evaluating him to be sure there aren't any organ or brain complications."

"What? What's that mean?"

"Parker doesn't think he was under very long, but Dr. Davenport says there can be problems when the brain is deprived of oxygen."

"Mummy," I said, the tears quickly flooding my eyes. "Will he be all right? Can't you find out?"

"We'll know soon. Dr. Davenport's optimistic, just concerned and doing the proper protocol." Her expression changed to one full of suspicion. "Now, tell me why you were so underdressed, Fern."

"I didn't think it was going to rain like that. Neither of us did," I replied, even though I knew she meant why I was wearing no bra and only a flimsy-looking tank top.

She stared at me, looking right through my words.

"How close have you and Ryder become, Fern? I don't want to hear lies or changes of the subject, either."

I lay back on my pillow and looked up at the ceiling. "We're close," I said. "We've always been close, despite Bea Davenport and Dr. Davenport."

"I'm talking about now, Fern. Has Ryder been visiting you when I'm not here?"

I didn't reply.

"Fern, answer me."

"He's visited me, yes."

"At night?"

"Sometimes," I said. I looked at her. "Yes. I told you. We like each other. A lot."

"A lot? What's that mean?"

"We're not just friends, Mummy."

"What have you done?" she demanded.

"Nothing terrible," I said sharply. "I told you. We like each other. We're more girlfriend and boyfriend now. His girlfriend dumped him—and because of me, too!"

She was just staring at me.

"Don't look so surprised. Why can't we be boyfriend and girlfriend? I'm old enough to have a real boyfriend, aren't I? Is Bea Davenport going to run our lives forever? Don't you think it's time you stood up to her? Even stood up to Dr. Davenport? We've lived like the unholy unwashed in this mansion too long, too long for me, at least. She can't keep Ryder and me apart. The first thing I'm going to do when I'm able is walk through this house and come in the front door whenever I want. If you won't quit, then I'll make her fire you."

My outburst nearly exhausted me again. I closed my eyes and lay back. When I opened them, she was standing by my window with her back to me.

"I want to go see Ryder," I said. "Mr. Stark will take me."

She turned. "Mr. Stark is home, asleep. Besides, Dr. Davenport wants Ryder to rest for now," she said.

"I want to see him. He surely wants to see me, to see that I'm all right. I'm going. If Mr. Stark can't take me, I'll call a taxi."

"He'll take you. He'll take you," she said. "Later. You get some more rest first."

"I don't need any more rest. We both almost died. He didn't see that I was saved, too. He must be asking for me. I want to see how he is for myself. Can he remember anything? He must be thinking about me."

She nodded. "He is asking after you. Dr. Davenport told me," she said.

"So? Good. I'll go. I'm all right now. I'm just a little sore. I'll call a taxi. If he's sleeping, I want to be there when he wakes up. I can do it, Mummy. I'm all right."

"Yes," she said. "You're all right."

"Good, then I'm going."

I had started to get up when she surprised me and sat on my bed, putting her hand gently on my leg. "Wait," she said.

"For what?"

"The truth," she said. She looked reluctant, perhaps changing her mind.

I lay back. "What truth? Tell me."

She nodded and first took a deep breath. "I'm going to start at the beginning so you'll understand."

"Okay, but after you're finished, I'm going to the hospital."

"Yes, yes. Now, listen. Dr. Davenport was very much in love with his first wife. Like everyone else, when I first came here to carry Ryder and deliver him, I thought Dr. Davenport had married her because everyone expected he would. According to the gossip, he was pressured by his parents."

"You told me that. You said it was an arranged marriage."

"Well, it was and it wasn't. Dr. Davenport's not a man who shows his emotions easily or even clearly. I'm not going to psychoanalyze him and tell you why that is. It's just his personality, a personality that probably works well with the career he chose for himself. I'm sure his parents and the way they treated him had a lot to do with the way he became."

"His parents never sounded very nice to me. Especially what they did after Holly died."

"No, they were not your typical loving mother and father. Both were quite selfish. However," she said, putting her hands on her lap and looking down, "Dr. Davenport didn't marry Samantha Avery only because that was what they wanted. He truly loved her, and he took her death very, very hard. Before the accident, I had begun to see how close they really were to each other. When you're part of people's lives the way I was, carrying their child, you witness things other people don't. I saw the affection between them, how protective of her he was. He worshipped her as much as he could. She was practically the only person who could make him laugh or let his guard down."

"Is that the truth you wanted to tell me?" I asked, disappointed. What did I really care how much Dr. Davenport had loved his wife? Why did it matter to me, to us?

"No. There's much more. About then, after Samantha Davenport's deadly accident, I began to see Franklin more frequently."

"Who was Franklin?"

"Dr. Bliskin."

"Oh. I never heard you call him that."

"I didn't in front of anyone else. Anyway, maybe I was more vulnerable than ever because I was witnessing Dr. Davenport's private suffering. Those were very sad days. Wyndemere was never as dark—and for all of us. Franklin brought some light into this house, brought some light to me. He was a very good friend of Dr. Davenport's by now, and he, too, knew how deeply in pain Dr. Davenport was, despite the facade of the stolid doctor he presented. In fact, that was how Franklin and

I first drew closer to each other. We'd spend hours together talking about Dr. Davenport, and eventually . . . well, you know what happened."

"You became secret lovers."

"Yes. The truth is, Franklin decided to move away and start a practice somewhere else because of what he and I had become. He believed, and to be honest, so did I, that we couldn't be near each other and not be lovers. It would come out, of course, and it would destroy his marriage."

"And because you had his child, right? Of course," I continued before she could respond. "How could he deny that? I sensed it when he was here."

She shook her head.

"What?"

"Let me finish. Dr. Davenport had become more or less a social recluse after Samantha's death. He went to work, but he went practically nowhere else. He had plenty of invitations, of course, especially that first year, but he went to only a few events that he felt were necessary for political reasons regarding the hospital. He was dreadfully lonely. He wasn't even paying enough attention to Ryder. Franklin was taking care of any medical needs Ryder had, and I was caring for him like a mother would, like Samantha had started to do. In my mind, he was my child."

"You did carry him and deliver him. I've read

about surrogates. They can feel like the child's mother even though they're not."

"This was different. I didn't feel that way in the beginning, especially when Samantha was there to play that role. But afterward . . . eventually, even Dr. Davenport was thinking of me the way he would think of his child's mother. Those were strange days, Fern. When he came home from the hospital, he even took to asking, 'How's our boy today?' He wouldn't buy the baby anything without buying me something as well. He even made sure flowers were delivered for me on Mother's Day. And he never forgot my birthday. He needed someone to care about, someone besides his patients."

"Oh. But that's sad, Mummy." I hadn't expected to hear something like that.

"Yes, it was. He had begun to insist that I sit at the dining-room table with Ryder in his baby seat beside me. I'd show him something new I had taught Ryder, and there was laughter back in the house. Anyone just entering Wyndemere, a stranger, would surely look at us and think we were a real family."

"It must have been uncomfortable for you."

"Very, but I didn't have the heart to refuse him or remind him that I was just his baby's nanny. In his mind's eye, he remembered me pregnant. He was there when Ryder was born, of course, and he saw me when I . . ."

"Breastfed him?"

"Yes. I even suspected that the way he had looked at me sometimes before Samantha's death bothered her. I think they even had an argument or two about it. I tried to keep myself deeper in the shadows, do what I had to do, and then get out of their daily lives, but Samantha was very social, too, and loved dressing up and going places. If anyone needed a nanny for her child, Samantha Davenport did. I could stay unnoticed just so much. In those days, I slept upstairs in Ryder's nursery, and when he was older and had his own room, I had mine, too. You slept in mine," she said. "Until Bea came to Wyndemere."

"Yes. I remember."

She was quiet. Was that it?

I wanted to go see Ryder, now more than ever. "Mummy, I think—"

"When I said Dr. Davenport was behaving strangely, treating me as if I really was Ryder's mother and having me at the dinner table, saying odd things, I was trying to get you to understand what happened, why it happened."

"What happened?"

There was an expression on my mother's face that I had never seen. It was an expression of abject terror. My mother always well hid whatever fears she might have, just as she kept her anger always below any boiling point. If something put her into a rage, it was a very short rage. She could catch her breath and keep everything in perspective.

"Dr. Davenport began to come to me at night. At first, it was simply to see Ryder, and then he came more and more to have me comfort him. I was the only one to whom he could reveal his emotional pain. I couldn't turn him away."

Now I was just staring at her, holding my breath.

"I knew he wanted me to pretend I was Samantha. I knew that gave him great relief. Of course, no one else knew, no one. And then one day, I realized what had happened."

"What?" I had to have her say it and say it clearly.

"I was pregnant with you," she said.

Can your heart really stop and start? Can you really feel something inside you crumble and fall like some ancient stone ruin? Can your blood really turn cold? Like a life preserver, my desperate thought rushed in to save me from what she was saying.

"But I could have been Dr. Bliskin's child! He was your lover."

"I knew the timing. I knew how far along I was. I knew who I had been with during the time that would make it possible. And although I have always played down the resemblances, I can see them clearly. It was why I was always secretly pleased to hear someone who saw you call you my clone."

"Are you telling me that Ryder is my half brother, that Dr. Davenport is my real father?"

She nodded. "For so many reasons, I hoped I would never have to tell you that, but it was my own blindness that prevented me from seeing the most important reason of all for telling you."

I shook my head. "No. I don't believe you. He never treated me like he would treat a daughter. Dr. Bliskin acted more like my real father in those few minutes we spent together than Dr. Davenport ever has. I've never felt . . . a connection. I would have; I should have. You're wrong. You just don't remember it right," I said a little louder. "You're ashamed that you slept with two men at the same time. And you're just saying this to be sure I won't be like you and sleep with Ryder and then other boys before I graduate from high school."

"That's certainly not my reason. I've never lied to you, Fern. I haven't told you everything I should have long before now, but I've never lied, and you know I haven't."

"No," I insisted. "Lies fly around here like dust. I'm not going to tell Ryder this. I'll never tell him."

"Dr. Davenport is telling him," she said. "As soon as he feels the moment is right this morning, he is going to tell him. As a result of this nearly tragic event, when he, like I, realized what was happening between you two, he came here, and he and I discussed it. I agreed with him that neither of us could keep the secret any longer."

"Wyndemere gives up one of its secrets," I said dryly like someone stunned, actually more like someone stung. "But how did you explain yourself, explain me, after I was born?"

"I'm ashamed to tell you that although I had never said it, I did act as if Dr. Bliskin was your father. Mrs. Marlene knew about our affair, as I'm sure some others in the house did at the time. They made assumptions, and I didn't do anything to dissuade them."

"Always protecting our precious Dr. Davenport," I said.

"And myself. I'm not going to offer any excuses, although there were clearly reasons. I've always questioned how much I did out of sympathy and how much was out of my own desire. That's quite a question for someone as young and as inexperienced in these matters as you. Maybe someday you'll help me find the answer."

I looked away. I wasn't crying. I was filled instead with a rage that overpowered sadness and disappointment. "He never would ask you to marry him, of course. He'd let you be seen as a woman who had slept with someone she couldn't

marry, and he let me be the fatherless child, the illegitimate child."

"I wasn't going to marry someone I didn't love
fully. There was sympathy and passion but not the
kind of passion that lasts a lifetime. I've always
warned you about that. It wasn't that I was beneath him or anything. He's not like that, despite
the airs he puts on."

"Did you ever sleep with him afterward, after
I was born?"

"No. I was faithful to Franklin then." She
smiled to herself. "Sometimes, during those early
days, I thought Dr. Davenport might have convinced himself you were Franklin's child. But he
was never one to refuse to see the truth. He sees
like an X-ray machine, sees everything and everyone like that, even himself," she said, looking past
me for a moment as her thoughts and memories
carried her off. Then her eyes seemed to click, and
she turned back to me. "Everything I've told you is
the truth."

"That's why he paid for so much and defied
Bea to keep you and me here when he married her,
isn't it?"

"Partly. I do my job well. She knows she's lucky
to have me despite how much she complains."

"But he lets her treat us like we're beneath
them both."

She was quiet.

"Why? Did he eventually convince himself that I wasn't his child? Did that make it easier for him to be so . . . so . . ."

"Aloof? No. Sometimes he doesn't have much choice. Bea knows more than I'd certainly like her to know, and she uses it to her advantage."

"How can he let her boss him like that? It's really blackmail. That's even worse."

"They are small sacrifices to keep the peace. You must remember you're not the only one who could suffer. There's Sam, too, and Ryder."

"I want to see him," I insisted.

"Dr. Davenport asked that you wait until he speaks with him first. He'll do that either this morning or during the day. If you go before he does that, Ryder will sense something, and if you tell him before his father can explain . . ."

"Then let him come and ask me himself," I said. "He's my father, too. He can explain it to me as well."

"Fern."

"You'll have to lock me in otherwise," I warned.

"Oh, Fern."

"I mean it," I said. "I want to hear it all from him. He owes me that. All these years, looking at me, talking to me like he was the king of the castle and I was merely a servant's daughter. He lived comfortably with the lie, and you let him."

"I did, but I'm not so sure I'd agree he was comfortable with it."

"What is he going to do about Bea when she finds out that you've told it all, that he's told Ryder the truth, too? She'll lose her high-and-mighty grip on him."

"That's not our problem, now, is it?"

"I won't ever let her talk down to me again. You can be sure of that."

She nodded with a small smile. "No, I don't imagine you will. However," she said, standing, "such defiance needs nourishment. Rest for a while. It's actually time for breakfast. Let me get some hot food in you. Please."

"I'm not very hungry."

She stood, waiting.

"Okay, but not a lot." I started to stand and felt a little wobbly, so I sat back.

"I'll bring it in, Fern. Give your body a chance to catch a breath. You're lucky you're not in the hospital, too."

Reluctantly, I gave in and lay back again. It wasn't only the ordeal on the lake in the storm that was doing this to me now. I felt as if I had been punched in the stomach and gone through another, even worse storm. My face had to be the face of disappointment and defeat.

"I'm sorry," my mother said.

My rage had not receded, especially the rage I

was feeling toward her. I wasn't prepared to forgive. Maybe I never would. "Why did you have
me? Why go through all this?"

"I had carried someone else's baby and delivered him. Something in me insisted I carry my own,
and I don't regret it one bit."

"But you stayed here. Why? There was always
the chance someone would find out the truth—Dr.
Bliskin, maybe."

"He knew the truth."

"And he still wanted to be with you?"

"Yes. He knew the whole truth, including how
and why it happened."

"Did he know some of the staff suspected
him?"

"Yes."

"And he was good with that?"

"He was good with being with me. That was
more important to him."

"But not more important than staying with his
wife and children."

"No, not more important than that."

"Did you stay in Wyndemere only because
of him? You could have lived somewhere else
close by and still seen him whenever you wanted,
couldn't you?"

"Staying here was something Dr. Davenport
wanted me to do very much. He trusted me with
Ryder, and it's not that easy out there for a young

woman with a child and no clear path to a means of self-support. I certainly wasn't going back to England. My father would have been beside himself with glee if I showed up with a child and had no husband."

"Did your mother and your sister really ever know about me?"

"After I learned my father had died, I sent them pictures of you. Someday you'll meet my sister, I hope."

"And Mr. Stark? Mr. Stark always knew the truth, didn't he?"

"Yes."

"That's why he's so devoted to us. He always felt sorry for us."

"I like to think it's more than simply pity. He's grown quite fond of you, of us both."

"And now Ryder will know," I said, more to myself than to her, as the realization of what all this meant sank deeper into me.

"Yes, and now you both know." She started out.

"You've got to hate it here," I said.

She stopped, thought a moment, and turned back to me. "For all its faults, all its dark history, this is still Wyndemere. It's too big and classic to disregard, and it gives you the feeling it's immortal and as protective as a fortress. The grounds are beautiful, and ordinarily the lake is a jewel. Maybe it will be that to us all again. Sunlight has a way of erasing ugliness. I guess I'd feel like Eve leaving the Garden of Eden or something if I left."

"Wyndemere? The Garden of Eden?"

She shrugged. "As one of our own English poets wrote, 'The mind is its own place, and in itself can make a heaven of hell, a hell of heaven.' "

She left.

I closed my eyes and once again saw Ryder looking down at me with such love in the rowboat. I listened to him making promises, and then I welcomed his kiss.

We were saved out there.

But we were drowned soon after we were rescued.

Epilogue

I DIDN'T GO to the hospital to see Ryder. After I ate
some breakfast, I fell asleep again. The weight of
the ordeal and the weight of the truth were too
much. I slept until almost two. It was very quiet
when I awoke. For a few moments, I lay there listening. I thought I heard someone moving out in
the kitchen.

"Mummy?" I called. I sat up.

A few seconds later, Dr. Davenport stepped into
my doorway.

As usual, he was dressed in a dark-blue suit
and a light-blue tie. Because he was so unexpected,
I gasped at the sight of him. I thought he looked
taller than ever. His face was in shadow.

"Didn't mean to surprise you," he said. "How
are you feeling?"

"Okay."

He nodded and stepped in, gazing around my room. "I can't remember when I was over here last," he said.

"I do. It was a long time ago. More than a year, in fact."

"Yes. My mother always wanted to do something with this section of Wyndemere, redecorate it some foolish way. My father wouldn't permit it, wouldn't waste a nickel if he could help it. He was very no-nonsense when it came to most of his spending. If he was flying anywhere himself, he'd never go first class. And he had his Mercedes for over ten years. Instead of buying new suits, he'd have his old ones tailored, and he was famous for putting new soles on old shoes instead of buying new ones. My mother did all the excess spending. Maybe that's why he was so frugal with himself. He was trying to balance the books."

"How's Ryder?" I asked. I was happy to hear him talk about his parents, something he had never done with me, but I was afraid he was doing it simply to avoid telling me something very bad.

"He's okay. Banged up a bit. I have him on an antibiotic to prevent any lung infection, but all the tests run on him were negative. There'll be no permanent physical damage, I'm sure. I had him released and brought home to his own room to rest. I told Parker we're even. I performed a bypass on him that saved his life, and he saved Ryder's."

"Why did you say 'no physical damage'? What other damage is there?"

"Well, aside from the guilt he's feeling for having risked your life as well as his own, he's learned some things, life-changing things you've learned as well. The combination is pretty heavy to bear for him at the moment, as I'm sure it is for you. Mind if I sit?" he asked, nodding at the chair by my vanity table.

"No."

He pulled it out and placed it beside the bed. I pulled my legs back and sat up against my pillows. I could never recall a time when he and I sat so close to each other. He clasped his hands and placed them on his lap. I hadn't noticed the thin, white strands invading his pecan-brown hair. Now, this close to him, I could see the fatigue in his eyes. It occurred to me that he must have been up all night, looking after Ryder, overseeing every test.

"You got a little bit scraped up, I understand. Blisters on your hands?" He reached for them. I held out my hands, and he looked at the palms. "They'll be fine. My grandmother used to have my grandfather soak his feet in green tea for his foot blisters. Actually worked. Modern medicine has some things to learn from the old household remedies."

He was still holding my hands. I looked at them and at him, and he let go and sat back.

"I sensed, of course, that things were beginning to develop between the two of you," he said. "Ryder was always very protective of you, something I admired in him, but lately, it began to take on other aspects. He's been a lot more emotional whenever anything referred to you or whenever you were mentioned.

"First, let me tell you that none of this is your fault or his. If anyone's to blame, it has to be me, solely me. Your mother is about as close to an angel as any human being could be. I guess I can say I've had the best of two worlds, because I've had you both here, under my roof, watching you grow and mature into a fine young lady."

"But not as your daughter," I said. "Until now."

"Yes, until now." He looked down at his hands, those long fingers entwined. He was silent so long that I thought he wasn't going to continue, but he looked up again. "What happened between your mother and me was not because she and I were lovers. She, as I know she has told you, was the surrogate mother who carried Ryder. After she was impregnated, she was everything a pregnant woman should be. She was vigilant when it came to protecting her health and the health of the baby she was carrying."

"Does Ryder know this now? That my mother carried him?"

"Yes. He and I talked for quite a while this morning. I described it all. My first wife was very fond of your mother, not because she was pregnant with her fertilized egg but because there was a genuine love and friendship between them. They hit it off immediately," he said, smiling as he recalled. "I used to be jealous of how well those two could get along. Samantha did far more with your mother than she did with me during those days and shortly afterward. They were more like sisters. In my mind's eye, I could never envision them separated. I was very happy your mother agreed to stay on past the time allotted.

"There was never any doubt in my mind that she took Samantha's death as hard as a sister would, almost as hard as I did. She was a great comfort to me. I don't think I would have gone on in my work if it wasn't for your mother. I was drawn to her for all those reasons, and then, well, she became something of a surrogate wife as well.

"Perhaps I took advantage of her. No, I definitely took advantage of her, and when she became pregnant with you, I felt an even deeper bond with her, but the love she sought for herself, the love she deserved, was not housed in me. It was her particular misfortune to fall in love with someone who couldn't be her life's mate. She tells me that you know who that is."

"I do. When I think of them parting, I want to cry."

"Yes, two very unselfish people. As long as I've known your mother, though, she's been that way. It was your mother's choice to keep our secret. What did I really have to offer to oppose that? Life as the wife of a man she didn't really love, a man who, when he faced the truth, admitted he was making love to his dead wife's memory? It wasn't fair to ask your mother, anyone, to be someone she's not just to make someone like me happy. You might be too young to understand that now; it might sound like I'm grasping for some excuse, but perhaps in time you'll understand. We human beings are a lot more complex than we think.

"I know you suffered because of the way we handled your birth. It's not enough for me to tell you that everything you need and will need has been set aside for you. That doesn't make it all disappear, but you should know that is true."

"I'm not as surprised about all this as you might think. I've always believed Wyndemere was a house full of secrets," I said.

"They do seem to enjoy it here," he said.

"Like the secret of your little sister?"

He looked up quickly. "Yes."

"Have you told Ryder that, too?"

"Not yet, but he'll know everything about Wyndemere and the Davenports now. I can promise you that. I just thought for now, he has quite a bit to digest. Truth is probably best learned and understood in small doses." He smiled. "I guess I can't help sounding like a doctor, prescribing.

"And so we come to this, you and Ryder. What am I to say about that? Here I am, a well-known and respected cardiologist who underestimated the power of the heart. I was too close to it to understand, to see what was right there in front of me, what was always right there in front of me.

"As a result, I've delivered quite a bit of unhappiness to people I should have protected and loved more. I can say I'm sorry, and someday I hope you and Ryder will forgive me. The truth is, I'm having a hard time forgiving myself. Only your mother has the will and the power to be compassionate enough for that. I'm so happy you have her and she has you. I hope you feel the same way and you don't blame her for anything."

"I love my mother. Nothing will change that."

He smiled and nodded. Then he slapped his knees and stood. "From this day forward, a bit too late, I'm sure, Wyndemere is your home, every part of it, anywhere in it you wish to go. Whenever your mother permits, I want you to have meals with your sister, Sam. She's going to need a real big sister, for sure. Ryder will be there from time to time.

He graduates soon, and he and I decided—actually, he decided—that he should do some traveling with some friends this summer before he starts college. It was something he had discussed with me a while back. I reminded him, and he thought that would be a good idea now. You both need a new start with a new identity, but yours involves being more of a Davenport."

"What about Bea?" I asked.

"Bea and I have drifted pretty far apart. We have some new understandings to develop if we're to continue. She'll be a challenge for us both. Bea never was much of that for Ryder," he said. "But the most important person in the middle of that is Sam. Her needs come before my own and my wife's happiness. And that's now true for you as well. So. Is there anything you need right now?" he asked.

He wasn't looking at me. He was looking sad and, for the first time, really sweet and warm to me. Gone was that pedestal on which he stood and looked down at all of us. He wasn't a doctor at the moment; he was a father.

"Yes," I said. I pulled away my blanket and stood. "Something I've waited a long time to get."

"Which is?"

"A hug from my father," I said.

His smile came like Ryder's often did, rippling through his face tentatively at first, frightened about being wrong, and then blossoming with a twinkle in his eyes that could rival stars. He embraced me and kissed my forehead and said, "Welcome home."

I watched him walk out, no longer looking ten feet tall and made of stone. He was, like everyone, desperate to be loved. That certainly made me his daughter.

I suddenly felt a new burst of energy and quickly went about getting dressed, doing my hair, putting on a little lipstick, and starting out through the hallway. I stopped after a few feet and smiled to myself. Then I turned around and went out the door.

What a contrast today was to the day Ryder and I chose to be on the lake. There wasn't a cloud in the deep azure sky. There was a warm breeze gently caressing branches and their vibrant green leaves. Yesterday the grass had been cut, and the air was perfumed with its scent. There were even more birds, robins and sparrows threading through trees, hummingbirds madly circling a rosebush, and two beautiful orioles floating over the front lawn. On such a day, Wyndemere's austere look retreated, and I could easily understand why my mother was so attached to it. Truthfully, I was, too. I simply hadn't been permitted to love it as much as I could, as I should, secrets and all.

I hurried to the front door, took a deep breath, and entered the house. For a moment, I stood there and looked at everything the way a stranger might. It was as if I was seeing it all for the first time. After all, it was my home now, too. When I looked at the Davenport family portraits, I no longer looked at them as I would look at some historical people whose pictures belonged in museums, their clothes and hairdos vaguely interesting to someone exploring a previous time in history. Now they were my relatives, too. Who had any resemblance to me?

I looked at every antique, every piece of furniture, differently, moving slowly through the large entryway toward the stairway. At the entrance to the sitting room on the right, I paused. Bea Davenport and my father were sitting on settees opposite each other. They had obviously been in deep conversation. They both looked at me. Bea's eyes widened with surprise and then quickly went back to normal. She looked at my father and looked away. He didn't smile. He nodded. I smiled, and then I hurried to the stairway and walked up. I turned right at the top and walked slowly to Ryder's room. The door was closed. I knocked softly, and then I opened it.

He was lying in bed, his eyes closed, but when he opened them, he sat up quickly.

"Fern! How are you?"

"How am I? How are you? You're the one who was in the hospital," I said, moving to his bed.

"It's like I can't remember much about it. I

mean, I remember how hard we worked at trying to get back, but everything after that is a blur."

I sat at his feet and gently rubbed his leg. "Maybe that's better. You'll have fewer nightmares than I will."

"I'm sorry. I was stupid."

"We were both stupid. You do know Parker saved you, though, right?"

"Yeah, sure." He lay back against his pillow. "And I know a lot more, too, as I know you do."

I nodded. "Dr. Davenport came to see me this morning, came to my room."

"You mean our father came to your room," he said.

"Yes."

He looked down and then up quickly. "I don't feel dirty or anything. I won't let anyone say that about me or about you. I was in love with the other half of you. That's how I see it. I mean, I won't stop caring for you more than I would any other girl, but . . ."

"It'll be different. Yes, that's a good way to think of it. I was in love with your other half, too."

"I think I always sensed it, sensed who we really were to each other. Everything fits now, especially why your mother is so important to me. I think of her as my mother, which only makes you more my sister."

I reached for his hand.

Neither of us spoke, and then he shook his head and turned away. "It's just not fair, is it? It's like a big joke was pulled on us."

"Yes, it does feel like that," I said.

"My father shouldn't have let this go on."

"No, and he knows it. There isn't much we can do about it except perhaps forgive."

"I'm not ready, but . . . I will," he said.

"Yes, you will. So. I understand you're going to do some traveling?"

"Right after graduation. Terry Hudson has been after me to join him on a trip to England, sightseeing, history. His father is the head of radiology at the hospital."

"England. How ironic. You're going to my homeland."

"You'll get there. I'm sure your mother will take you to see her sister, see where she lived."

"She said she would. I'll look forward to that."

We heard someone open the door and saw Sam move tentatively into the room.

"Hey," Ryder called. "Whatcha doing?"

"Nothing. You drowned," she said, close to tears.

"No. Just a big, deep dip in the lake. Come on in. Fern and I were talking about having a picnic next weekend. I'll set up the badminton net. You love that."

"Really?"

"Sure. Right, Fern?"

"Absolutely. You and I will beat his pants off."

Sam laughed. I reached out for her, and she took my hand. I patted the bed, and she sat beside me.

"Look at us," Ryder said. "The Wyndemere children."

"Houses don't have children," Sam said.

Ryder and I looked at each other.

"Sometimes they do," I said. "It's just another secret."